THE VISCOUNT BESIEGED

Elizabeth Bailey

SAPERE
BOOKS

THE VISCOUNT
BESIEGED

Published by Sapere Books.

20 Windermere Drive, Leeds, England, LS17 7UZ,
United Kingdom

saperebooks.com

ISBN: 978-1-80055-025-4

CHAPTER ONE

Dissension raged in the drawing-room at Pusay. Not that this was unusual, for the activities of Miss Isadora Alvescot frequently drew down upon her head the noisy complaints of the rest of the family. But in a house of mourning, where the expectation was for quiet and solemnity, Society might consider such argument inappropriate, unseemly even.

This did not occur to the combatants, who were indeed engaged in debating the matter of appropriateness, but only concerning the performance of theatricals in the present circumstances.

'It must be counted quite irregular, Dora, with your poor papa barely cold in his grave,' said the plaintiff with dismaying bluntness. 'You would not wish your conduct to be thought shocking.'

'By whom?' demanded the defendant, suppressing the sting stirred by the cruel choice of words, for Isadora would permit none to see her wounds. 'Except for ourselves and Harriet, who is to know anything of my conduct? Besides, as you know very well, Cousin Matty, I do not give a fig for anything anyone may say of me.'

'Yes, more's the pity,' responded Mrs Matilda Dotterell, the indigent relative who had resided at Pusay with her two children since her widowhood many years ago. 'But you might give something for what is said of your poor mama.'

Isadora eyed her with dangerous calm. 'I do not take your meaning.'

Her friend Harriet intervened. 'Now, Dora, don't get upon your high ropes. All Mrs Dotterell is saying — and I must say I agree with her — is that Mrs Alvescot may well be blamed for not guiding you better.'

She had struck the right note. Whatever Isadora's failings, she was acutely conscious of her mother's ineffectual nature. It would be grossly unjust for Mrs Alvescot to shoulder the responsibility for anything she might choose to do. Why, her mama could no more prevent her from doing as she wished than fly to the moon.

To Isadora's chagrin, Cousin Matty then chose to broach the matter directly to the lady of the house.

'Ellen, I appeal to you,' Matilda said, crossing the room. 'This performance of Dora's will not do at such a time.'

It was plain to Isadora that until her cousin's intervention, her mama had not given the matter a thought. Why should she, accustomed as she was to the impromptu plays got up by her daughter? Her mama had never seen in them anything either untoward or out of the way. Isadora noted that she had taken her usual chair across from the bare expanse of carpet by the central window that constituted the improvised stage where the argument was in progress, settling her plump person in the indolent manner habitual to her, a comfortable expectation of enjoyment in her pretty, matronly features.

It was pitiful to see this ready acceptance shattered as Matilda descended upon Isadora's poor mama before ever Isadora, and the small company she had dragooned into performing with her, could begin upon the poignant little piece she had fashioned out of the tragedy of Lady Jane Grey.

'If Dora will not mind what I have to say upon the matter, then it is in your part to correct your daughter, Ellen. Pray talk some sense into her head.'

This command, thrown at her seemingly out of the blue, evidently startled Mrs Alvescot, for she blinked at Matilda's large person standing over her.

'Me, Matty? But Dora will not listen to me. Besides, what has she done?'

'It is not what I have done, Mama,' Isadora put in, 'but what I am about to do.'

She came across to perch on the arm of the chair next to her mother's, careless of any creasing to the high-waisted black satin mourning-gown she had decided would suit very well for the purposes of her role. She had swept her dark curls up into a Grecian topknot banded about with black ribbons, satisfied that the costume lent her tall figure the necessary elegance, although she was aware that her current martial attitude was decidedly inapposite to Lady Jane.

'Cousin Matty thinks we shall all be accused of impropriety if we perform the play,' she said scornfully. 'It is quite absurd. As if Papa would have minded.'

'Now that is very true,' said Mrs Alvescot, throwing a pleading glance at her cousin. 'Indeed, Matty, I was just now conscious of a little ache at my heart that dear Aubrey is not here to enjoy the piece. He was so proud of Isadora's talent, you know.'

'Yes, and even if he was not,' put in Isadora triumphantly, 'I know he would have had not the least objection.'

Isadora's papa had encouraged her to the last, suggesting tomes from his library where she might find the information she needed about Lady Jane. Why, even through the months of dreadful pain and weakness, he would have her perform in his bedchamber rather than not see her play at all.

'I am quite sure he would not have objected,' agreed Matilda in the tone of one willing to make concessions, and taking the chair to the other side of her cousin, 'but I fear that it is not Aubrey we must consider just at this time.'

Isadora gazed at her blankly. 'What in the world can you mean, Cousin Matty?'

Her friend, following her across the room, took it upon herself to answer. Harriet Witheridge was, Isadora considered, deceptively pretty. Under instruction, she was clad in a half-robe of blue sarcenet over a muslin gown in a similar pastel hue in deference partly, as her friend knew, to the full black of mourning worn by all in this house and, at Isadora's request, to the role she had agreed to take on. The sweetness of her looks hid an unexpected strength of character, for she was inclined, to Isadora's occasional annoyance, to treat her very much as a younger sister in spite of the other's slight superiority in both height and years.

'Now, Dora, you know very well Mrs Dotterell is only concerned with how it must appear to people,' Harriet said severely. 'I confess I had not thought about it before myself.'

'Fudge, why should you?' demanded Isadora impatiently. 'You have known me forever, and I have been performing since I don't know when.'

No one could argue with that. Isadora had been, from childhood up, an indefatigable actress — off the stage as well as on it, as she suspected some of her acquaintance held. So much so, indeed, that she was not nearly as concerned about the way the family was now circumstanced following her papa's death as were the rest. If only the family might be suitably taken care of, her secret plans could go forward. If not...

Well, there the matter rested. For until the wretchedly recalcitrant heir to the Alvescot estates chose to show himself there was no saying what might befall any of them. But to suggest that she might be censured for performing a play was absurd. She looked back at the instigator of this fetch.

'Great heavens, Cousin Matty, I wonder at you! You have lived with us for years and years, and you must be quite as certain as I that Papa did not give a fig for the proprieties in his own home.'

'That's very true, Matty,' nodded Mrs Alvescot. 'Dear Aubrey—'

'Yes, Ellen,' cut in Matilda smoothly, 'but Aubrey — God rest his soul — is no longer with us, and, much though it pains me to remind you of it, we are all of us obliged to look to a different source for our standards of conduct.'

Isadora had no difficulty in interpreting this speech. 'If, Cousin Matty, you are referring to Lord Roborough —'

'Oh no,' groaned Fanny Dotterell, one of the younger members of the group. 'Not the Errant Heir again.'

Fanny would object, of course. At fourteen, she was thin with a sulky pout about the mouth that bid fair to turn into the pinched look of perpetual anxiety that characterised her mother, Matilda. Unsuitable though she was, Isadora had lured her into portraying the young Princess Elizabeth in the play only to keep her from complaint. Up to now her young cousin's attention had been firmly on settling on her head the elaborate crown she had devised of silver filigree and coloured beads, and no doubt practising the words of her important final line. Mention of Lord Roborough, however, drew Fanny back into the family circle.

Isadora could not blame her for groaning. His lordship, although as yet unknown to the inmates of the Pusay household, had become a thorn in their collective flesh. Indeed, Isadora could scarcely endure to hear the sound of his name.

'Of course I am referring to Lord Roborough,' Matilda returned, ignoring her daughter's interjection.

'And just why should he presume to censure my conduct?' demanded Isadora ominously, taking the comment entirely to herself as she knew had been her cousin's intent.

'Well, it is his house now, after all.'

'That is true, Dora,' fluttered Mrs Alvescot, her plump features crumpling into lines of worry.

'And,' pursued Matilda doggedly, 'he is the head of the family.'

'Oh dear, so he is. Do you indeed think he may take exception to Dora's play?'

'Take exception?' echoed Isadora with heat, jumping up from her perch. 'He had better try!'

'I should be much astonished if he did not take exception to it,' declared Matilda. 'These great men, you know, Dora, are sticklers for punctilio.'

'Are they indeed? In that case, perhaps you will enlighten me as to why we have not seen hide nor hair of the wretched man these many weeks since poor Papa passed on. If he is so concerned with punctilio, I would have supposed that, if he did not find it convenient to visit us, he would have had the common courtesy at the very least to have written to Mama instead of sending word by Mr Thornbury.'

This was undeniable. Even Matilda had been extraordinarily put out — on behalf of her cousin, she had said — by such a piece of rudeness. The family lawyer had written to his lordship at Barton Stacey in Hampshire expressly to inform him that, Mr Alvescot having died, the estate had now fallen, by an obscure family connection, to his lot. Receiving no response, Mr Thornbury, urged thereto by the unsatisfactory state of affairs at Pusay, had again written requesting the viscount's pleasure, and received only a brief note in reply, the contents of which had been dissected ad nauseam by the Pusay residents while they waited in vain for the heir to appear in person.

'Dora is quite right, Mama,' put in Fanny fairly, unusually taking her cousin's part. 'Lord Roborough has shown himself in a very poor light.'

'Thank you, Fanny,' Isadora said, a trifle surprised. She added, 'Let me tell you, Cousin Matty, that if Lord Roborough has any idea of coming the head of the family over us I shall very soon make him think better of it.'

Harriet laughed. 'I should think you will, Dora. But you might consider poor Mrs Alvescot's sensibilities. She is looking quite alarmed.'

Isadora stepped back to her mother's side, her manner softening at once. 'Now, Mama, you know very well I will never do anything to ruin your chances. Only I cannot undertake to kowtow to the ordering of my life by a complete stranger.'

'No, my love,' agreed her mother, briefly taking Isadora's hand between both her own, 'but perhaps he will not attempt to order your life, and so we may all be comfortable.'

'Judging by the utter lack of interest he has so far shown,' Isadora said drily, 'I should think that is all too likely.'

At this point they suffered an interruption. Isadora's young cousin Rowland, all of twelve years old, who had been standing all this time, ready for his brief part as the headsman, muffled in a black cloth helmet that concealed everything but his eyes, grew impatient. Tearing off the helmet, he strode forward, somewhat red-faced from the heat of the summer sun that came at him through the glass of the central window.

'Here, Dora, are we going to do this Lady Jane of yours or not? Because if we aren't —'

'Yes, we are,' interrupted Isadora in a determined tone, fixing Matilda with an eye that dared her to intervene.

That lady opened her mouth to retort, and, encountering a desperate plea in the eyes of Mrs Alvescot, closed it again with a sigh.

Triumphant, Isadora whirled about, ushering her cast into position. 'Come, Fanny, Harriet. Take your places.' Behind her she heard her mother's whispered plea.

'Oh, Matty, pray don't enrage her any more. Her temper is particularly uneven just now, for she misses Aubrey dreadfully, though she will never let any of us see it. Perhaps it is wrong, but at least it keeps her amused.'

Grateful for her mama's sensitivity, Isadora mentally dismissed the nonsensical idea that her preoccupation with acting was merely an amusement. It overrode everything else, for no sooner was she embarked upon her first line than all became as nothing to the present moment as she lost herself almost entirely in the poignancy of the role.

What difficulties she had experienced in her determination to do this play had all to do with coaxing from her relatives and friend performances that would not altogether disgrace her. She had compromised on the matter of dress, agreeing that mourning garb would in general provide an appropriately sombre note, so that only representational headgear denoted Harriet's queenly role and Fanny's princess. Rowland was content enough, having blackmailed Isadora into allowing him, if he wore the helmet, to use a real axe for his part as the headsman.

But Isadora demanded, at the very least, that these indifferent players create around her a suitably grave ensemble against which her own portrayal would be the more telling.

She was relieved to note, in that small percentage of her mind remaining free to take in what was going forward around her, that this requirement was being met. She felt the hushed expectancy that fell over the room as Queen Mary condemned Lady Jane Grey to an early death — although why Harriet in that role should sound a degree tearful was a puzzle. She had not time to ponder this, however, for she must launch into her final emotional speech.

Mrs Alverscot sighed deeply as she did so and Isadora was satisfied for she had hoped her haunting rendition might go straight to the heart. She had planned to cut a truly tragic figure, but she had not bargained for Queen Mary's demeanour. Out of the corner of her eye, Isadora thought she noted the flutter of a pocket handkerchief, and in the background of her mind she heard a distinct sob.

An admonishing and fierce whisper was next to be heard. 'Harriet!'

Poised for the climactic moment of her dramatic speech, which would signal the movement into the final tableau of execution and Fanny's telling line to complete the play, Isadora ignored the slight distraction. 'I have lived only to love,' she uttered painfully in the character of Lady Jane, 'and I have loved only to die.'

Another muffled sob broke from Queen Mary, producing an instant loud whisper from the Princess Elizabeth. 'Harriet, stop that!'

Somewhere in the periphery of her vision, Isadora saw Harriet start, and it came to her belatedly that Fanny had shifted from her position and was now stationed at Harriet's elbow. Desperately, Isadora tried to ignore the unscheduled sotto voce dialogue going on in her rear, thankful that she knew her lines well enough to be able to continue without effort.

'What is the matter?'

'Nothing is the matter with me,' snapped Fanny. 'It's you. You're not supposed to be crying.'

'Hush,' warned Harriet. 'You are troubling Dora.'

But the leading light of the Alvescot theatricals, thrusting down her understandable annoyance, refused to allow the disturbance to interfere with her performance, although she did falter a trifle.

'I commend... I commend me to my Maker, to He in whose bosom at this moment rests —'

'I like that,' came from Fanny in a piercing whisper. 'It was not *I* who was sobbing loud enough to be heard all over the house.'

'— my soul, my heart, my love, my husband,' Isadora persisted, raising her voice over the top of the background hubbub.

'For goodness' sake, Fanny,' exclaimed Harriet impatiently, 'will you be quiet?'

At this point, completely losing the thread of Lady Jane Grey's discourse, Isadora paused uncertainly, casting about in her mind for the line she had lost, whereupon the twelve-year-old headsman, glancing wildly round in the sudden silence, became convinced that he had missed his cue. Uttering his only line, a hoarse grunt that he had rehearsed until his throat ached, he hefted his axe on high.

'Rowland, no!' shrieked his sister Fanny.

Harriet screamed. Isadora jumped violently. Rowland started and lost his grip. And two petrified pairs of audience eyes watched the heavy axe fall from the nerveless hands of the confused headsman and land with a thud on the carpet.

Instant pandemonium broke out; cries of dismay and alarm, a concerted movement away from the axe — for the handle bounced and shuddered as it hit the floor — and a sound like a rushing wind as Matilda leapt from her chair and dashed across the room. 'Rowland, you stupid boy!' she shrieked, and boxed her son's ears.

Mrs Alvescot, apparently under the impression that this was all part of the play, broke into enthusiastic clapping.

Isadora, standing blinking and confused in the ruined chaos of her tragedy, was turning from one to the other of her fellow players as if seeking guidance. Oddly, it was the expression of applause from her mother that brought her out of her stupefaction. Applause? They had not even finished the play! She whirled to face her young cousin. 'Great heavens, Rowland, what in the world were you thinking of? I had not finished my speech.'

'Yes, and I have not had a chance to say my line,' accused Fanny, glaring at her erring brother, who was massaging his tender ears. 'Princess Elizabeth does have the last word.'

'Well, if you wish to complain of that, Fanny,' put in Harriet severely, 'you have only yourself to blame. You would keep talking.'

'I?' gasped Fanny, outraged. 'You began it, Harriet —'

'I could hear both of you chattering behind me, if you want to know,' Isadora interrupted, irate. 'And never mind your line, Fanny. What about my play? It is utterly ruined!'

'I told you not to let him loose with an axe, Dora,' said Matilda, lifting the offending article and placing it carefully against the wall out of harm's way.

'Let him loose? He had only to lift the thing at the right moment. A child could have done it.'

'He *is* a child, Dora,' Harriet pointed out, removing the simple cardboard crown from about her brow.

'I'm not a child,' protested Rowland hotly, the words belied by his chubby countenance. 'Only Fanny startled me by shouting. I thought I'd missed my turn.'

'It wasn't *me* shouting. It was Harriet. Anyway, *she* started it. She was crying.'

'So it *was* you sniffling,' Isadora broke in despairingly, diverted from the main issue. 'How could you? After everything I said in rehearsal.'

'But you do it so well, Dora,' her friend pleaded excusingly. 'How could I help it? Even the thought of sending you to the scaffold upsets me.'

Isadora cast up her eyes. As if they had not been over this a thousand times. 'Harriet, Mary could not possibly have cared about Lady Jane. This is Bloody Mary we are talking about. She went on to slaughter I don't know how many Protestants.'

'Yes, I know,' agreed Harriet. 'You told me so. And I said I did not like it. I wish very much that you had not made me play her.'

'Indeed, so do I,' said Isadora frankly. 'I should have given it to Fanny, except that she is not old enough.'

'I'm fourteen,' protested Fanny. 'And I certainly would not have cried.'

'Cried?' echoed Isadora, raising her brows. 'No, indeed. You would rather have relished condemning me to have my head chopped off.'

Both Fanny and Rowland burst into laughter at this, but Harriet was shocked.

'For shame, Dora, how can you talk so?'

'Yes, you should not jest about such things, Dora,' agreed Matilda.

'I'm not jesting.'

Matilda clicked her tongue and came up to lay a protective arm about her daughter's thin shoulders. 'Anyone would suppose that Fanny is not at all fond of you.'

'She isn't,' claimed Isadora flatly, and her dark eyes went to her cousin's. 'Are you?'

Fanny grinned. 'Well, I wouldn't exactly send you to the scaffold.'

'Dora, my love,' came Mrs Alvescot's voice plaintively from the armchair across the room. 'Do you tell me something has gone wrong? Oh dear, and I thought it went off so well.'

'Yes, Mama dearest, something has indeed gone wrong,' Isadora agreed, sailing across the room. 'What should happen is that when I finish my speech I walk around in a circle and the others follow me. I kneel, Rowland raises the axe, and Fanny says —'

'But, my love,' interrupted her mother in a horrified tone, 'you were surely not going to have poor Rowland drop the axe on you?'

'Fanny would have done,' put in Rowland, grinning as he followed Isadora across the room.

He hovered by the door a moment or two and then sidled from the room. Isadora noticed but kept mum, realising Rowland probably hoped his lapse from grace might be better repaired in his absence.

'The thing is, Mrs Alvescot,' Harriet explained, coming across the room towards her, 'that Rowland should not have dropped the axe at all. I'm afraid both Fanny and I are to blame for that.' She glanced at Fanny, who was muttering in protest. 'Yes, we are, Fanny. I have the grace to acknowledge it, even if you do not.' Turning to Isadora, she took her hands, saying penitently, 'I am so sorry, Dora. Between us we have spoilt it for you.'

Isadora squeezed the hands she held. 'No matter.' She grinned impishly. 'It only goes to prove that Cousin Matty was right, and fate has decreed that the performance was not to be. I dare say it is for the best. It is only a trifle of a play, after all.'

'Oh no, Dora, don't say that. It is a very good little play.' Harriet turned back to Mrs Alvescot. 'I do wish you might have seen the end. The raised axe was all to be part of the final tableau, you understand. Dora had conceived it quite brilliantly, I think.'

Fanny had by now joined the party, and, the excitement having begun to die down, she and her mother, together with Harriet, disposed themselves in sofas and armchairs, choosing from out of the unmatched collection seemingly set higgledy-piggledy about the room in homely comfort those seats conveniently close to Mrs Alvescot's chair.

As Isadora knew and valued, a sense of fashion and order was entirely lacking in this large family drawing-room in the house at Pusay. Portraits and paintings had been hung around the walls with no logical or aesthetic plan. A baize-covered table at one end served equally for card games, letter-writing or the tea-tray — indeed, any occupation that happened to suit at a given moment. A pianoforte and a harp stood against one wall, the one sometimes utilised by Mrs Alvescot and the latter suffered over by Fanny.

An air of general untidiness prevailed, for books or embroidery, and the other impedimenta of daily life, were left lying where they had been used. Only the large empty square by the central window was uncluttered, since this area served

— and had done so since time immemorial, so it seemed to the family — for Isadora's stage.

Here the family congregated. More so lately, for in the household's mourning state their visitors were few. Only their lifelong friends and neighbours came: Harriet, and her brother Edmund Witheridge, together with Harriet's betrothed, Mr Joseph Caistor, who was staying with them at present.

'Well, I don't think it is brilliantly conceived,' said Fanny judiciously. 'I mean, what was Queen Mary doing at the execution? And as for Elizabeth —'

'You had no objection to Elizabeth when I said you could play the part,' interrupted Isadora, pausing in her aimless perambulations about the room, for alone among the company she had not taken a seat. Which, she reflected, as Harriet at once joined issue with Fanny, arguing the merits of the play, was perfectly true. She had written the part of young Princess Elizabeth into the play precisely because she had known that her cousin's forthright criticisms would only be withheld if she herself had an important role.

Not that it had stopped Fanny's tongue. Nothing could. Cousin Matty put no real restraint on her, and she was inclined to say exactly what came into her head.

Wandering towards the windows that flanked her improvised stage, Isadora heard only vaguely the discussion continuing as both her mama and Cousin Matty took sides. There seemed little point in entering into it herself. Besides, if she spoke, she would only make everything worse by saying that the play was less at fault than the actors were.

Of course, there might well be a better way to depict the tragedy of Lady Jane Grey's life. No doubt Shakespeare would have found it. But, since Shakespeare had inconveniently omitted to chronicle the story, Isadora had to fend for herself, drawing on what little knowledge she had of the time, culled from her papa's books. Besides, she was less interested in historical accuracy than in the tragedy of a young girl, innocent and in love, and quite literally cut off in the flower of her youth.

That she was herself capable of bringing off the poignancy of the scene Isadora never doubted. But she felt the background personages must enhance it. Otherwise, why waste time and energy in dragooning her relatives and Harriet into participating?

She sighed inwardly. She might just as well not have done so, as it turned out. Should she have stuck to her guns and insisted on Edmund performing?

The thought of Edmund, who admittedly had at seventeen the same good looks as his sister, did not move Isadora with anything other than the desire to use him as an actor. But Edmund had declined to participate, since the only part available to him would have been that of Lady Jane's husband. He had confessed to his sister that to portray such a role could only remind him of the prize beyond his reach in real life. Harriet, most improperly repeating his words to Isadora, had recommended that she write his part out of the play.

'For you do not want him dangling after you, I know, and he is bound to feel encouraged if he is permitted to act as your husband.'

Isadora had regretfully agreed with this dictum, for she had no desire to give Edmund the slightest encouragement. It was quite ridiculous that he should have conceived this *tendre* for her. How could he suppose she would consider marrying a fellow three years her junior? A boy she had known almost from the cradle too.

Her attention was recalled by Harriet, who had risen to leave.

'I must go, Dora. We are to dine out tonight and Joseph will be wondering what has become of me.'

Mrs Alvescot smiled comfortably at her daughter's dearest friend. 'It is so kind of you, Harriet, to have helped Dora to amuse herself in this way.'

Isadora paused on her way to accompany Harriet to the door. 'Amuse myself? It is more than amusement, Mama. It is acting.'

'Exactly,' chimed in Matilda suddenly. 'And you see what has come of it. I do trust, Dora, that you will be more circumspect in future. Especially when Lord Roborough arrives.'

'Oh, we are back to him, are we?' said Isadora bodingly.

'Lord,' groaned Fanny. 'Mama, pray don't start again on this subject.'

'Be quiet, Fanny,' snapped Matilda. 'I shall start on any subject I choose. Besides, I hold to it that for all our sakes Dora must take care not to give Lord Roborough any cause for offence.'

'Offence?' cried Isadora, firing up. 'He is the one who has given offence.'

'Let me tell you, Dora,' said Harriet, intervening as she usually did to pour oil on the troubled waters, 'whatever the rest of us may say, Edmund at least insists that, for his part, he cannot think that Lord Roborough will be able to find any fault with you.'

'He would not say so if he had to live with her,' Fanny asserted.

Isadora was obliged to laugh. 'Well, Fanny, if by some remote chance I do suddenly have pretensions to be liked by the new lord and master of all our lives, I know I can depend entirely upon your support.'

Harriet smiled. 'At any rate, you may depend upon mine. I will leave you to quarrel over Lord Roborough in private.' But once she was outside the room with Isadora, who had elected to walk with her to the door, she added in a low voice, 'Don't think I don't know what you're planning, Dora, for I am too well acquainted with you. I shall come and see you tomorrow when we may be alone.'

'You may do so, but you will not change my mind,' Isadora responded, aware that Harriet, who knew all about her secret plans, heartily disapproved of them.

'I can at least try. No, no, don't accompany me. I know my way very well.'

'You should, after all these years,' Isadora laughed. 'Very well, I shall go back and face my cousin's warnings.'

'Yes, but don't lose your temper, Dora.'

'I shall try not to.'

But this promise was put severely to the test. Matilda was waiting only for Isadora's return into the room to take up the argument again. 'I cannot understand you, Dora,' she complained. 'Your poor mama has been left with little enough of her portion, but you have none at all. While as for myself and my children —' She broke off, whisking a handkerchief from her sleeve and applying it to her eyes.

Mrs Alvescot instantly threw out a hand in distress. 'Oh, poor Matty, don't cry. You know you will always have a home with me, no matter what happens.'

Isadora would not have argued with this. The Dotterells had ever been so much a part of the family it had never occurred to her to consider a life that did not include them. For the first time she realised that Cousin Matty must be entertaining some very real fears for her own future. Who was to say Viscount Roborough would consider himself responsible for these relatives, even supposing he was prepared to assist her mama out of her difficulties? Her mama, of course, would not dream of abandoning her cousin. But how would they all live?

All the more reason, then, for Isadora to pursue her own schemes.

'But you cannot afford to keep us, Cousin Ellen,' Fanny pointed out, as if she had read Isadora's mind. 'For my part, I think you should write to Lord Roborough and tell him the true situation.'

'Mr Thornbury told him the true situation,' Isadora said, taking a seat by her mother. 'He even wrote to warn him months ago, before he wrote that Papa had died, for we all knew very well Papa would not recover.'

Mrs Alvescot nodded vehemently, setting aquiver the frill of her pretty mob cap, the only touch of white in the otherwise strict severity of her mourning costume. 'Now that is true, for Aubrey instructed Thornbury to do so because the connection is so remote. Dear Aubrey. He knew so well what a toll his illness had taken on our finances. It distressed him particularly that you, Dora, could not have your season.'

'Oh, fudge, as if I cared for that.'

A season was just what Isadora did not want. It would ruin all. She must not enter Society in that guise. But in any event nothing would have induced her to leave the house in such circumstances — what with her papa so ill and her mama so distressed. Her papa had wanted her to accept Lady Witheridge's invitation to her to come out with Harriet in London last year, but she had resolutely refused.

'But Aubrey told me I had nothing to concern myself about,' went on Mrs Alvescot cheerfully. 'He was certain Lord Roborough would come to our rescue.'

'If he doesn't, we shall have nothing to look forward to but penury and disaster,' prophesied Fanny gloomily.

'Well, you had better steel yourself to them, then,' said Isadora frankly, 'for I have no expectation of his coming to our rescue.'

'But, my love, your papa said it was his duty to do so,' protested Mrs Alvescot.

'I quite agree,' said Matilda.

'Well, Papa had every reason to be sanguine,' Isadora offered, 'because he clearly knew nothing of this viscount.'

'Nor do you,' Fanny pointed out.

Isadora ignored this obvious truth. 'Besides, Lord Roborough probably sees no reason why he should rescue us, nor even why he should keep a fatherly eye on us, as you seem to think he must, Cousin Matty. He is only distantly related to us, after all. And Thornbury says he has children of his own to think of.'

'That is true, my love,' agreed Mrs Alvescot, 'but you forget that his note stated he clearly understood our predicament and that we need not move from the house.'

'*As yet*,' quoted Isadora, adding cynically, 'and that is all he said.'

'For my part, I am thanking God for this small relief,' said Matilda devoutly. 'Imagine if he had requested our instant removal. What in the world would we have done?'

'He may yet tell us to remove,' Fanny reminded her.

'No, no, Fanny,' argued Mrs Alvescot. 'Remember that he has a title. He has estates of his own — very substantial ones, I imagine — so what need can he have for this one?'

Isadora curled a sceptical lip. 'I have no wish to distress you, Mama, but I fear that a man who is so callous he cannot even write a letter of sympathy is not going to concern himself over whether he needs another estate.'

Fanny gazed at her with narrowed eyes. 'I see what it is, Dora. You don't wish him to rescue us at all. What you want is an excuse to take up acting in earnest.'

Matilda exclaimed in horror, but Isadora had no answer to make to this beyond a look cast at her young cousin that boded her no good at all. It was left to Mrs Alvescot to express the opinion of the family.

'Indeed, I have often thought what a pity it is that you might not tread the boards, as they say, Dora. I am sure you could have become quite as great a tragedienne as Mrs Siddons. Only it is quite ineligible, and I am sure Lord Roborough will not countenance such a thing for a moment.'

At this, Isadora jumped up and moved to the door, uttering dangerously, 'Will he not, indeed? Well, if he chooses to show his face here and tell me so, I shall be ready for him, believe me.' With which, she whisked herself out of the room. Arguing over whether the heir would do anything to help the family out of their predicament was one thing; being reminded he had the power to stop her pursuing her plans was quite another. Well, he might have that power. But not for long, for she was but a few months short of her majority.

Passing along the upper corridor, Isadora headed for the stairs, hoping she would not run into Rowland outside. She wanted to be alone. Hopefully, he would be in the stables, as usual, trying to persuade old Totteridge to allow him to ride Titian. Totteridge could be trusted to be steadfast in refusal. Rowland could never hold her papa's restive mount.

A pang smote her. Was it only a matter of six weeks? It felt like a lifetime.

Come, Isadora Alvescot, this will not do. She had promised her papa she would not grieve — not unduly. Death, he had insisted, would come as a merciful release. She must hold to that. In general, she could do so, plunging herself into her acting. Only, when Cousin Matty would insist on bringing up the question of their possibly having to leave home...

She pushed the thought away as she ran lightly down the long staircase that curved to the hall. That would not happen. Yet if she was wrong, if the viscount did turn them penniless from their home, then it was only a matter of time before she would be in a position to put the family back on its feet. For Fanny was right, infuriating though that was. Whether or not Lord Roborough came to the rescue of the family made no difference to Isadora. Not only did she wish to become an actress in earnest, she was going to become one. Not as Isadora Alvescot, of course. She would have to think of another name.

Fanny might have nosed her secret out, she thought, as she crossed the hall to the front door and let herself out of the house, but she did not think her cousin really believed she would do it, any more than did her mama or Cousin Matty. They had not seemed surprised to hear Fanny accuse her. No doubt the wretch had told them already. She had probably been listening at the keyhole when Isadora had been discussing the matter with Harriet.

She wondered, as she sped across the wide expanse of lawn to the gazebo that headed the start of the flowering gardens, if that was what had made Cousin Matty harp on and on about Lord Roborough.

But all thought of the Errant Heir left her as she reached the leafy bower that invariably formed the background to those performances she gave out of doors, and where, alone, she practised her speeches, peopling the lawn with an imaginary audience of vast proportions. She had headed here by instinct rather than design, knowing the best cure for the disturbing thoughts awakened by the discussion in the drawing-room was to devote herself to her art.

Disenchanted with Lady Jane after the fiasco upstairs, she chose instead to try out again that speech of Juliet's before she took the drug that was to make her appear dead in order to escape with Romeo. It was a section of the play that was still giving her a little trouble, and she meant to have the entire role of Juliet perfect for her launch on an unsuspecting public.

As always, no sooner did she throw out the lines, 'Farewell! God knows when we shall meet again', than she was lost in a world of her own. The uncertainty of Juliet grew into fear, the girl's imagination stirring at all the hideous possibilities that might ensue. 'What if it be a poison…?' With one hand, Isadora held an imaginary vial away from her at the full length of her arm, gazing upon her empty fingers as if she truly saw there this thing that might, while it promised happiness, deceive her into death.

As she began to enumerate the visions of waking in the tomb among the bones of her ancestors that filled Juliet's mind — 'Where bloody Tybalt, yet but green in earth, Lies festering in his shroud' — the horror of the image was reflected in her voice, which shook with fear as her breath came short and fast.

Her voice grew in power with the further embroidery of Shakespeare's persuasive text, so that at the last she was almost shrieking out the plea. 'Stay, Tybalt, stay!' Her hand came close as she raised the imagined vial and cried out, 'Romeo, I come! This do I drink to thee.' With which, she thrust her fingers to her mouth, threw back her head, and swallowed. Her eyes closed, the invisible vial dropped from her fingers, and she began to sway.

But before she could fall, supposedly drugged, to the ground, an alien sound penetrated her absorption: a slow hand-clap that echoed in the still summer air.

Isadora blinked, opening her eyes. Bewildered, she looked about for the source. It was not difficult to find. Almost directly before her, although several feet away, stood a total stranger. He was some years her senior, strong-featured, and from his head to his heels strikingly attired in black.

CHAPTER TWO

Isadora gaped at the man stood before her. His hands rested together as they ceased to clap. 'Bravo!' he said. 'I have seldom seen a more startling demonstration of grief.'

Isadora was shocked out of her bewilderment into instant reaction. Grief? What was he thinking of? 'It is not grief Juliet is feeling,' she said unthinkingly. 'I should have thought even an idiot would recognise it as fear. One would suppose I had mistaken the entire speech. And I know I am a better actress than that.'

The stranger bowed slightly. 'Better, and considerably more mature than is called for in the part.'

Isadora bridled. 'I beg your pardon?'

He smiled. 'It was meant for a compliment. It takes a degree of maturity to enact the drama of Shakespeare, no matter the age of the character.'

'Well, that is certainly true,' Isadora agreed at once. 'Fanny is just the right age. Fourteen, you must know. But I cannot imagine anything less dramatic than the way —' She broke off, suddenly struck by the oddity of this conversation. One did not talk like this to strangers. And where had he sprung from? He had appeared out of nowhere. Who in the world was he?

Glancing round at the empty lawns about her, she realised to the full the peculiarity of his being here at all. She frowned. Perhaps he was only part of her imaginary audience. She put out a tentative hand. 'I suppose you are real?'

The stranger laughed. A solid, reassuring laugh. At least he did exist. Lifting a hand, he swept off his black beaver hat, and the sun burnished on auburn hair cut fashionably short and arranged in a deliberately disordered style. The sudden brightness to his face softened the strong features — or was it the smile? — and Isadora was conscious of a tug somewhere in the region of her chest that she did not recognise.

Involuntarily she smiled back as he came towards her and took her hand. He was taller than most males of her acquaintance and she had to look up at him. A novel — and disconcerting — experience.

'I am real enough,' he said, and she became aware of light eyes that crinkled at the corners with warmth. 'Enough, that is, to appreciate your very considerable talent. I beg your pardon if I startled you, however. I simply could not help expressing my very favourable response.'

Inexplicably breathless all at once — why she could not have said, unless it was that such frankly expressed praise did not often come her way — Isadora gave a somewhat self-conscious laugh. 'Th-thank you,' she managed. 'You are very good, sir.'

'No, you are very good,' he countered. Then he replaced his hat and leaned back a little. 'I must confess, though, that I think you overplayed the climax a trifle.'

Isadora's feeling of cordiality faded and her tone became frosty. 'Oh, indeed?'

'All that rhetoric about "loathsome smells" and —'

'And shrieks like mandrakes torn out of the earth,' quoted Isadora in a metallic sort of voice. 'Yes, what about it?'

'Well, what about it?' said the stranger, frowning. 'The imagery is enough by itself, I would have thought. There can be no need for you to reinforce it in that shrieking tone you chose to adopt. Rather more the *Macbeth* witches than Juliet, don't you think?'

'No, I do not,' Isadora snapped. Witches indeed! How dared he? Immediately after paying her that compliment too. It was like a douche of cold water. Forgetting the difficulties she had been experiencing with this very part of the speech, she demanded crossly, 'Who are you to tell me how to act? And just what do you know about the matter?'

'Not much,' he responded quite mildly. 'But this I do know: you will never make much of an actress if you are not prepared to listen to constructive criticism.'

'Constructive? You said I sounded like a witch!'

'Only in the climax. I cannot fault the rest of the speech.'

'You astonish me,' retorted Isadora. 'Let me tell you that I don't give a fig for your opinion, favourable or otherwise.'

Infuriatingly, he grinned at her. 'How should you when you profess not to know who I am?'

'Profess? I don't know.' Great heavens, but she would hit the wretch in a moment! 'Who are you? Tell me at once. And while you are about it you may also explain why you are lurking about our grounds, and why you crept up on me only to make impertinent comments about my acting.'

Instead of complying, the gentleman merely tutted in a mock-reproving way.

Isadora glared at him. 'Stop that!'

He raised his brows. 'My dear girl, I am simply expressing my disappointment that you find my comments on your acting impertinent. I thought I had made it clear how much I approved of your performance. In fact, that is why I am here. I was wandering around the gardens and, hearing you begin, was irresistibly drawn to listen.'

Isadora tried not to be mollified. But that was very difficult when those crinkling eyes invited her to be so. And his comments were so acceptable. She pulled herself together. This would not do. An explanation was still wanting. 'But why were you wandering around the gardens? And you still have not told me who you are.'

'I would have thought that was obvious. I guessed your identity at a glance.'

'Did you indeed? How extremely clever of you, when I am in *my* garden.'

'And you are dressed in mourning,' he agreed, ignoring the point of her remark. 'Added to the fact that there is only one young lady in residence.'

'That is where you are mistaken,' announced Isadora triumphantly, 'for there is also my cousin —'

'The Dotterell girl?' he queried, breaking in. 'But she is not, I understand, of an age to concern me just yet.'

Isadora frowned at him, puzzlement creeping in under the annoyance she still felt. 'Concern you? How in the world —?' She broke off, staring at him blankly. He knew about Fanny? Why should it concern him? No! But… No, he couldn't be.

The stranger grinned again. 'I see you have guessed it.'

'You can't be…' Isadora said in a dazed way. 'It isn't true.'

'I'm afraid it is, though,' he said, and bowed. 'I am Roborough, ma'am. And you are Miss Alvescot.'

Isadora was incapable of speech. Roborough? The viscount? Impossible. This was he? No, no. She was asleep, dreaming. A nightmare! How could he be Roborough? The viscount was — well, not this kind of a man.

'I see the news comes as something of a surprise to you,' he said in an apologetic tone.

'Surprise…?' repeated Isadora vaguely. She drew a breath, trying for coherence. 'No, indeed, it is not surprise.' She flung up her hands to her head suddenly, blurting out, 'I am utterly bewildered!' Her hands dropped. 'You are truly the viscount? Lord Roborough?'

The gentleman nodded, saying lightly, 'I am desolated to be obliged to reiterate it, since it obviously troubles you so much, but yes, Lord Roborough.'

Isadora gazed at him in a good deal of consternation. What had she done? What had she been saying to the man? And she had promised her mama she would do nothing to ruin the family's chances. She ought to apologise. Placate him. Only it went so much against the grain she did not know how she could even begin to form the necessary words. Great heavens, how was she to know? It had not been her fault. He was to blame, not she. What did he mean by creeping around incognito in that way?

A soft laugh interrupted her thoughts, and his face came back into focus. Isadora frowned at the amusement in it. 'What in the world is so funny?'

'Have you any idea how much of what is passing in your mind is mirrored in your countenance?'

'Yes! It is the mark of an actress.'

'A natural actress, yes. Believe me, you are far more effective when you are natural. You should cultivate the trick of it in your playing.'

All desire to placate this man vanished instantly. Isadora's chin came up. 'Are you at that again? I should like to know where you come by your expertise, my lord. I suppose you must have seen dozens of better actresses in order to be able to offer me the benefit of your no doubt excellent advice.'

'Sarcasm doesn't suit you, Miss Alvescot,' said Roborough, his tone mild. 'But yes, I have seen many actresses. None, however, as good as you. Except perhaps Mrs Siddons.'

The matter-of-fact way in which he made the statement lent it a sincerity that laid Isadora's ruffled feathers. He really meant it. And he probably had seen dozens of actresses. Softening, she was about to speak and thank him prettily. But his lordship was not finished.

'It is a pity,' he added, 'that you will never display your talents further afield than your own garden.'

The feathers fluffed up again, and Isadora opened her mouth to challenge this opinion in no uncertain terms. But wait. It would not do to blurt out her plans to him. She must be discreet. Particularly when she did not know what he intended. Let him believe her docile for the moment.

Suppressing with some difficulty the hot words that had risen to her tongue, she turned towards the house. 'I had better take you in and present you to Mama and the others.'

Roborough seemed tacitly to accept the change of subject. He fell in beside her. 'I only hope they don't suffer from as great a shock as you evidently did.'

Isadora glanced up at him. 'Well, I was not expecting you to be —' She halted all at once, realising just what it was that she had not expected. What a fool she was not to have questioned it before. 'You cannot be Lord Roborough.'

He stopped and turned, raising his brows. 'Why can I not?'

'You are not old enough.' Which was true. He was scarcely a boy, for his countenance had the stamp of maturity and his figure was too athletically moulded, but he could not be more than thirty, and he did not behave like a family man. And that was not all. 'Besides,' she added, running her eyes down the fashionable cut of his black cloth frock-coat and breeches, with their accompanying black waistcoat and cravat, 'you are in mourning.'

'Like you,' he agreed. 'Did not Thornbury tell you?'

'He told us only what you wrote in that stupid note,' Isadora said, quite forgetting her vow not to spoil her mama's chances.

'Was it stupid? I dare say it was, for I know I was distracted when I wrote it.'

'Distracted?'

'Extremely so. I had only just come into the title —'

'Good heavens! Then you are not —'

'I am not the Lord Roborough you were expecting, obviously.' He gave a shrug of resignation. 'Of course, I had forgotten. Thornbury told me I had not mentioned it in the letter I wrote. The case is, Miss Alvescot, my father died but a week or two after your own.'

Isadora stared at him as enlightenment dawned. 'Then he did not even receive Mr Thornbury's first letter?'

'If he did, he was not in any condition to acknowledge it. By the time I received what must have been the second letter, I am afraid everything was at sixes and sevens and I simply had no time to deal with it properly. So —'

'This is terrible,' Isadora broke in, quite appalled. 'You have no idea of the truly shocking things we have been saying about you. We thought how very uncivil of you it was, you see, not even to write a letter of sympathy to Mama. Particularly when you had known all along that Papa was not going to recover. At least, your father must have done so, for Thornbury wrote to him at Papa's bidding, and —'

'That will do,' said Roborough firmly, catching at her unquiet hands and holding them strongly. He smiled. 'Miss Alvescot, I much preferred it when you were railing at me. Pray don't spoil your effect by this effusive apology.' He paused, releasing her hands as Isadora eyed him uncertainly. 'I suppose it is an apology, of a sort?'

She had to laugh. 'Lord Roborough, you are quite abominable. You must know very well that it would positively choke me to be obliged to apologise to you.'

He grinned. 'Yes, I rather gathered that. But don't address me so formally, I beg of you. Roborough will do. We are in some sort related, are we not?'

'Distantly,' Isadora said, eyeing him warily now.

His brows went up. 'Why are you looking at me as if I were a coiled snake? Do you dislike the relationship?'

Isadora drew herself up. 'That depends upon how much you intend to encroach upon it. I may as well tell you at once that I do not consider myself to be under your jurisdiction.'

Roborough looked amused. 'Why should you?'

'Well, Cousin Matty insists that as head of the family you have all sorts of powers over us all,' Isadora said in a goaded voice, 'and everyone else seems to think you may order our lives as you see fit.'

'Whereas you do not?'

'No, I do not.'

'I wonder why I am not at all surprised to hear that?' he said musingly. 'Let us hope I am not obliged to order you to do anything at all.'

Isadora hardly knew what to make of this. It seemed as if her fears were unfounded. She must revise all her ideas about him, all because he was himself and not his father. The hint of amusement that seemed constantly to underlie his words was encouraging. He seemed pleasant enough. Yet he had given nothing away of his intentions. Perhaps he might?

'Lord Roborough,' she said impulsively, turning once more towards the house.

'Miss Alvescot?' he responded, again falling into step beside her.

'What do you —? Have you decided —? Oh, great heavens, I shall just have to say it. What *are* you intending to do?'

'At this present, Miss Alvescot,' he answered seriously, 'I have no very precise idea. That must depend upon circumstance.'

She glanced at him. 'You will not turn us out, then?'

Roborough halted abruptly, moving to face her again.

Isadora, pausing herself, saw the light eyes flash.

'Turn you out?' he repeated in accents of disbelief. 'Is that what you supposed I should do?'

Isadora was conscious of a measure of discomfort, but she did her best to ignore it, doggedly pursuing the question. 'Well, you only said we need not think of removing *as yet*,' she said, laying emphasis on the words she had filled with so much hidden meaning, 'and seeing how little interested you appeared to be in our predicament —'

'You naturally wrote me off as a monstrously callous individual, with no thought for anyone but himself,' he finished, in a tone clipped with bitterness.

Isadora, remembering how she had used the very word *callous* only today when speaking of him, at once rose up on her high ropes to conceal her instant guilt. 'How in the world was I to know what sort of man you were? I went on the evidence to hand. It is not my fault you were mistaken for your father.'

It seemed to Isadora, from the way Roborough compressed his lips, that he was biting down on a sharp retort. She braced herself for battle. But instead of the rebuking words she was expecting he turned towards the house and started off again.

'We had better go in,' he said coolly. 'I imagine Thornbury will by now have apprised your mama of my arrival.'

'Mr Thornbury is with you?' asked Isadora, diverted.

'Certainly. In fact, we rode here in his gig. I did not wish to burst in on you all unannounced.'

He might never have expressed himself in that earlier bitter tone, Isadora thought. He was calmness itself. Oddly, it annoyed her, but she thrust the feeling down. She ought to be grateful he had not chosen to take his umbrage further. The desire to goad him was almost overwhelming, but she fought it valiantly. For her mama's sake, she must not antagonise him.

'That is why I was wandering in your grounds,' he offered, flicking a glance at her.

'*Your* grounds, you mean,' said Isadora before she could stop herself. She saw his eyes narrow and at once exclaimed crossly, 'Oh, you are nothing but a shrew, Isadora Alvescot!' She added, contrite, 'I beg your pardon, sir. I promise you I did mean not to say one word out of the way.'

But Roborough was laughing. 'Never mind it. I dare say I shall become accustomed.'

They had arrived by this time at the steps leading up to the front door of the house. He paused a moment and his gaze ran over her features.

'Isadora,' he said, savouring the name on his tongue. 'An enchanting name. It suits you.'

A rush of air to her chest quite startled Isadora. That odd breathlessness attacked her once more. It was almost as if she could feel her own pulse beating, far too fast. Fortunately she was not required to say anything, for Roborough spoke again.

'We are two families in mourning, Miss Alvescot. I cannot think anything much will be settled before the necessary period of inactivity is over. Will you lead the way?'

You would not have supposed, Isadora thought crossly, anyone had ever thought of the Errant Heir as anything but charming. Not that one could accuse him of behaving towards her mama with the easy style he had adopted towards herself. He was treating Mrs Alvescot with all the proper deference and gentleness due to an inconsolable widow. Overly so, in Isadora's opinion.

'I would not for the world have distressed you by an ill-timed visit, Mrs Alvescot, but, Thornbury having assured me you would receive me without ceremony, I ventured to allow him to bring me here without prior notice. I hope you do not mind?'

'Oh, dear me, no,' fluttered Mrs Alvescot, pressing a hand to her bombazine-covered bosom. 'I am only too happy — that is — it is not for me to object. And we have been waiting for you forever.' Her colour rushed up and she threw out anxious hands. 'Oh dear, I did not mean that — and it is not you we have been expecting. Except that we did not know it. But Thornbury —'

Here the lawyer, a sensible family man approaching his middle years, intervened. 'I have been advising Mrs Alvescot of the error, my lord.' Turning to the lady, he prompted, 'His lordship's chaise, ma'am, is following us. I did suggest to his lordship that I believed there would be no difficulty about his putting up here at Pusay, but he insisted —'

'I insisted,' interrupted Roborough with what Isadora felt to be an unnecessarily ingratiating smile, 'that this must depend upon your wishes, ma'am, and if there is the slightest objection to my doing so I beg you will not put yourself out. I can very well stay at an inn.'

'An inn?' chimed in Matilda, who had been gazing at Roborough in a state of semi-stupefaction almost since the moment of his entry. 'I should think not indeed. What, with a house this size at your disposal? And your own establishment at that.'

'That is very true,' said Mrs Alvescot in her usual fashion, nodding vehemently as she looked up at the unexpected features above her. 'We could not think of you staying anywhere but here. Indeed, I had better show you about the place so you may choose where you would prefer to sleep.'

'I would very much like to see around the house, ma'am, at some convenient time,' said Roborough, putting out a hand to stop her as she came anxiously to her feet, 'but there is no question of my choosing a chamber. You will, if you please, continue to treat the place as your own. I am merely your guest — for the moment.'

Aha! Isadora caught at the caveat even as her mama and Cousin Matty fell over each other's words in their expressions of relief and thanks for this generous concession. There was an ominous ring in that *for the moment*. Just as there had been in the simple phrase *as yet*. For all his soothing outward manner, Roborough had plans of his own.

It had not taken long for the introductions to be performed, Thornbury having already prepared the ground. It was evident he had carefully primed Roborough, for the Errant Heir had astonished Fanny and Rowland — the latter having been hastily sent for to the drawing-room — in greeting them by name. They had since sat — looking, to Isadora's critical eyes, unbelievably angelic — side by side and silent, on a sofa next to Matilda, simply drinking Roborough in. If he had deliberately set out to captivate the family, he was certainly succeeding.

Except, Isadora decided, for herself. Until she knew what he intended to do with them all, she would reserve judgement.

But one thing she knew already. Roborough was a man of decided opinions, and if his conduct in the gardens was anything to go by he was unlikely to be swayed by anyone else, least of all her dear but docile mama, no matter how much he pretended to defer his preferences to her judgement. Toady how he might, Isadora was not deceived.

She was, however, curious. Just as curious as her cousins, it turned out. For no sooner had the door shut behind Lord Roborough and Mrs Alvescot — for nothing would do for the lady of the house but to show him to the best spare bedchamber immediately — than they turned, as one, to Mr Thornbury, who had risen to leave, their tongues loosening on the instant.

'How old is he?' demanded Fanny, getting in first.

'He looks a first-rate sportsman,' said Rowland, hard on the heels of his sister. 'Does he box with Mendoza?'

'He is a man of fashion, one can see that,' came admiringly from Matilda. 'Does he have a house in town?'

'Is he married?' asked Fanny eagerly.

'He must be, he's a viscount,' said Rowland scornfully.

'What has that to say to anything?' Isadora put in, despising herself for showing any interest at all in the matter.

'Dora's in the right of it,' conceded Fanny. 'Though I dare say he is married. The eligible ones always are.' She turned eagerly to the lawyer. 'Is he married, Mr Thornbury?'

'What does it matter?' exclaimed Isadora impatiently, making up for her previous error.

'It does,' came anxiously from Matilda, 'for if he is, his commitments will be heavier, and there will be less room for us.'

'Pooh!' scoffed Rowland. 'I don't think he means to abandon us. He's too much the gentleman.'

'What, merely because he has an air of fashion?' Isadora put in. 'That means nothing at all.'

'Very true, Dora,' Matilda said, for once in agreement with her cousin, 'but he has shown himself to be both thoughtful and considerate.'

'Mr Thornbury,' said Fanny despairingly, jumping up from the sofa. 'You say nothing. Tell us about him, pray.'

'Patience, I beg of you,' said Thornbury, laughing and throwing up his hands.

'Yes, but surely —' began Matilda.

'Mrs Dotterell,' he said firmly, 'there is very little use in your asking me all these questions. I assure you I know little more than you do, least of all what his lordship intends.'

'Yes, but you must know how old he is,' insisted Fanny. 'Or whether he is married.'

'How should he know?' put in Isadora scornfully. 'I don't suppose Mr Thornbury wasted time asking Lord Roborough such unimportant questions.'

'And most impertinent ones on my part,' Thornbury added severely. 'You may believe, Miss Fanny, that I confined myself to unravelling the odd circumstance of our mistaking his lordship's identity, and in answering his questions.'

'I knew it,' exclaimed Isadora. 'He discovered all our names in advance just so that he might appear in an agreeable light.'

'Oh, that must be nonsense, Dora,' said Matilda irritably. 'He is a most pleasant man — thank heaven!'

'And terribly good-looking,' added Fanny, glancing slyly at Isadora. 'Don't you think so, Dora?'

Isadora declined to answer this. She had just remembered Roborough had evidently not known her own name before she had mentioned it herself, and she was looking frowningly at Thornbury. 'What did he ask about us?'

The other three were too eager to hear the answer to this to interrupt the lawyer with further questions.

'Only what might have been expected,' Thornbury answered.

'Well, what was that?' demanded Isadora, adding impatiently, 'Do sit down again, Mr Thornbury. You cannot suppose they are going to let you go before their curiosity is satisfied.'

Thornbury smiled. 'Their curiosity?'

'Well, I don't care what he asked. I learned everything I ever want to know about the viscount when we met in the gardens.'

'Why, what did he say to you?' asked Fanny eagerly.

'Never you mind,' Isadora responded darkly.

'I'll wager it was Dora who did the talking,' guessed Rowland, grinning.

'For heaven's sake,' said Matilda on a querulous note. 'For my part, I am more concerned with what Mr Thornbury can tell us.' She turned to the lawyer again. 'It pains me to trouble you, sir, but I am so anxious.'

With obvious reluctance, Thornbury resumed the seat he had been occupying on the sofa until Roborough and Mrs Alvescot left the room. He sighed at the expectant faces all about him. 'There really is very little to tell. Lord Roborough had not assimilated the contents of my letter, beyond the fact the family were situated in extremely difficult circumstances. His enquiries were in the main connected with the details, which you all know, and the number of persons with whom he must concern himself.'

'He wanted to know how old we all were, I dare say,' Isadora put in shrewdly, recalling what Roborough had said about not having to concern himself with Fanny as yet.

'That, yes,' agreed Thornbury, casting her a glance of surprise. 'It is relevant, in the light of any future arrangements he may choose to make.'

'Arrangements?' echoed Isadora suspiciously. 'What sort of arrangements?'

Thornbury shrugged. 'I have no idea, Miss Alvescot.'

'You mean he has forbidden you to speak of them,' guessed Isadora.

Thornbury coughed. 'Not precisely. Although naturally I would be obliged to respect his lordship's wishes if he had done so.'

'Great heavens, one would think the matter was no concern of ours at all!'

'I think his lordship is aware of how very much it is your concern,' Thornbury said in a reproving tone. 'But the truth is, he has not confided in me with regard to any plans he may have.'

'But you spoke of arrangements?' Matilda ventured.

'I was speaking only as one who understands what question must arise in his lordship's mind.'

'What question is that?' pursued Matilda.

'Yes, we aren't lawyers,' stated Fanny practically.

'Fanny, you shouldn't be so brassy,' butted in Rowland suddenly. 'I dare say Mr Thornbury will refuse to tell us anything if you talk like that.'

Fanny looked daggers at her brother, and then turned sweetly to the lawyer, saying unctuously, 'I beg your pardon, Mr Thornbury.'

'So I should hope,' said Matilda severely. 'Now hold your tongue, do, Fanny. You were saying, Mr Thornbury?'

The lawyer raised his eyebrows. 'Was I?'

'Arrangements,' Isadora prompted.

'Ah yes. What I meant was that, should Lord Roborough choose to take responsibility for the family — and from his discourse I will say at least I have every expectation that he will — he can only gauge the likely form and expense of this if he knows the ages of the parties concerned.'

Matilda was gazing at him with painful enquiry. 'You think, then, that he will include us?'

Thornbury gave her a reassuring smile. 'It certainly did not seem to me that his lordship gave any indication he would do otherwise. But,' he added carefully as the Dotterells brightened, 'that can only be my guess. I do not know the viscount and he will have to speak for himself.'

'Which he will, mark my words,' said Isadora with a kindling eye. 'He is nothing if not outspoken.'

Matilda was visibly relieved. 'For my part, he may say anything he chooses, as long as he provides for me and my poor fatherless children.'

Isadora got up abruptly. 'He shall do so, Cousin Matty. For if he refuses I promise you I shall have a great deal to say about it. He will not withstand my demands.'

'Oh no,' groaned Fanny. 'If you are to speak for us, Dora, we may as well abandon hope immediately.'

Rowland burst into rude laughter at this, but Matilda paid no attention, being fully taken up with the need, as she evidently believed, to bring Isadora to her senses.

'Dora, pray don't take your usual manner with Lord Roborough. You will only alienate him, and then where shall we be?'

'I will do nothing of the kind,' snapped Isadora, incensed. 'Besides, I have already quarrelled with the wretch — but that was before I knew who he was. But if you suppose I have any intention of kowtowing to him as you and Mama have done, you may think again. I have already told him he has no authority over me, and —'

'You did what?' burst out Fanny.

'Oh, Dora, how could you?' moaned Matilda.

'*And*,' continued Isadora pointedly, 'he did not appear to mind my saying it in the least. In fact, I was quite in charity with him. So you may make yourself easy.'

'I am not in the least easy,' stated Matilda in a tone of foreboding. 'I have the most dreadful presentiments already.'

'With Dora on the loose, Mama,' chimed in Fanny matter-of-factly, 'you could not help but do so. Depend upon it, she will ruin all our chances.'

Isadora slammed out of the room. Really, if the family wanted her to remain in charity with Roborough, they were going quite the wrong way to work. She could see how it would be. Nothing but flattery and sycophancy from morning to night. Well, she was not going to behave in that nauseous fashion. She would rather die. Ruin all their chances, indeed. Fudge! As if Roborough — little though she knew him, this much was obvious — would be taken in by any expression of docility on her part. Had he not himself said he liked it better when she railed at him? Well, if he chose not to assist the Dotterells, rail at him she would, with a vengeance.

But, to say truth, she did not really think he was going to refuse to help them. She remembered the bitter anger that had slipped from his control when she had merely suggested he might turn them out. Did not that argue for a favourable outcome? And Thornbury believed he would take responsibility for the whole family, did he not?

Excellent, let him do so. Then she might take to the boards with a clear conscience. In this, of course, she must be circumspect. If he had not expressed the idea that it was a pity she would not act out of her own environment, Isadora might almost have been tempted to confide in him. For he had thought her acting worthwhile. Her heart warmed unexpectedly at the remembrance of the compliments he had paid her. But, she reminded herself, approving of her acting was a far cry from allowing her to take it up professionally.

Ladies of her class simply did not do that, which was why she had not wanted to appear in Society. No one need know she had ever been Isadora Alvescot. As long as no connection was made, no breath of scandal would redound upon her family. In truth, this was why she needed Roborough to take care of them all.

It was one thing to put herself in that situation — from which there would be no going back, for once known as a famous and, she hoped, splendid tragedienne she could kiss goodbye to her former identity forever — but quite another to drag her unwilling family along with her into exile from polite society. For that was what it would mean. She had never pretended otherwise. She was neither as cruel nor as selfish as that, whatever Fanny thought.

No, if she was to accomplish her plans, Roborough's role must be to take on the family, in whatever fashion he deemed most suitable. The only difficulty would be in finding the way to her own destiny before Roborough chose one for her.

The thought froze her on the short stairway in the path she had taken towards her bedchamber — for it was almost time to change into her habit for her accustomed early evening ride

— which lay in the additional side-wing that had been built on to the old house in her papa's young days.

Would Roborough acquiesce in her plans? No, he would not. Oh, fudge, she must think!

No solution had yet occurred to her as she went off down the back way towards the stables, to find her horse already saddled and waiting. The cooling air was refreshing as she cantered down the bridle-path, her Juliet neck and neck with her papa's Titian, ridden by the hardy old groom Totteridge, and the anxiety that had been building up began to wane.

The horses slowed as the woods thinned out, and they turned to take the scenic route back to the estate. She and her papa had always called it that, she recalled with one of those unexpected pangs. It was near two years since her papa had been able to ride it with her. At first, it had been merely that he had not been well enough to ride, and Totteridge had been detailed to accompany Isadora in his stead, both to exercise the stallion and to keep her safe. Later, there had been no question of him riding ever again.

Tears pricked at Isadora's eyes as she automatically guided Juliet to pick her way through the brambled edge of the fields that bordered their home ground. The familiar view across the estate blurred, and she reined in her mount at the top of the hill. Through a haze she saw the Jacobean house squatting in the unrolling valley, below the clusters of interrupting trees dotted here and there, a two-storeyed, low-lying bulk, the single wing snaking out the side, ivy encroaching up the walls.

A tear sneaked over her lashes as she remembered her papa's laughing words: 'Such an ugly building. I cannot imagine what possessed my great-grandfather to employ such a poor architect.'

Ugly, yes, but it was *home*. Somehow, its very ugliness, its lack of line and form, seemed all of a piece with the spirit of the inhabitants within. There was no order to their lives, no beauty of shape or design, although the servants managed to keep the shut saloon downstairs in some semblance of tidiness. All was chaos and comfort. And, to say truth, the arrangement of the rooms inside the house only added to the sense of disarray.

From the big drawing-room at the front, which benefited from the many windows, one might penetrate at either end into smaller rooms. One of these had been her papa's sitting-room in the first throes of his illness, when he had not been confined to bed, and was now given over to the sole use of her mama who was wont to doze there in the afternoon. The other had ever been Cousin Matty's sitting-room, in use most of the time as a playroom for her two children.

All the other rooms — bedchambers, most of them, except for the informal family dining parlour — were of the oddest shapes and sizes, and could be entered by only one door from the central corridor. Downstairs, as well as the one good saloon, was the library, the formal dining-room, a couple of musty parlours and the range of domestic offices in use by the servants. The wing comprised the bedrooms of the younger members of the family, and housed those privileged servants who were not obliged to sleep in the attics.

The groom's gruff voice interrupted her mental wander through the house. 'Hadn't ye better stop your dreaming, Miss Dora? We'll be late.'

Isadora blinked hastily and looked round at Totteridge. 'I was thinking of Papa.'

'Oh, aye?' uttered the man sceptically. 'I guessed you was thinking of yon lord, come to tak' the place over.'

'I am not thinking of him at all,' stated Isadora crossly. 'At least, I wasn't. Now you have made me do so, and I had as lief not.'

'Aye,' agreed Totteridge feelingly, 'Especially if you're goin' to stamp about in one o' your tantrums, Miss Dora.'

'I do not have tantrums,' objected Isadora, urging her mount onward and heading down the hill alongside the groom.

'Oh, aye? And I don't have no horses to look after neither.'

Isadora ignored this heavy sarcasm, reflecting that at least Totteridge had succeeded in diverting her out of those dangerous memories. She wondered if that had been his intention. Ever faithful, he rode with her whenever she wished, night and morning, when either Rowland or Fanny on the pony did not accompany her instead. The elder ladies never ventured out on horseback, but would instead take the air in the only unsold open carriage.

It was not so odd, she supposed, that she should be thinking of all this now, on the brink of change. She had never thought much about home and the life they all led. Not until now, when everything she knew might be snatched away from her. It was not the same as if she had married, or indeed if she had left to become an actress. They were choices. It was a very different thing to have the place torn from her by an outsider.

Unconsciously, she put spurs to Juliet's side, and the mare increased her pace to a canter. It was as well they had already negotiated the steepest part of the hill. They crossed the greensward that ran past the orchard at the same speed, and then Totteridge called out to her as the wall surrounding the back gardens loomed up.

'Don't ye put her at that fence, Miss Dora! Hold hard and I'll ope' the gate.'

Isadora reined in to wait for the gate to be opened wide. Then she trotted Juliet through and on to the stables. Totteridge dismounted and gave Titian into the charge of an under groom, and was just assisting his mistress to alight when voices caught her attention.

She turned from the horse in time to see the entire family coming around the corner of the house towards the stable-block. With them was Roborough.

'Oh, here's Dora,' exclaimed Rowland. 'I told you she would be out riding, Cousin Ellen.'

Mrs Alvescot threw out her hands. 'Dora, my love, what a pity you were not with us. Here we have all been, showing Lord Roborough over his new property.'

Something clutched within Isadora's heart. Her eyes darkened as they went to Roborough's face. How could they? How could he? Her voice shook. 'Already? You don't waste much time, do you?'

CHAPTER THREE

Roborough met the reproach in Isadora's brown eyes and inwardly cursed. He might have known it. Very well to allow the rest of the family's persuasions to prevail, but he should have anticipated this.

For it had not been his choice to set off immediately on an inspection of the place. How indelicate of him it would be to demand it almost upon his arrival, as if he could not wait to take possession. Particularly after the length of time he had taken to come here at all.

Not that he could have avoided the delay. Indeed, if it had not become imperative that he look over the possibilities at Pusay, he doubted whether he would have been able to find the time to come here even now. But the Pusay residents had not given him any choice. He did not know if he was glad or otherwise when they stated this fact in no uncertain terms.

'It wasn't his fault,' protested Rowland.

'We decided to take him about,' said Fanny, adding in a superior tone, 'and you might have guessed it, Dora, if you weren't so ready to take offence.'

'You ought to apologise at once, Dora,' proposed Matilda severely.

'Good God, no,' interrupted Roborough involuntarily. 'Don't ask her to do that, for pity's sake!' He saw, as he spoke, that Isadora's eyes had softened. A muscle twitched in her cheek. Was she trying to keep from laughing? He had spoken unintentionally, but it seemed as if it might have served a useful purpose.

'Matty, pray don't enrage her,' he heard Mrs Alvescot begging of her cousin in an undertone. Aloud to her daughter she said, 'Dora, you know the stables better than any of us. Why do not you show Lord Roborough the horses?'

'Pooh!' broke in Rowland. 'As if she would. I'll show him the stables.' As he spoke he ran into the entrance to the block, calling back to Roborough, 'Come on, sir. We've a few tidy good 'uns in here.'

Roborough hesitated, glancing across at Isadora. 'Won't you join us, Miss Alvescot?'

Isadora had swung from anger to remorse and back again, in so violent a fashion she had been unable to find speech. Then, just as anger threatened to get the upper hand, this infuriating man not only cast her to the brink of laughter, but overrode her cousin to invite her participation in the tour of the stables. Must he be so unfailingly pleasant? And must he smile at her in that irritatingly irresistible manner?

Within an ace of announcing that she had to go and change out of her cloth habit of dark blue, she relented. 'Very well.'

She heard her mother sigh and almost retracted. But Roborough was standing at the entrance to the stables, waiting, and Matilda was nodding encouragement. Fanny's sour pout decided her. She walked into the stables, to find Rowland ready and eager to discourse on Titian's manifold points as the under groom rubbed the horse down.

Roborough listened with only half an ear. He found himself thinking how well a riding habit became Isadora. The jacket, tight to the waist where the petticoats flared out, emphasised her curves as the black satin gown, with its high waist, so popular at this time, did not. Her height enhanced the costume too and her black locks, now coaxed to the side under a beaver hat, curled attractively over one shoulder.

Why in the name of all the gods was she still unwed? What was she — nineteen? Twenty? Not less. Perhaps more. No, she could not be more, for Thornbury had told him she had still not attained her majority.

Not that it mattered. Even were she more than one and twenty, he had still to provide for her somehow. As he must for them all, God knew how!

His thoughts ran on as Rowland continued his eulogy, Roborough interpolating a suitable word or two at convenient moments. But his mind was far from horses. He had been with this unfortunate family for less than an afternoon, yet already he was aware Thornbury's guarded comments had by no means given him a full picture.

Mrs Alvescot, now. A helpless creature, if ever he saw one. Anxious she might be, but it was plain she was used to someone else taking responsibility for her and it had not been at all difficult to allay any fears she had expressed.

Having shown him to his bedchamber, she had insisted on summoning Hampole, the butler — a frail and doddering individual who seemed only to add to the general helplessness of the Alvescot household — to warn him to expect Roborough's chaise, and to instruct his valet on arrival where to bring his lordship's accoutrements.

'Now I dare say you would like to see around the house,' she had said, glancing up and down the corridor in a vague way as if she sought enlightenment on a mammoth task. 'Oh dear, I wonder where Matty is. She is much better than I at this sort of thing.'

'I beg you will not inconvenience yourself, ma'am,' he had said immediately.

'Yes, but you will wish to know your way about at once, for it is your house. It is not true that you are just a guest, and perhaps if you take your place straight away we may all of us be more comfortable.' Her rounded countenance had gazed anxiously up at him. 'Or don't you think so?'

Roborough had smiled. 'My only wish is to see you comfortable, Mrs Alvescot.'

A great sigh had escaped the lady. 'There now; if I did not say to Dora over and over again that it must be so.' Then she lowered her voice a trifle, glancing over her shoulder as if she feared to be overheard. 'I must tell you, Lord Roborough, that, though it may make me more comfortable, I cannot answer for Dora. I only hope you will not take it amiss if she — if she...' Her voice had petered out, and she cast him a look imploring his understanding.

Roborough had concealed his amusement. It was easy to see who had the ordering of things here — not Mrs Alvescot but her strong-minded daughter. He leaned conspiratorially towards her. 'To tell you the truth, ma'am, I had already surmised Miss Alvescot does not view my coming with any very great enthusiasm.'

Mrs Alvescot sighed. 'Dear me, no. She is used, you see, to do very much as she chooses and she did not take at all kindly to Matty's suggestion you might take it into your head to—' Then she had broken off, evidently recognising that these intimacies were addressed to one who was little more than a stranger. 'But I must not run on so. Let us go at once to the drawing-room and engage Matty's good offices. She is a dear creature. Such a comfort to me.'

Roborough had begun to realise that *comfort* constituted the sum of Mrs Alvescot's ambition. He knew the type: so indolent, so easy-going that any undue exertion or call to tax their very limited brainpower became a strain upon them, yet so universally pleasant and easy to please they were invariably surrounded by loving families who did everything they could to encourage their laziness. Isadora, in every way opposite, must, he supposed, have taken after her father.

Although there was a resemblance in feature here. About the eyes, he thought. For Mrs Alvescot's brown orbs were set in the same wide hollow that characterised her daughter's vividly expressive eyes, topped by the same arched brow. Her hands, too, were given to gestures that found an echo in Isadora's own movements. And, for all her plumpness, Mrs Alvescot moved with a flow similar to that which added so much grace to her daughter's carriage.

He would not have noticed so much but for the fact of having watched Isadora performing her Juliet in the gardens. A rare opportunity. It was not often one had the chance to study a female unconscious of one's gaze. Although, he recalled with a quickening of interest, she had not laid on any arts to attract even when she had become conscious of his presence. A refreshing change.

And she did not do so now, he reflected, glancing again at her as she stroked the muzzle of her mare. Far from it. She was much too involved in talking of her horse, and, he noted in passing, of her father, for it seemed Mr Alvescot had chosen the animal.

Roborough could not tell if her joy in the beast or her patent admiration of her father's knowledge of horseflesh was uppermost. Mr Alvescot had evidently been a man beloved in his family circle. How different from his own case.

But this was no moment to be reminding himself of the horrors he had left behind. He had something of more importance to hand here, for the present. And an agreeable interlude it was proving to be, before the fell hand of fate moved inexorably on. Because Isadora Alvescot — a mercurial creature — had eased into warmth, and he wished, if he could, to sustain that.

'What do you call her?' he asked Isadora of the horse.

'Juliet,' she answered, and instantly laughed. 'Now you will say that you should have guessed it.'

'Had I thought about it, yes,' he agreed, smiling. 'But then I have only seen you do the one role. You might as easily have named her Lady Macbeth.'

'Oh, indeed?' said Isadora, firing up. 'Is that supposed to reflect upon my character?'

'Not unless you are driven to murder the unwelcome guest under your roof.'

Isadora let out a crow of laughter, her quick flare of anger dying down. 'Let me tell you, it will not be your fault if I don't. Murder you, I mean. You are quite the most abominable man I have ever met.'

'As I don't know what other men you have met, Miss Alvescot, I am unable to judge the worth of your estimate,' he retorted. 'You will notice I make no attempt to return the compliment.'

Isadora found herself smiling warmly at him, only half aware that Rowland watched the quick give and take of words in frowning puzzlement.

'That is because you are stronger than I,' she told Roborough, 'and you must know how unfair it would be to enrage me into engaging in hand-to-hand combat. But I can be fair, too. I will save you the trouble. I know I am abominable.'

'What an admission.'

'You are supposed to deny the charge, you know,' Isadora told him frowningly.

'You jest,' he said, brows raised. 'Nothing would induce me to do so.'

Isadora began to think that in Roborough she had met a foe to be reckoned with. She was quite unused to be spiked at her own game. No one in the family had either the wit or the will to challenge her thus. They moaned at her, nagged at her and called her unlovely names. But they could not engage in this sort of cut and thrust. She had to admit to a feeling of exhilaration.

It faded rapidly as she came out of the stables to find the rest of the family waiting. As she noticed her young cousin run up and whisper in Fanny's ear, she began to regret having allowed herself to become engaged in such banter with Roborough. Rowland would tell his sister. She would report to Cousin Matty and her mama, no doubt, that Dora had threatened to murder Roborough. Then she would be obliged to endure Cousin Matty's recriminations and her mama's lamentations.

Great heavens, why must they be so blind? Could they none of them see the man had something up his sleeve? She felt it, even had it not been obvious. If the family would but look, instead of fawning all over him, they would see it too.

She watched Roborough's face surreptitiously, taking little part in the noisy argument that accompanied the showing of the house to its new owner. She could not have been said to gain by it — no clue as to his intentions, certainly. That strong countenance, firm at the jaw for all the ready laughter, its lean lines animated enough, and the light eyes, alive with interest, nevertheless gave little away.

Roborough, had Isadora but known it, had as little idea as she of his intentions. As the tour continued, wending its way into the added wing, back through the kitchens and thus, room by room, up the stairs to the living area most frequented by the family, he brought his wayward attention to bear on his surroundings. They were extraordinarily apt for this family. Had he a choice, he would leave them living here as they always had done. But the estate, Thornbury had told him, could not sustain them. What was he going to do?

His preoccupation kept him silent, although he was aware of the argumentative voices of the family all about him as he walked.

He came to himself to find he was standing at his bedchamber door, down the hall from the big drawing-room, and all the members of the Pusay household — with the exception of Isadora, whose features were once more tight and closed against him, he noted — were gazing at him expectantly.

'We dine in an hour,' Matilda said helpfully.

'Dear me, yes,' fluttered Mrs Alvescot, reminded of her duty. 'You will wish to change. We will all do so now.' She looked hopefully at her cousin. 'Matty, is it the dining parlour upstairs, or —?'

'Yes, indeed, Ellen,' said Matilda at once. 'Lord Roborough will not wish for any formality. Not on this first day.'

Formality, Roborough thought, had long gone by the boards. Which was all to the good. Let it be more so. 'Indeed, no,' he said reassuringly, addressing himself to Mrs Alvescot. 'And I do wish you will drop the title. My given name is Titus, if you care to use it, but Roborough will do.'

'Titus?' repeated Fanny. 'What an odd name.'

'Be quiet, Fanny,' begged Matilda in a strangulated tone. 'You will not use it, be sure.'

'Perhaps we can call him Cousin, as we do you, Cousin Ellen,' suggested Rowland brightly.

'Yes, yes,' said Matilda hurriedly. 'Now that will do, both of you. Go away and leave Lord — I mean, Cousin Roborough — to his toilet.'

'Yes, I thank you,' agreed Roborough, his eyes crinkling with that innate warmth. 'I would not wish to make a performance of it. I do not have Isadora's talent.'

Matilda instantly scattered her offspring, and Mrs Alvescot hurried away, leaving only Isadora standing her ground. She was staring suspiciously at him. He eyed her, a hint of a question in one slightly raised brow. Now what was troubling her?

At length, he said resignedly, 'I see I have been relegated to a coiled snake again.'

'Why are you being so pleasant to everyone?' Isadora burst out.

So that was it. Well, he could counter that one. He allowed a slight frown to crease his brow. 'Do you think there is anything to be gained by being rude and offensive?'

Isadora flushed. 'Which is to say that I am offensive.'

'Strange to say,' he said mildly, 'I meant no such thing.'

Mollified, Isadora said grudgingly, 'I suppose I have been rude.'

'Very.' Then, not quite deliberately, he grinned. 'But not without provocation, I confess.'

She tried, but the bubbling laughter would not be contained. In spite of herself, Isadora warmed to him again, feeling her suspicions melting away. But not entirely. It could be he was just as he appeared. But she could not rid herself of the conviction there was about everything he did, everything he said — if not to her, to the rest of the family — a calculation, as if he meant to achieve something by it.

Roborough, aware of the changes in her thoughts because they were reflected by the expressions flitting across her face, wondered at her a little. That she did not trust him was certain. But she could not help herself enjoying this sort of bantering exchange — as he did himself, for God knew it came as a welcome diversion from the relentless gloom he had left behind him at Barton Stacey. Really, he did not know why he was making this effort with her. It did not matter what he decided. It was plain Isadora was going to be difficult.

'What are you going to do with us?' she asked on an almost plaintive note, almost echoing his line of thought. 'And pray don't fob me off with your *depending upon circumstance*. You have not come here without any plans, for all you may try to make the rest of them believe that.'

'Isadora…' he began, then, realising what he had said, added quickly, 'If you will permit me to call you so?'

'I don't care what you call me,' she said impatiently, 'if only you will tell me what I want to know.'

He grinned. 'That is a considerable concession, I hope you realise. I have a very fertile imagination — especially when it comes to name calling.'

'Don't try to turn the subject. I will not be put off so, Cousin Roborough, so do not think it.'

'I don't.'

Though he had hoped to divert her, the persistent little devil. What in the name of all the gods was he to answer? Scarcely the truth. Heaven help him if she learned what he had in mind. She must eventually, if it proved the way forward. But not now.

'Isadora,' he said in as non-committal a tone as he could summon to his aid, 'you are an intelligent female. Look at the thing from my point of view. I scarcely know the situation here. I have not seen the accounts. I have not been around the estates. I cannot possibly make any value judgements until I have some facts upon which to base them.'

It was not working. Isadora's eyes had narrowed and the enmity, which seemed to slide in and out of her in wayward fashion, was back. 'Fudge! You do not mean me to know, and that is the matter in a nutshell.'

He was silent. It was true. What could he say? For a moment Isadora held his eyes, a dangerous light in her own. Then she turned abruptly and walked off down the corridor towards the entrance to the wing.

Roborough watched her out of sight, beset by the oddest feeling of depression — an echo of that which he had been enduring at Barton Stacey. Was Pusay to become unbearable too? Shrugging off the threatening mood, he went into his allotted bedchamber and gave himself up into his valet's capable hands.

CHAPTER FOUR

'But what an extraordinary coincidence,' said Harriet Witheridge, amazed.

True to her promise, she had hunted Isadora out in the little end-parlour downstairs, a retreat to which she was prone to escape, either to practise her roles or when she did not want anyone to know where she was. Harriet was privy to this hiding place only by virtue of the fact that she had once, walking across from the squire's house, come upon Isadora entering by a side-door to the house which led directly into this room.

The only other person who knew of it was the elderly butler Hampole, who had discovered the young daughter of the house shivering in there one winter morning, and, without betraying her, had taken it upon himself ever since to order the fire made up for her. Today, however, Isadora had escaped not to work but to think furiously, so she would be ready with a counterplan the moment she learned what Roborough intended.

Not that she could have been said to have profited by it. Nothing had occurred to her. Instead she had found herself going over everything that had happened since his arrival, recalling the truly infuriating manner in which the family had taken him to their collective bosom.

Rowland and Fanny had rapidly passed from awe to downright devotion, as far as she could see. Roborough might have been their long-dead father! Cousin Matty apparently regarded him as some sort of hero. While as for Mama... Well, if she had not placed her future fair and square in Roborough's lap, then Isadora did not know her own parent. And Roborough himself was plainly amused by the whole thing. Yes, and very obviously amused — great heavens, how she was beginning to loathe the wretch! — by her own disgust at her family's voluntary subjugation. Amused, too, for all she could tell, by her stubborn determination not to swell the number of his Pusay conquests.

It was therefore with distinct relief that she greeted the arrival of her friend Harriet, and proceeded to regale her with every detail of the event that had turned their lives around in the Pusay house in the less than twenty-four hours since Harriet had left them yesterday.

'What is a coincidence?' demanded Isadora, picking up her friend's remark.

'That Lord Roborough should also have lost his father, thus giving rise to all your nonsensical speculations about the poor man.'

'He is not a *poor man*. Anything but, in fact. I have never met anyone more capable of holding his own. Nor of making himself agreeable. Why, the rest of them are positively berserk with admiration.'

'So why not you?' demanded Harriet, arranging her muslin skirts as she sat next to Isadora on the small sofa on which she was perched. 'What is he really like?'

Isadora's eyes kindled. 'He is abominable, if you must know. A teasing wretch. He chooses to joke with me, but I suspect it is only to bring me around like the others.'

'For goodness' sake, Dora,' exclaimed Harriet impatiently. 'I mean, what does he look like? Is he young? Is he handsome?'

'I will allow him to be attractive,' Isadora said grudgingly. 'But he is neither young nor handsome. At least, I dare say he is not above thirty. But he is not pretty like Edmund.' She paused a moment, and added almost as an afterthought, 'His eyes smile.'

'Dora, you do like him,' Harriet accused.

'Like him?' echoed Isadora, jumping up the better to face her friend. 'You must be mad, Harriet. I am well on the way to disliking him intensely.'

She might as well not have spoken for all the notice Harriet took of her words. Eagerly, she asked, 'Is he married?'

'Harriet, you are as bad as Fanny.'

'But what else is there to know about such a gentleman? We know he is a viscount. You have yourself confessed he is agreeable, and attractive, and,' she went on very firmly as Isadora opened her mouth to respond, 'his eyes smile.'

'Yes, I know, but —'

'What is more, he is less than thirty. He must be quite the most eligible gentleman to come your way in all these years.'

'Come my way? Just what —?'

'And if you are not the fool I take you for, you will at once cease to prate about this nonsensical dislike you say you have taken to the man and be at pains to attach him immediately.'

For a long moment, Isadora merely gazed at her friend in utter stupefaction. Had Harriet run completely mad? She to set her cap at Roborough? She would rather die. What, was she to be counted a traitor, to take the usurper of her home to husband? A traitor not only to the family, to her papa's memory, but also to her own ambition. Besides, she had every expectation they would find him to be married after all. Not that she cared. It made no difference to her.

'Harriet,' she said at last with a calm born of astonishment, 'you have quite taken leave of your senses.'

'On the contrary, Dora, you must be counted quite crazy if you cannot see —'

'Fudge. Even were such a thing remotely possible, I should not marry Roborough — not if he were the last man in the world. I dare say I shall never be married. Not, in any event, to anyone of that social standing.'

Harriet eyed her ominously. 'I suppose I need not ask what you mean by that remark. Now, Dora, you must listen to me —'

'Not if you mean to prose on at me about marrying Roborough, for a more stupid —'

'Dora, you have got to stop this nonsense about going on the stage. I know that is what you think you may do, but you are living in a fantasy. This is real life, Dora. There is only one life for you — just as there is for me, and —'

'Well, then, why don't you marry Roborough?' cut in Isadora, exasperated.

'I am betrothed to Joseph,' Harriet reminded her with dignity. 'Besides, I am only thinking of your future, Dora.'

'I know, and I do wish you would not,' said Isadora despairingly. 'I have my future well in hand, Harriet. Besides, you know me well enough to know I will not be deterred.'

'Yes, I do,' agreed Harriet. 'But, Dora, I cannot and will not stand by and let you ruin yourself without a fight.'

Isadora laughed. 'Well, believe, my dearest Harriet, there will be a fight. Particularly if you mean to try and marry me off to the Errant Heir. I only hope the wretch is married already. That will put your ideas firmly to bed.'

'I wish I could remember,' Harriet said, frowning. 'Only I never did meet him, for all we must have been attending the same parties. At least — what was his name before he came into the title?'

'I haven't the least idea. Nor do I care.' Isadora moved to the door. 'However, since you are so determined to find out all about him, I will introduce you and then you may question him to your heart's content.'

'I shall do nothing of the kind,' Harriet protested as they left the little parlour together.

'Well, you need not refrain on my account. For my part, I will be only too happy if you plague him beyond bearing.'

'I was thinking of his account rather than yours. I would not be guilty of such a piece of presumption as to question him about anything at all. I only hope you will not put me to the blush by quarrelling with him in my presence.'

'Never fear,' Isadora told her with mock-meekness. 'I shall be as good as gold — just for you. But if —' She broke off, halting suddenly in the middle of the hallway. Harriet, almost bumping into her, began to ask what was the matter. 'Hush!' said Isadora urgently. Had she heard what she thought? Voices in the library. Men's voices. Yes, there they were again.

She saw by Harriet's face that she was hearing them too now. The low tones had filtered through just as they were passing the library door on the way to the main staircase. Creeping on tiptoe, Isadora sneaked closer and put her ear to the woodwork, ignoring Harriet's shocked look.

Yes, it was Roborough and Thornbury. She could hear them clearly now.

'You are sure there is no alternative?' Thornbury was saying. 'It must be the estate?'

'I'm afraid a sale will prove inevitable.' That was Roborough. Apologetic, but determined. 'Perhaps you could begin by putting out some discreet feelers. I do not wish it generally known just yet that the property is on the market.'

He was going to sell the estate! Isadora reeled in shock, moving away from the fateful door without even being aware she did so. He was going to take their home from under them and pass it on to strangers. How could he be so cruel?

'Dora, what is it?'

Harriet's concerned tones brought her a little out of the oddly unreal sensation she was experiencing, as if she were not actually there.

'He is going to sell,' she said blankly.

'*What*? What do you mean?'

'Roborough. He is going to sell the estate.'

Harriet stared. 'Sell this house?'

'Yes, I tell you. He is just instructing Thornbury.' Without thinking, she put her ear back to the door.

'Dora, for God's sake,' hissed Harriet.

'Hush!' whispered Isadora again, for she had just heard her own name spoken. What more? Great heavens, what more?

'You have some query concerning Miss Alvescot, my lord?' asked Thornbury.

'It is rather a delicate matter, Thornbury. I only wondered if there might be a local suitor.'

'A suitor?' echoed Thorbury, evidently surprised.

'Yes. Surely it is not a strange idea Isadora could well be married off in the near future?'

Isadora, listening behind the door, very nearly burst into the room on the instant. Married off? *Married off?* 'So that is what he intends, is it?' she said aloud, her tone wrathful. 'We'll see about that.'

But Harriet, seeing her reach out towards the door-handle, seized her wrist and began to run back the way they had come.

'Harriet, let me go!'

But it was plain Harriet had taken fright, and nothing would do for her but to bundle her friend back into the little parlour, shut the door firmly — but quietly — and lean against it, half panting with effort.

'Harriet, come away from that door!'

'No!'

'Harriet!'

'Dora, I know you. You will say dreadful things and this Roborough of yours will be furious and your poor mama will be distracted and everything will be terrible.' She ended this rattling speech on a rising note that in itself gave Isadora pause. But it did not assuage her fury. She swung away across the parlour.

'That man!' she raged. Oh, but she would like to murder him with her bare hands. 'How dared he? How *dared* he?'

Harriet relaxed away from the door, though she remained in front of it, as if she suspected Isadora might make an unexpected dash to get out. 'Dora, calm down,' she pleaded. 'You have not even told me what he has said to cause you such distress.'

'Distress?' echoed Isadora, whipping about to face her. Could not Harriet see what was the matter with her? 'I am not distressed, Harriet, I am livid. Do you know what he said?'

'No, I don't,' Harriet snapped. 'I have just said so.'

'He asked Thornbury if I had a suitor,' Isadora told her, biting out the words. 'Because, if you please, he wants to parcel me off in marriage.'

'He said that?'

'Well, not exactly that.' Really, why must Harriet quibble? She knew what she had heard. 'But it is what he meant, you may take it from me.'

'That,' said Harriet sceptically, 'is what it seems to me I can't do. I know you, Dora. You always manage to make something out of nothing. What exactly did he say?'

'How in the world should I remember it exactly?' exclaimed Isadora impatiently. What did it matter, in any event? She knew what Roborough was about. 'It is plain enough what he intends. He means to sell the estate. That much I did not mistake, I assure you. And if I don't miss my guess he is looking to marry me off as soon as he may, and so be rid of the whole concern of us.'

Harriet blinked. 'Dora, what are you talking of? How could he possibly get rid of all of you by your getting married?'

'Easily. My husband would assume responsibility for the rest of my family, would he not? In the circumstances, he could scarcely refuse. That is, of course, presuming the existence of this local suitor Roborough has invented for his purposes.'

All at once Harriet's eyes widened. 'Oh, Dora, you don't suppose Thornbury will tell him about Edmund, do you?'

'I should not be at all surprised.'

'But Edmund could not possibly afford to take responsibility for your family.'

'No, and I would not wish it on him either, be sure.'

For a moment or two Harriet gazed at her friend, an appalled expression on her face, while Isadora paid no heed, instead pacing to and fro about the little parlour, her mind full of Roborough's iniquities.

Now she understood why he had been so pleasant to them all. He was trying to curry favour, to put himself in a situation of sympathy with the family, that he might the more easily persuade them to accept this hideous decision to sell off the only home they had all of them known. Such duplicity! Such a barefaced, unmitigated liar! He did not know what he would do. It must depend upon circumstance. Yes, on the circumstance of finding someone stupid enough to wish to buy this ugly old house.

Well, let him try. She would be very much interested to see what he would do when he discovered that no one in their right mind would give him so much as a penny piece for the place. She had almost forgotten the presence of Harriet until her friend, dropping into the nearest chair, spoke at last in accents of reproach.

'Really, Dora, you are dreadful. You are making me think as absurdly as you do yourself. As if you have any real idea of what Roborough intends. You cannot take a few words overheard through a shut door and assume an entire history upon them in this way.'

'I don't see why not. And if he did not wish me to make such assumptions he should have told me to my face what he intends — as I asked him to.'

'And what did he say?'

'He would not tell me, of course. Now I see why.' Isadora nodded in a determined manner. 'Well, he will find he has made a very serious mistake.'

'Yes,' agreed Harriet drily, 'when he discovers there is no suitor — except Edmund. And he must guess at once that he doesn't count.'

'I don't mean that. It is plain enough he does not wish to take responsibility for us all. He may or may not be planning to foist it all off on to me. But I shall spike his guns, see if I don't. My plans may serve the family just as well as his.'

Harriet groaned. 'Your plans? God help them all!'

'They will be safer in my hands than in Roborough's.'

'I strongly doubt that. What do you suppose you can do? In any event, you cannot stop him selling the estate if he chooses to do so, you know.'

Isadora tossed her head. 'I may not be able to stop him selling the estate, but I can, and will, stop him selling me.' She moved purposefully towards the door.

Harriet jumped up. 'Where are you going?'

'Have no fear, I am not going to thrust myself into his meeting with Thornbury. There will be time enough to tell him what I think of him. But I am not going to let the family remain in ignorance of his dastardly intent.'

But the family, confronted with Isadora's plan to rescue them from Roborough's plot, greeted it with an discouraging silence.

'But what in the world is the matter with you all?' demanded Isadora, standing arms akimbo in the middle of the drawing-room, flanked on one side by Harriet. Her glance went from one to the other. They had not looked like this when she had told them of Roborough's scheme to sell.

Mrs Alvescot, ensconced in her usual chair, seemed vaguely apprehensive, lines of worry creasing her countenance. But Matilda's frankly disapproving gaze and Fanny's superior smirk were quite unwarranted. Only Rowland, a slight frown marring his chubby features, appeared to be giving Isadora's idea consideration.

'Anyone would suppose you had rather trust to a stranger than your own flesh and blood,' Isadora pursued, a little hurt in her voice.

'Dear me, no, my love,' said her mother at once. 'It is not that.'

'It is when the flesh and blood is Dora,' put in Fanny with devastating candour.

'Fanny!' reproved Harriet, forgetting her own condemnation of Isadora's plans. 'That is a horrid thing to say.'

'Don't mind it, Harriet. I am quite used to hearing that sort of thing from Fanny.'

'Fanny, that was uncalled for,' Matilda told her daughter sternly, throwing a minatory glace at her but returning her gaze almost immediately to Isadora's face. 'However, I cannot help but feel — in this instance — there is much to be said for trusting in Roborough rather than a chancy scheme like yours, Dora.'

Isadora bridled. 'Chancy? You do not believe me capable, then, of becoming a successful tragedienne?'

'Even if you did,' broke in Harriet, 'bringing the family into it with you is quite ineligible.'

'Exactly,' said Fanny. 'You may choose to tread the boards if you wish; there is no need to drag the rest of us into it.'

'I'm with you, Dora,' chimed in Rowland. 'Perhaps I could get a position in the theatre where you're acting. Maybe I could lift the scenery on and off.'

'Yes, and drop it on the actors' heads,' sneered Fanny unkindly.

'Don't be foolish, Rowland,' said Matilda irritably. 'You will be going to school.'

'Yes, but if I was working in the theatre with Dora I need not go to school, and —'

'That will do,' said Matilda firmly. 'Dora is not going to work in the theatre.'

'Am I not?' said Isadora dangerously.

'Certainly not. I hold to it the whole notion is ridiculous, and I am sure Cousin Roborough will put a stop to it on the instant.'

'Oh, Matty, pray,' pleaded Mrs Alvescot feebly, glancing at her daughter's face as if she thought to see storm clouds gathering there.

Her intervention was in vain. Eyes snapping, Isadora said bitingly, '*Cousin* Roborough will put a stop to us all doing anything but what he chooses if he is allowed to sell this house. Is that what you want?'

'But Dora, my love,' came plaintively from her mama, 'we are in any event obliged to do what Roborough chooses. And if he is planning to sell the house I am quite sure he has already decided where we are to live. He only wants us to be comfortable, dearest.'

'Comfortable? Where are we to be comfortable? In any event, I may make you just as comfortable when I am able to afford a house, Mama.'

'Yes, my love, but Society will be closed to us if you are an actress, and so we should have no need of your house. We had as well live in a cottage.'

Isadora was silenced. She had not seriously expected any of them to acquiesce in her designs, but she had thought at the least they might be moved on hearing the estate was to be sold. But Roborough had so bewitched them all that the wretch could do no wrong. 'You are all besotted,' she said in a defeated tone. 'I only hope you may not be in line for a rude awakening.'

'Even if they are, Dora,' Harriet said persuasively, 'and Lord Roborough proves not to be as good as his word, you must see that even this unknown future is safer than the certain scandal you would bring down upon their heads with this actress scheme of yours.'

'It is well for you to take everyone else's part,' Isadora retorted crossly. 'I dare say you will not be so complacent when you find Roborough is pressing Edmund to marry me.'

'*What?*' gasped Matilda, and Mrs Alvescot looked startled.

Harriet grimaced at them, saying apologetically, 'She has taken it into her head, only from a word or two she overheard, that Lord Roborough plans to marry her off.'

'He did say so,' Isadora insisted.

'Oh dear,' fluttered Mrs Alvescot in her helpless sort of way, but she added sensibly, 'Only Dora, my love, what else is he to do with you?'

'Very true,' agreed Matilda. 'Although it's my belief Dora has misinterpreted the whole thing.'

'That is what I think too,' Harriet chimed in. 'In any event, I know you will never marry Edmund, Dora.'

'I'll marry Edmund,' piped up Fanny eagerly. 'That will save the family just as well as Dora's silly scheme.'

'Pooh!' scoffed Rowland. 'As if Edmund would marry you when he is head over heels for Dora. Even I can see that —'

'What I want to know,' interrupted Harriet, 'is whether Lord Roborough is married.'

'Don't we all!' said Fanny despairingly.

'Because it seems to me —'

'Harriet!' cut in Isadora warningly.

Matilda and Mrs Alvescot caught the meaning at exactly the same moment.

'You don't mean Dora and Roborough?'

'Oh, dear me. Dora and Roborough?'

At this precise instant, the door opened to admit Roborough himself, Thornbury in close attendance.

Dead silence greeted this inopportune entrance. Roborough glanced from one guilt-ridden or embarrassed face to another. Now what? Automatically his eyes went to Isadora. The colour in her cheeks was heightened, but she met his gaze full-on. What in the name of all the gods had he done to deserve that look? The brown eyes were positive daggers.

It was Thornbury who saved the day, stepping forward to present Harriet to the viscount. 'I believe you have not met Miss Witheridge, my lord.'

Roborough smiled as he greeted this strange new countenance. A pretty girl. Witheridge? Ah yes. The name of the local suitor Thornbury had given him. This must be a sister. Good God, if the boy bore any resemblance to her in feature, Isadora must surely be smitten. Though Thornbury had seemed doubtful.

There was no time to pursue this thought, for Thornbury was once more seeking his attention. 'My lord, would you wish me to return after luncheon?'

Roborough's was forestalled by Matilda, who had recovered her wits.

'Oh, but if you still have business with his lordship, Mr Thornbury, you must stay and eat luncheon with us. Must he not, Ellen?'

'Oh, dear me, yes. Forgive me, Mr Thornbury,' apologised Mrs Alvescot. 'Matty is so much better than I at these arrangements.'

Isadora hardly heard this little interchange for, after that one killing glance at Roborough, she had retired to the windows, where she was joined in a moment by Harriet.

'You must be mad,' whispered Harriet in a stunned tone.

'What do you mean?'

'Roborough, of course.'

'What about him?'

'Dora, he is practically ideal. Why in the world can none of you find out if the man is married?'

Before Isadora had an opportunity to respond to this, the scathing words were halted on her tongue by the opening, yet again, of the drawing-room door. Hampole, the butler, barely standing on his unsteady legs, peered about out of short-sighted eyes for his mistress. Seeing her at last, he stood aside, revealing a stranger waiting in the aperture.

'Mr Syderstone, ma'am,' Hampole announced.

There entered a man of middle age, with a mottled countenance, a portly bearing, and even more fashionably attired than the new master of the house. His prune-coloured broadcloth coat, buff breeches and gaily striped waistcoat could not help but form a startling contrast to the almost unrelieved black in the room. He had evidently followed the direction of the butler's look, for he addressed himself at once to Mrs Alvescot.

'Forgive this intrusion, ma'am, I beg. I am come in search of Lord Roborough.'

'Oh!' exclaimed the lady, bewilderment in her voice.

Isadora's eyes went instantly to Roborough's face. He was looking both astonished and, if she was any judge, none too pleased. Yet as he stepped forward he spoke with all his usual calm.

'You have found me, Syderstone.'

'So I see, my dear fellow,' said the other man in a hearty tone. 'And delighted I am to have done so.'

'No doubt,' Roborough responded on a dry note. His voice hardened slightly as he added, 'Perhaps you will oblige me by telling me just how you knew where to look.'

Mr Syderstone smiled. A rather cynical smile, Isadora thought. Cynical, and even — sinister? 'Ah, my dear fellow, it does not take a genius to discover that. I have been at Barton Stacey, you must know. Lady Roborough was kind enough to furnish me with your direction.'

'Was she indeed?' returned Roborough smoothly.

Isadora, intent on trying to read the thoughts behind Roborough's words — for there was something odd in his manner, so unlike him — noticed only in the background of her mind the pricking up of several ears about the room.

But it was outspoken Fanny who put these separate thoughts into words. 'Lady Roborough? Does he mean your wife?'

Preoccupied, Roborough barely glanced at her as he answered, 'No, my mother. I am unmarried.'

Isadora heard this statement with the oddest sensation — as of a leaping of the heart in her chest. Well, she knew what that meant, she decided, over the subsequent flurry of her pulse. Apprehension. For now they would give her no peace.

Her flicking glance confirmed this. Yes, there were her mama and Cousin Matty, exchanging looks Isadora found no difficulty in interpreting. Fanny and Rowland, too, whispering. It needed only Harriet's knowing dig at her ribs and the expectant look she met as she turned to her friend to set the seal on her instant determination. These designs she would thwart with even more energy than that she was reserving for Roborough himself.

Oh, dear heaven! Had Roborough caught the immediate wild glances between her family upon learning of his bachelorhood? Her eyes went to his face, that apprehensive heartbeat accelerating again. No, for his attention was all for the newcomer. The relief was intense. For all she might resist any attempts of her family and Harriet to drive her into Roborough's marital orbit, nothing could be worse than to have him recognise their object.

By this time Mrs Alvescot had risen to greet Mr Syderstone, and was proceeding to present him to the assembled company. 'Any friend of Lord Roborough is welcome here,' she was saying in response to the gentleman's renewed apologies for arriving uninvited.

But Isadora, whose eyes were still on Roborough, saw a slight curl twist his lip instead of the usual smile. A friend? She did not think so. An acquaintance perhaps. One, what was more, whose coming was both disagreeable and inconvenient to him. She saw Roborough turn to say something to Thornbury, who glanced at Syderstone — now exchanging inane how-do-you-dos with Fanny and Rowland — and nodded.

Then the stranger was moving in Isadora's direction and she was obliged to give him her attention. She noted, as she greeted him politely, that his eyes strayed rather to Harriet, softening with evident admiration. They were intelligent eyes, oddly vivid in a rather heavy setting. For Syderstone's features were weighty, puffing unattractively under the eyes and between the graven lines running from nose to mouth. Age or dissipation? It was difficult to tell. He wore his own dark hair, shorn even closer than Roborough's and greying a little at the temples. What attractions he might once have had were certainly hidden. Not that it appeared to deter him from flirtation, for Harriet was now being subjected to the sort of regard that invited response.

She was blushing, poor Harriet, but she was not long disconcerted. With a brief, 'You must excuse me,' to the man, she turned to her friend. 'I must be going, Dora. Joseph —' she threw a sugar-sweet smile at Syderstone — 'my betrothed, you must know, is expecting me to accompany him out this afternoon.'

The shaft went home. The light in the visitor's eyes was quenched, and he bowed. 'You must not let me detain you, ma'am.'

Isadora tucked her hand in Harriet's arm. 'I will come with you to the front door.' They were no sooner outside the drawing-room than she added on a laugh, 'That was superbly done, Harriet.'

Harriet shuddered. 'What a dreadful man. I cannot think how Lord Roborough comes to have such a friend.'

'Oh, he's not a friend,' Isadora said positively.

'How do you know?'

'Did you not see how Roborough looked at him?' She pulled at her friend's arm. 'But come. We must not stand here gossiping. They will come out at any moment.'

'Dora, what are you talking of?' demanded Harriet as she was hustled along the corridor to the end of the stairs.

'I am talking of the Errant Heir and this man, of course. If I don't miss my guess, Roborough is furious at his coming and will certainly demand an explanation before he sits down with him to luncheon. Which he must do, for Mama is bound to invite him.'

'But how can you have an idea of anything of the kind?' Harriet asked in a bewildered tone as she hurried after Isadora down the stairs.

'Because I have my eyes and ears on what is important, Harriet,' Isadora told her drily, 'rather than being bowled over by the quite unimportant fact that Roborough is single.'

She instantly regretted having reminded Harriet of this piece of news, for that young lady took it up at once. 'Oh yes, isn't that fortunate?'

'Fortunate!'

Harriet halted at the front door, turning determinedly on her friend. 'Now, Dora, you must —'

'Harriet, don't,' begged Isadora, opening the door and stepping outside.

'But —'

'You are wasting your time. Why in the world should you suppose Roborough has any notion of marrying me when you know very well he is set on marrying me off to someone else?'

'Dora!' exclaimed Harriet. 'I had not thought. Perhaps he was asking Thornbury about you because he has taken a fancy to you and he wished to know if you were heart free.'

'Ingenious, Harriet, but hardly credible.'

'Why not? After all, you wanted to know if he was unattached.'

'I?' gasped Isadora. 'The question never occurred to me!'

'Well, it ought to have done. Why, *attractive* does not begin to describe him. I have always thought how well red hair becomes a man.'

'Red?' echoed Isadora, unaccountably put out. 'It is not red.'

'Oh well, russet, then,' conceded Harriet.

Isadora frowned. 'Like autumn, you mean.' Her memory dwelled a moment on the image of Roborough's head and an odd sensation stirred in her chest. Yes, like autumn. Warm and friendly. Without realising it, she nodded. 'Chestnut, that is it. Just like Titian's coat. Though it did go a kind of bronze in the sun, I recall.'

'I wonder if you will produce red-headed children?' mused Harriet.

The agreeable vision splintered instantly, and Isadora exploded. 'That is precisely the kind of remark I do not wish to hear on your lips. Great heavens, Harriet, you must have taken leave of your senses! What am I, a brood mare?'

'But only think, Dora,' pleaded Harriet, quite unrepentant. 'What better solution could there be to all your difficulties? You may be sure Mrs Dotterell and your mama will have thought of that.'

'Yes, thanks to you,' said Isadora bitterly. 'Now they will nag me from morning to night.'

'Never mind it,' Harriet said soothingly. 'We may all of us wish for it, but nothing will come of the idea if Roborough does not wish it himself.'

'Which he quite clearly does not, thank heaven.'

'No, unless you will make an effort to change his mind.'

'Which I will not. You forget, Harriet, I am going to become an actress.'

'Not that again,' Harriet groaned. 'You may just as well cease this silly daydreaming, Dora, because there can be no doubt Roborough will forbid you.'

'Undoubtedly, were I to ask for his permission. But I shall do nothing of the sort.'

Harriet eyed her suspiciously. 'What do you mean to do?'

'I don't know yet. But you may believe I shall think of something.'

'For goodness' sake,' cried Harriet, exasperated. 'You would be far better employed in thinking how you might attach Roborough than doing the very thing likeliest to incur his enmity.'

Which remark so much annoyed Isadora that she parted from her friend on the curtest of terms and stalked back into the house, only to be brought up short by the sight of the three gentlemen entering the library.

All thought of Harriet's stupid notion vanished immediately. Here at last was the possibility of a clue. Roborough would give nothing away. But why should she not learn something in spite of him?

She did not, it was true, feel altogether comfortable about a deliberate attempt to overhear a conversation to which she was not meant to be party. The earlier occasion had been rather different. She had heard something on passing the door. She need not, she was persuaded, altogether reproach herself for that time.

This, however, presented a temptingly fresh opportunity. Yet she shrank from the task. It would be putting herself on a level with Fanny, whom she had condemned for listening at keyholes.

As she hovered uncertainly in the hallway, the matter was decided for her. The library door opened and Mr Thornbury came out. Catching sight of Isadora, he halted, his hand still on the handle of the closed door. His eyebrows rose.

'Miss Alvescot?'

Isadora beckoned, backing away to the bottom of the stairs. Thornbury followed her, throwing a brief glance at the library door.

'Mr Thornbury,' said Isadora in a commanding whisper. 'Now you may tell me exactly what Roborough is planning. He means to sell the estate, does he not?'

Thornbury frowned. 'You have not, by any chance, been guilty of eavesdropping on a private conversation, Miss Alvescot?'

Isadora could not prevent a giggle from escaping her lips. 'Well, yes. But only accidentally.'

'Indeed? I am to infer, then, that this little display of hesitation betokens another accident?'

Isadora had to laugh. 'Very well, then, I confess I was thinking of it, but I could not quite bring myself to the sticking point.'

'I am glad to hear it,' Thornbury smiled, relenting a little.

'Dear Mr Thornbury,' said Isadora, tucking a friendly hand in his arm and urging him up the stairs, 'you know I would only do so in circumstances of the direst need. Which these are. It is so very important to me to know what is going to happen.'

Thornbury tutted. 'Cajolery, Miss Alvescot, is wasted upon a hardened lawyer. Particularly from an accomplished thespian. And no,' he added firmly as she opened her mouth to respond, 'I will not repeat my conversation with his lordship. I will say, however, that neither you nor the family need fear for your future.'

'Only for our home,' Isadora said bitterly.

'Would it distress you so much to leave it?' asked Thornbury gently, pausing at the top of the stairs.

Isadora looked at him. So Roborough did intend to sell. But the question, put in that kindly way, pierced through her anger to the core of her hidden vulnerability.

'It is not the h-house,' she said, a catch in her voice. 'Only that Papa —' She could not go on. Even had speech not failed her, she did not know how she could have explained. Her papa's presence, though she did not mean it in a supernatural way, seemed to pervade the place. Without it, she must lose all she had left of him.

But it seemed as if Thornbury did not need the explanation. She found that an avuncular arm was about her shoulders, giving her a hug. His voice, however, was bracingly matter-of-fact. 'You will have to let him go some time, Miss Alvescot. And it is not the house. Everything you need is in yourself. Your memories will serve you just as well, if not better.'

Isadora, the mistiness receding from her eyes, looked gratefully up at him. 'You do understand.'

He smiled. 'I was very much attached to your father. And you, Miss Alvescot, remind me of him every day. It is sometimes as if I hear him talking, you are so much alike.'

Isadora grimaced. 'It is not a resemblance remarked upon by the rest of the family.'

As if he felt her return to normality, Thornbury removed his arm from about her shoulders. 'They are too used to you to see it.' He laughed. 'Even Lord Roborough immediately supposed you must have your character from that source.'

Oh, he did, did he? Evidently she had been much under discussion. Well, two might play that game. Perhaps it could prove worth her while to cultivate this Mr Syderstone.

CHAPTER FIVE

'You will allow me to point out,' said Roborough in curt tones, 'that your visit here is neither well-judged nor necessary.'

'Oh, come, come, my dear fellow,' protested Syderstone. 'You will scarcely deny the matter is of some moment.'

'To you, yes.'

'And should be to you,' came the silky response. 'A debt of honour, I may remind you, Roborough, is sacred.'

'I am not likely to forget.'

Aware that he was allowing his bitterness to show, Roborough dragged his emotions under tight control. A welcome interruption came in a knock at the door. Ah, the butler. Thornbury had rung for him before he had left the two of them alone. He ordered suitable refreshment, reflecting that the imminent luncheon would give him time to recover his sangfroid.

'Tell me how you left everything in town,' Roborough said, summoning a friendly tone.

Syderstone's lips smiled, but his eyes showed his understanding. Nevertheless, there was an undercurrent of warning in his tone, as if to say he would not long be deflected from the subject nearest his interest.

'You have been too long out of public life, my friend. The season has long been over. I have not come from town but from Kent.'

'Your estates, of course,' Roborough said, dredging up a light laugh. 'Silly of me. I'm afraid the business of taking over from my father has put me out of touch with time.'

'No doubt.' Syderstone coughed with mock-delicacy. 'Speaking of your father…'

Roborough held up a hand. 'Excuse me on that head, if you please.'

The other man frowned. 'All very well, Roborough, for you to be so nice, but I must speak of him.'

'Pray don't. In fact, there is no need to discuss the matter at all. I have all the facts as you gave them in your letter, and there was really no necessity for this journey. Did you suppose I should not pay you?'

Syderstone spread his hands. 'My dear fellow, perish the thought. My fear is rather than you cannot pay me.'

Roborough fought down his instant ire. Damn the man. Of course, he was right. Where was he to find the half of such a sum in the wasted inheritance into which he had fallen? But that did not mean his creditors should come hounding him in this way. 'Not at the present moment, no,' he conceded frankly.

'I thought not.' Syderstone suddenly beamed at him. 'Then I heard of your second inheritance.'

'Did you indeed?'

'I did, my dear fellow. And I thought, how excellent well young Roborough has done for himself. He will not, I feel sure, fail to remember his obligations. And you see, I was right.'

'If you mean that you supposed I should sell this estate merely to pay off a debt to you, Syderstone, you are wide of the mark. I have other calls on my purse to consider besides yours.'

Syderstone's urbanity did not desert him. He smiled. 'But none, I would guess, quite as immediately heavy.' His guess was accurate. But that made it no more acceptable.

'It comes to something when a man may be dunned in his own home!'

'Dunned? My dear fellow, you entirely mistake me. There is a difference, I protest, between dunning and looking to one's interests.' Syderstone's quick eyes glanced about the library. 'Is not that just what you are doing? Or am I again mistaken?'

No, he was not mistaken, damn his eyes. Unless one could claim the interests of all one's dependants marched with one's own, Roborough thought, as another knock on the door signalled the arrival of the burgundy from Alvescot's cellars. As he poured the liquor and handed a glass to his unwanted guest, he was aware of a greater intensity of emotion bottled up inside him than he had thought existed. True, there was reason enough for resentment. But in speaking of the matter this morning to Thornbury he had not been nearly as conscious of it. Then again Thornbury, besides having the lawyer's logical mentality, was a man of enormous common sense. He had readily understood the pressing need to sell the Alvescot inheritance.

'But was there nothing left at all, my lord?' Thornbury had asked, a measure of sympathetic concern in his voice that had warmed Roborough to the heart. He found himself confiding far more of the situation than he had intended.

'The estate has been squeezed dry.'

'Could no one have stopped it? Had your father no advisers?'

A harsh laugh had escaped Roborough's lips. 'As if he would have listened to them! Our own man of business tried, I tried. I even called upon my uncle who is now my heir. But it was as if my father were possessed of some incurable disease.' He had met the lawyer's eyes. 'This is to go no further, Thornbury.'

'You may rely on me, my lord.'

On the whole, Thornbury had taken the news well. It was not easy being obliged to tell the dire truth of one's father's activities to an outsider. But he had realised that if Thornbury was to appreciate his position he had no real choice, unless to be thought an outright rogue himself.

They had discussed alternatives, but at length Thornbury had agreed there really was no other way.

'If I am to provide for this family as well as my own, I don't see what else I can do.'

'Nor I, my lord,' Thornbury had said flatly. 'I do not know what commitments you have, but these here are enough in themselves. Do you suppose the sale would furnish you with sufficient means?'

'I doubt it. You have said Mrs Alvescot has a little money of her own, but her cousin is in her train, together with the children.'

'What would you propose for them, sir?'

'School for the boy, and some gentlemanly profession, I suppose. The girl may have to settle for a companion or governess, I'm afraid, for I cannot find four dowries.'

'Four?'

Roborough had smiled wryly. 'Miss Alvescot, for one. And I have two young sisters at home. But Fanny may be lucky. If I can recover the estate in the next few years, who knows? But I need the proceeds from this one to begin, Thornbury.'

Only now, it appeared, he was being pressed to use them for quite a different purpose. He looked over to where Syderstone sat, leaning at his ease in one of the two big cushioned chairs, savouring the wine. There was nothing else for it. Roborough must persuade the man to wait. If he paid him, there was not a hope in hell of providing for even one impoverished family, let alone two.

'How badly do you need the money, Syderstone?' he asked abruptly.

Syderstone looked up, smiling. 'That, my dear fellow, is irrelevant.'

'Not to me. And pray don't remind me again that it is a debt of honour.'

'I was not going to.' Syderstone finished his wine and rose, giving a little bow. 'I have every faith in you, my dear fellow.'

'In that case, you will oblige me very much by leaving here this very day.'

'Oh, I couldn't do that. Not after I have accepted Mrs Alvescot's very kind invitation to me, as your friend, to remain.'

'Mrs Alvescot will excuse you,' said Roborough, almost grinding his teeth. The man was a human leech.

'I could not possibly disappoint her. Besides, I am of a mind to pursue my acquaintance with Miss Alvescot.'

'*What?*'

Syderstone's eyebrows went up. 'You have some objection?'

'None at all,' said Roborough, an edge to his voice.

'Ah, but you must be in some sort her guardian, and I would not dream of —'

'Her mother is all the guardian she needs. In any event, she is very nearly one and twenty.'

'Yet you must have some say in her future,' persisted Syderstone. 'I would hesitate to encroach without your permission.'

A flame of anger was burning in Roborough's chest, but he maintained a cool front. What in the name of all the gods Syderstone meant by this fetch was beyond him. 'Miss Alvescot,' he said, as evenly as he could, 'is as yet barely known to me. But I am already perfectly certain she will take care of her own future without any assistance from me.' And let them see if that did not spike any schemes the man might have to use Isadora in some way against him. But the arrow misfired. 'Ah, excellent,' came Syderstone's urbane voice. 'In that case I may interest myself there without let or hindrance.'

With difficulty Roborough refrained from inflicting physical violence upon the man. What sort of game was he playing? Some scheme to force his hand, probably. Perhaps Syderstone thought to seem to threaten Isadora's safety so that he would do anything to get rid of him. Even pay him.

All he needed was another battle of wills on his hands. One would have supposed Isadora to be sufficient for any man to contend with. Still, let Syderstone try his hand against her, then they would see. God knew he had enough difficulty with her himself. Though at least it was an invigorating battle. And her protestations were honest, unlike Syderstone's. Besides, Isadora was... The very thought of her seemed to calm him a trifle. Isadora was endlessly amusing. He could not help but admire her, on so many counts. Fearless, quick-witted; a rebellious little monster, but endearing with it. Not to mention her truly amazing talent.

'A penny for them, my dear fellow.'

Roborough blinked. Syderstone's face came back into focus. He had entirely forgotten the man's presence. Mentally thanking Isadora for the brief respite, he poured the man another glass of burgundy.

'Syderstone,' he began, returning more easily now to his usual mild tone, 'why don't you go away, there's a good fellow? It will take me some time to settle my affairs, but you may rest easy that when the money is available you shall have it.'

'I shall, my dear fellow,' said the other silkily. 'I mean to make very sure of that.'

CHAPTER SIX

No opportunity had yet presented itself for Isadora to draw the attention of Mr Syderstone for the purpose of discovering what she might about Roborough. What with church and the general gathering on Sunday, there was no chance of privacy.

She was therefore delighted, a couple of mornings later, to find him breakfasting alone when she came in from her ride. She smiled involuntarily. 'Oh, Mr Syderstone, how fortunate. I mean,' she corrected herself hastily, 'how glad I am that someone is still here. Usually I am last in and obliged to enjoy a solitary meal.'

'Then,' Syderstone smiled, with a little bow, for he had risen at her entrance, 'I beg you will allow me to keep you company.'

She saw then that his place was already being cleared by the housemaid who had been assisting Hampole to serve from the various dishes laid out on the sideboard.

'But you have finished already,' she said on a deliberately disappointed note. 'Then I must not keep you.'

'I shall not, I protest, be guilty of deserting you.' He waved a hand at the housemaid. 'This kindly wench will perhaps indulge me with another cup of your excellent coffee.'

'How thoughtful of you.'

Isadora was glad of his courtesy. For how else was she to attract his interest? She knew herself to be unremarkable in looks, except when she was acting, for she was aware some transformation took place in herself that made her stand out. She had no woman's wiles. She had no leisure for that sort of absurdity. Among their acquaintance it was Harriet who had the admirers — apart from Edmund, of course.

'Not at all,' Syderstone responded, resuming his seat. 'You have rescued me from the dilemma of deciding what to do for the morning.'

'I have saved you from boredom, you mean,' Isadora said drily, turning to help herself from the dish of ham and eggs the butler was proffering. The silver serving-dish shook in his unsteady hands, and she added quickly, 'Do put it down, Hampole. There is no necessity to hold it for me.'

But Hampole, evidently on his mettle before a stranger, merely gave her a reproving look and stubbornly maintained his grip.

'You wrong me, I protest,' said Syderstone urbanely. 'Only everyone appears to have business on hand. Roborough was before me, and has gone. Your cousin has taken her two children off for their lessons. While as for Mrs Alvescot —'

'Oh, Mama never rises for breakfast,' Isadora interrupted.

'There you are, then. Now, if fortune favours me, I might persuade you, Miss Alvescot, to take a turn about the grounds with me.'

Fortune, Isadora thought, accepting with alacrity, had instead favoured her. He looked to her for amusement as a last resort, it seemed. Not that she gave a fig for that, if only he might not prove as close-lipped as Roborough and Thornbury.

Not very much later, they were walking about the lawns — in full sight, Isadora ensured, of the schoolroom party who had brought their books out under the trees on this warm day. Matilda had unfortunately been obliged to attend to her own children's education ever since the family were obliged to let Isadora's governess go and Rowland's lessons with the vicar had to be given up. These retrenchments had been hard. No wonder Cousin Matty was so set on Roborough's taking them all under his wing.

For a few moments, the realisation stopped Isadora from beginning the enquiries she fully intended to make with regard to Syderstone's business with Roborough. But it would not do. She must find out something about Roborough's situation. If this man's visit could throw any light on the subject, then she must not shrink from her self-appointed duty.

But before she could turn the conversation into this channel they suffered an interruption. Someone was walking purposefully towards them across the lawn from the house. It did not take long for Isadora to recognise him. A fair youth, boyishly slim, with handsome looks very much akin to Harriet's, although he lacked her strength of character.

Edmund! What a nuisance, just when she had a chance to begin her investigations. What in the world did he want?

She was not left long in ignorance. Young Mr Witheridge, his breath short, Isadora saw, less from exertion than from some strong emotion under which he was evidently labouring, came up with them in a moment.

'Dora!'

'Good morning, Edmund,' she responded in a repressive voice. Great heavens, what was the matter with him? Could he not see she had a visitor? 'Allow me to present you to Mr Syderstone.'

Edmund started, as if he had not seen the man. Then, to Syderstone's evident amusement, judging by the cynical smile on his face, he gave the other the curtest of greetings.

'Harriet's brother, sir,' Isadora explained. 'You met her the day you arrived.'

'Yes, I see the resemblance.'

Flushing, Edmund looked anything but gratified by this comment. He addressed himself pointedly to Isadora. 'It's on

Harriet's account I have come, Dora. She — er — she needs your advice.'

'My advice?' repeated Isadora, gazing at him. Since when did Harriet require her advice?

'Something about her wedding-gown,' Edmund said, so fluently Isadora almost believed him.

'She wishes me to come now?'

'Immediately.' Then, apparently realising the infelicitous nature of this remark before Isadora's guest, Edmund added on a stammer, 'At least — I mean, that is, if — if it ain't inconvenient.'

Her curiosity now thoroughly aroused, Isadora abandoned Mr Syderstone with some appropriate words of excuse and went off on Edmund's arm.

'Edmund, what is all this?' she demanded as soon as they were out of earshot. 'And don't tell me again that Harriet desires my advice, because —'

'I will reveal all, but not here,' Edmund said in a tone of ill-suppressed urgency, fairly pulling her along around the side of the house towards the back. 'Let us get to the stables first.'

Mystified, Isadora allowed herself to be hurried in the direction of the stable-block, all sorts of speculations arising in her mind. 'Harriet is not ill, is she?'

'No, nothing of that sort.'

But as they came within sight of the stables she frowned. 'But where is your carriage?'

'I didn't come in my carriage,' Edmund responded. 'I rode.'

Indeed, Isadora could now see his horse tethered near the mounting-block. He was, besides, attired in a blue frock-coat and buckskins, his boots a trifle dusty from the roads. 'But Edmund,' she protested, 'I am not dressed for riding. Besides, I have only just eaten.'

'It's all right. We're not going home.'

Isadora looked round at his set young features. 'Then what —?'

'Wait, I pray you!' Edmund halted at the stables and, bidding her again to wait, quickly went inside. Isadora could barely contain her impatience when he came back out a moment later.

'Edmund, what are you doing?'

'Making sure no one is there.'

'Of course no one is there,' Isadora responded in an exasperated way. 'Totteridge has gone to eat his breakfast and smoke a pipe, I dare say. While as for the boys, if they have dealt with Juliet and Titian, they are free until feeding-time. What is the matter with you, Edmund?'

'I will tell you,' Edmund promised. 'Only come inside for a moment.'

'In the stables? Are you mad?'

'I must be alone with you. If you please, Dora.'

Shrugging, Isadora allowed him to drag her into the comparative shadow of the harness-room. This was a low-ceilinged apartment abutting the stalls, its rows of benches against the three walls decked with the debris of grooming — brushes and cloths, sacking and saddle-soap, along with a bit and bridle in the process of being mended. Livery jackets jostled for position on the wall-pegs between saddles and stirrups and reins looped carelessly over wooden bars. Here, as in the rest of the house, a general air of disorder prevailed.

Isadora, naturally enough, noticed nothing amiss. Beyond holding her petticoats a little away from the straw-strewn floor, she paid no heed to her surroundings. Her attention was all for Edmund Witheridge's extraordinary air of suppressed excitement.

'Well?' she demanded.

Edmund swallowed, squared his shoulders, and set his jaw. 'Dora, Harriet has told me all!' he announced dramatically.

'Oh, fudge,' groaned Isadora, guessing now the purport of all this determined mystery.

'Dora, you shall not marry Roborough!'

The commanding tone did not impress Isadora. 'Well, I could have told you that. Really, Edmund, your conduct is absurd.'

His pose of knight-errant collapsed. Flushing darkly, he stuttered, 'You c-call it absurd that I have come to — to rescue you from the importunities of one who — who —'

'Edmund, I do not know what Harriet has said to you, but I assure you I am suffering no importunities.'

'But you are in the power of a stranger.'

'I am nothing of the kind. If you must know, Roborough has offered me no sort of annoyance — except provocation to my temper.'

'Aha!' Edmund pounced, seizing her by the shoulders. 'He has angered you. Harriet said so.'

'Yes, he has,' agreed Isadora with asperity, 'but so are you just at this moment, Edmund. I wish you will stop being so foolish. Release me at once!'

'But I'm offering for you, Dora,' protested Edmund on a note of desperation, tightening his hold in spite of her command.

'Don't be stupid,' Isadora said shortly, dropping her hold on her skirts so that she might push at his chest.

'It's not stupid. I want you to marry me.'

'Well, I'm not going to. Pray think a little. Your mama would have an apoplexy if I agreed to marry you.'

'Hang Mama! I love you, Dora!'

'No, you don't,' Isadora said, trying to pull away. 'Now let me go!'

She had expected to cow him into obedience, for he was weaker than she in spirit. But not, it transpired, in body. Edmund, too impassioned to heed her, pulled her closer and attempted to kiss her.

Isadora, furious, wrenched herself away and dealt him a stinging slap. 'How dare you, Edmund? What in the world has come over you to conduct yourself in such a brutal fashion?'

But Edmund, who had started back with one hand flying to his cheek, was looking past her, an expression of intense horror on his face.

Isadora turned quickly — and froze. Standing just inside the stable doorway, blandly surveying the scene, was Roborough.

Hot with embarrassment, Isadora found herself unable to utter a word. Her mind was all chaos. Had he seen? How much had he heard? Why, oh, why did he have to walk in just at that precise moment? It was typical of the man. What would he think of her?

But Roborough's face gave nothing away. And his voice, when he spoke — the first to break the seemingly unending silence — was as cool as ever.

'You must be Mr Witheridge,' he said calmly, addressing himself to Edmund, and adding, much to that young gentleman's evident discomfiture. 'No doubt you are just leaving.'

'Leaving?' Edmund gasped out. 'No, I —'

'Don't let me detain you,' pursued Roborough in the pleasantest of tones. 'I will look forward to meeting you on another occasion.'

There could be no mistaking his message. Isadora, seeing Edmund redden under this comprehensive dismissal, however politely phrased, almost felt sorry for him. But, reflecting what Roborough must have seen, she was easily able to refrain from pity. This was all Edmund's fault, and Roborough was the last person she would have wished to catch her out in such a compromising situation.

Edmund looked at her, the expression in his eyes compound of entreaty and apology. Isadora understood. He was not going to admit his fault before Roborough, but he recognised himself to be at fault. She swallowed her resentment and spoke as calmly as she could. 'We will talk some other time, Edmund.'

Obviously reluctant, Edmund glanced again at Roborough, who smiled slightly and pointedly stepped aside, leaving the doorway free. Isadora saw Edmund's lips compress tight shut. Then, without another word, he marched out.

Isadora was left wondering what to say. This was the first opportunity she'd had since overhearing Roborough's plans to speak to him alone. She ought to demand an explanation. Only her position was, to say the least, invidious. Here he had caught her in the embrace of the very person Thornbury had no doubt told him was her suitor. Now he must either believe her willing, or realise that he must think of something else — depending upon how much he had seen and heard.

Willing she was — to murder rather than marry Edmund. For how could she take up a righteously indignant stance against Roborough after this? Indeed, she could not even look at him, much less confront him with his iniquitous plot. Instead, she fell to lifting her black muslin petticoats a little to check whether they had acquired any dirt or straw.

'No, it is hardly the ideal garment for a stable,' came Roborough's amused tones.

Isadora's eyes flew up. Was he laughing at her? She could see no trace of laughter in his features.

He raised his brows enquiringly at her fierce look, but all he said was, 'I am glad you are in here, though, for I hope you may be able to advise me.'

'Advise you?' What in the world was the man at?

'Yes,' he said, and, turning in a leisurely way, just as if nothing untoward had occurred, he wafted a hand towards the stalls. 'I was hoping to ask your head groom if he could select a mount for me. But you, Isadora, are even better placed to tell me which horse I may ride.'

'May?' echoed Isadora with an ironic inflexion. 'You do not need anyone's permission.'

'Needing and seeking are two very different things,' he responded easily.

'Ah yes. I had forgot your determination to make yourself agreeable at all costs.'

'Not to you. I have quite abandoned any hope of that.'

Isadora was betrayed into a laugh. She met his gaze and saw that the warmth of his tone had spread to his eyes. Her pulse quickened — inexplicably, for what had she to be nervous of in his presence? Except that he had seen Edmund...

The thought blanked. What had he seen? Whatever it was, whether it ruined his plans or not, he had delicacy enough to refrain from embarrassing her further. For that at least she must be grateful. Unconsciously she smiled at him. 'You are mistaken. There are moments when I do find you agreeable.'

His brows rose. 'There are? Good God, Isadora, you overwhelm me!'

'I wish you will not be so absurd. It cannot matter a jot to you whether I find you agreeable or not.'

'Can't it?' he countered, the light eyes holding hers.

Isadora's breath caught. She eyed him uncertainly. What in the world did that mean? Nothing, in all probability. He was a teasing wretch and he wanted only to set her at a disadvantage by saying absurd things.

Amusement crept into his gaze as he read the puzzlement in her countenance. Was it so impossible for her to conceive of his desire only to be on friendly terms? How long was she going to persist in this determination to regard him as a usurping enemy? It would serve them all a deal better if he could find a way to reach her. To allay her suspicions. To make her see him for what he was, and not what she imagined him to be. Keep it light, he told himself. Keep it easy.

'Come, let us settle this business of a suitable horse,' he said, turning away from her. The bait hooked.

'There is only one suitable for a man of your weight,' Isadora told him, following him towards the stalls.

'Titian?' he guessed, turning to her. He added as she nodded, 'I was hoping you would say so.'

Isadora halted. 'Then why did you not ask to ride him in the first place?'

'Because I am not so insensitive,' responded Roborough calmly. 'He was your father's horse.'

The sharp pang took Isadora unawares. She gasped in air, clutching one hand to her chest. A sobbing breath left her lips, and as the unexpected tears pricked at her eyes she felt her flailing fingers clasped in a firm hold. She clutched the hand thankfully, hardly knowing whose proffered help this must be. His voice was soothing.

'Steady, now, steady.'

Isadora recovered in a moment. She found Roborough had led her back to the centre of the harness-room, away from the horses. She looked up into his face, and the concern she read there quite startled her. Meeting his eyes, her own gaze became fixed. The strangest sensation passed through her, as of a current of warmth that seemed to flow from her fingers where they were in contact with his. Confused, she drew them away, and the contact broke.

'All right?' he asked softly.

'Yes, th-thank you,' she responded, faltering a trifle. 'I — I don't know why it hit me like that. Papa had not in fact ridden Titian for near two years before —' She stopped abruptly.

'Before his death,' Roborough finished for her.

She glanced at him again, conscious of a drop inside her chest, for he had spoken in a hard voice.

He must have read her reaction for he grimaced. 'Yes, I know that is harsh. But it does not do to avoid the word, Isadora. You will become accustomed.'

Isadora stared at him in perplexity. She had forgotten his own recent bereavement. 'Have you?'

His lips twisted into that bitter curl. 'My grief, ma'am, is all outward show.'

Dismayed, Isadora blinked at him. What oddity was this? How could he not grieve for his father's passing? 'I do not understand you.'

The strangely disquieting look did not leave his face. 'How should you? You do not know me, Isadora.'

'Well, that is scarcely my fault.'

Roborough recollected himself. She was right. It was not her fault. None of it. Banishing the emotions that had arisen despite his iron control, he smiled again. Here was the very opening he needed. 'The matter is susceptible of remedy.'

'Is it? In that case, you can tell me what you intend to do about us all.'

'I did not mean that.'

'Well, if you wish me to become better acquainted with you, it would be a start.'

'Possibly an end too. But,' he added quickly as she opened her mouth to retort, 'why not begin with a ride together this evening?'

Isadora tossed her head. 'So that you can cozen me into showing you over the estate, I suppose.'

'Not at all,' he responded instantly. 'Thornbury will do that.'

'Then you need not ride with me.'

'For pity's sake, Isadora, all I want is some company! I am itching for the exercise, and it is so tedious with only a groom behind. Come, humour me this once. You may at least show me the best rides, and if you do not enjoy it I promise I shall never tease you to ride with me again.'

'Well, you need not talk as if I am utterly churlish.'

'You are not churlish, only contrary. Perhaps I should have done better to forbid you in any circumstances to accompany me on a ride.'

'Forbid me? You may try!'

He grinned. 'I thought so. Very well, then. Don't you dare attempt to ride with me this evening, Miss Alvescot. On pain of — of —'

'Of what?'

'I don't know yet, but I shall think of something in good time, I promise you.'

'I should not wish to put you to such trouble,' Isadora said sweetly. 'So I shall obey you without question.'

He sighed. 'I see I cannot win. I shall have to settle for Fanny, I suppose.'

'Fanny? Great heavens, no, she will drive you demented! She does nothing but carp and refuse to take jumps. You had much better ride with me.'

'But what an excellent notion. I wish I had thought of it for myself. I thank you, Isadora.'

Isadora burst into a peal of laughter. 'What an abominable man you are, Roborough.'

'So you have several times informed me,' he agreed, smiling. 'Shall we say four o'clock?'

But by the time four o'clock came Isadora had found ample time to remember Roborough was her enemy who meant to sell her home. Moreover, he had interrupted that embarrassing scene with Edmund and she, fool that she was, instead of seizing the opportunity to find out whether he meant to marry her off, had let him trick her into this agreement to ride.

She was sorely tempted to cry off, she thought, as she hooked the habit at the bodice over her cotton chemise, particularly as he had thwarted her plan to pump Syderstone for information by taking the man off with him when he had gone to meet Thornbury. Crossing to the mirror, she set her beaver at a rakish angle on her dark curls, which she chose to wear loose for comfort under the hat.

On the other hand, he had rescued her from Edmund very neatly. He had understood her distress too, and helped her — without sentimentality, which she would have hated — with that strangely comforting current of warmth. It would be a pleasant change to ride again with a companion, rather than only Totteridge.

Nevertheless, she greeted him with some reserve as she mounted, with Totteridge's help, upon Juliet's back. Totteridge, about to swing up on to one of the hacks, was forestalled by Roborough, waiting in the saddle on Titian.

'You need not accompany us, Totteridge. Miss Alvescot will be safe enough with me.'

'Aye, my lord,' agreed the groom, although he cast a doubtful glance at his mistress.

Isadora, unaccountably finding her reserve melting away, wondered what this betokened. Her frowning glance went from Totteridge to Roborough, and she noted that he, like herself, had dispensed with mourning to ride. Green suited him, she found herself thinking as her gaze dwelled on his coat and his waistcoat where the colour was repeated in a lighter hue.

She gave herself a mental shake. What was she doing, thinking of Roborough's attractions? What did he want with her, in any event? To be sure, she did not need an escort other than he; not even for the sake of propriety, for they were cousins and he was in some sort her guardian. But deliberately to seek privacy with her? That was odd indeed.

Intrigued, she led the way to the gate at the back which one of the stable-lads was already running to open. Once through, she trotted towards the border of the estate, heading for the bridle-path. 'This is my usual route,' she called.

'I am in your hands,' Roborough responded. 'Shall we get a gallop?'

'Beyond the bridle-path, if you wish for one.'

'More than anything.'

That meant they must bypass the bridle-path and take to the open lands on the other side. They would come up again at its further end, taking a circuit around the small forest through which the path ran.

It was exhilarating to ride unchecked, to sail over ditch and fallen log, to fly with the mare, pounding neck and neck against the stallion — Roborough had to be holding him in to stay with her, for he had by far the stronger horse. To know, too, that the person with her rode from enjoyment and not from duty. She felt that. Roborough's presence at such a time came close to the sensations she had experienced riding with her papa. The man had been right. There was a deal to be said for companionship.

At length he called out — just like her papa — that he must give Titian his head for a space. Then the chestnut stallion streaked ahead, hooves rattling across the open ground. Isadora reined Juliet in a little, watching with unconsciously admiring eyes the figure upon the horse's back. He rode well, she had to give him that.

When she saw him slowing, she flicked the mare's side and caught up at a canter. Roborough's light eyes were shining as he turned to greet her.

'How much I have longed for that!' He patted the stallion's neck. 'This is a splendid fellow.'

'He is, isn't he?' agreed Isadora enthusiastically. 'Have you such a horse?'

'Oh yes. He is a black, though. I call him Othello.'

'But of course,' cried Isadora, laughing as he grinned provocatively at her. 'So expert on the works of Shakespeare as you are.'

'I am sure I cannot compete with you,' he protested as their horses fell in beside each other again. 'Tell me, though, what other roles have you perfected?'

Isadora slid a look at him. 'I was under the impression that you did not think I had perfected my Juliet.'

'I am never going to be permitted to forget that, am I?'

'Well, you meant it.'

'I also meant it when I said you were an excellent actress. That, however, does not appear to mitigate my criticism.'

'No,' agreed Isadora, 'it does not.'

'Alas! Forever doomed for one unthinking remark.'

'But it was not unthinking,' protested Isadora.

'Is that what rankles?'

'What rankles, sir, is that you were not asked for your opinion. I did not even know who you were. Furthermore, I had been rehearsing, not performing for an audience.'

'Yes, that is fair comment. On the other hand, had you been aware of my presence, you might not have performed so unselfconsciously — nor so charmingly.'

Amazed, Isadora gazed at him. 'It is apparent you know little of acting.'

'Tell me about it, then,' he invited, with the utmost cordiality. 'I am very willing to be enlightened.'

Isadora was silent for a moment or two. No one besides her papa had ever shown any real interest in the workings of her craft. Even he, she believed, had only listened to indulge her when she talked excitedly of this or that problem. Was Roborough truly interested? Or was this another of his ploys? Somehow, it did not matter. The urge to talk about her acting was overwhelming. 'You may regret having asked me.'

'Possibly.' There was the faintest of laughs in his voice. 'But we shall never know unless you try me.'

'Well,' Isadora began dubiously, 'I do not always understand it myself. It is as if — when I am acting, you understand — I become another person. I am no longer Isadora Alvescot. At least, only a little of me remains. I feel with another's feelings. I think with another's thoughts. And I am no longer here, but in some imaginary place where I see only the people concerned with that other self. It does not seem to matter who it is — Juliet or Lady Jane Grey, or even,' she revealed with a laughing glance across at him, 'Lady Macbeth. For the time, I live them — as if they live in me.' She stopped and her eyes searched his face. 'Can you understand me at all?'

Roborough's eyes had never left her countenance while she spoke. There was such animation in her features, such a glow in her voice. There could be no doubt of her intense involvement in this favourite pastime. Talking like this, she was positively captivating. A creature of many moods, this girl.

'I don't know if I understand how it should be so,' he answered. 'But I have heard Garrick felt the same. Perhaps all great actors do.'

Isadora stared at him, only half aware she had brought her mare to a halt, and that he had followed suit. Great? Was it possible he believed she had a claim to the word? No, it could not be. But if it was so... Dared she confide in him? Tell him what she planned?

'But what have I said?' he asked, half-laughing.

'Garrick was a gentleman, was he not?' Isadora found herself saying.

'I believe so. What of it?'

What of it, indeed! A man might do what a female dared not attempt. Involuntarily, she burst out, 'I wish I were a man!'

Roborough broke into laughter. 'What next will you say? Let me tell you, Isadora, as a female, you are refreshing, to say the least. I cannot think you would do any better as a man.'

'Yes, I should,' she said crossly, thoroughly put out by his unwarranted amusement, 'because I should be able to call you out.'

'You would not need to, for if you were a man I should not be here in the first place.' He frowned suddenly. 'Or is that what you meant?'

'I meant nothing of the sort, as it happens. But, now that you come to mention it, I should certainly have preferred it. At least I would have told me what I intended to do.'

He could not control his laughter, although he was aware Isadora was incensed by it. Really, she was a most unpredictable female.

'I cannot imagine what you find so funny. Either you laugh at me, and say the most infuriatingly teasing things, or else you turn aside my questions as if they are of no account. You are hateful, Roborough.'

His eyes still alight with laughter, he glanced round at her, doffing his hat ironically. 'I thank you. And what am I to say of you, Isadora? You storm and rail at me, and persist in saddling me with various motivations of which I am quite unaware. And, if I am not very much mistaken, you are determined to thwart me whatever I decide to do. Therefore it is in my best interests to keep my mouth very firmly shut.'

Then, very unfairly, he urged Titian onward, speeding rapidly to a canter so that Isadora was unable to continue the conversation. It was with some satisfaction that she caught him up, for she was able to take him immediately at fault.

'You are going the wrong way,' she called. 'We must turn for the forest here.' With which, she wheeled her own mount and sped away, obliging Roborough to chase her at the gallop. But the trees soon thickened, and they had to slow down, picking their way through to the bridle-path. A short trot along this and Isadora brought them out on to the estate, with the squat shape of the unsightly Alvescot house nestling in the valley below.

Isadora reined in, and gestured widely with her whip hand. 'Behold your domain, sir. And if you suppose you will find anyone with little enough taste to purchase the ugliest house in England, then you must have windmills in your head.'

Roborough was not looking at the view. He was eyeing Isadora, his expression grim. She had no difficulty in interpreting the look.

'Yes,' she said defiantly. 'I know what you intend. What is more, I have told the family.'

'Have you?' he said flatly, his jaw set and hardness in his eyes.

Isadora was conscious of a flutter in her stomach. He was angry. It gave her a curious sense of pleasurable satisfaction to know she had succeeded in moving him to something stronger than mere amusement. Yet she could not help a slight feeling of apprehension. She fought it down. 'Yes, I have.' She might have added she had gained nothing by informing the family of his plan to sell, but she did not wish him to know that.

'Are you in the habit of distressing your family by giving them unnecessary information?' he asked bitingly.

'Am I in the habit…?' Isadora glared at him. 'I am in the habit, sir, of telling the truth. I do not prevaricate, and flatter, and toady my way into favour so that anything I do may be found acceptable, no matter how unpalatable it is.'

'You are treading on dangerous ground, Miss Alvescot.'

'Oh, indeed? Is that a threat, my lord? Will you banish me to my room? Beat me, perhaps? Or merely rid yourself of a tiresome charge by marrying me off to Edmund Witheridge?'

Roborough's expression altered abruptly. 'Have you run mad, Isadora? If you showed any disposition to marry that unfortunate boy, I would have you placed under restraint!'

'*What?*' Isadora fought for breath. 'You — you take it upon yourself to — to dictate whom I may marry?'

His brows rose. 'A moment ago you were accusing me of forcibly pushing you into marriage. You don't wish to marry the Witheridge boy, do you?'

'Of course I don't wish to marry him, but —'

'Then what are we arguing about?'

Isadora nearly screamed. 'The point is,' she said, with careful restraint, 'that if I did wish to marry him you would have no right to interfere.'

'Oh, I wouldn't do that.'

'Then why did you say you would have me placed under restraint?'

'A mere figure of speech. Though I dare say it is what a careful guardian ought to do. Really, Isadora, you should not be permitted to roam at large. You are far too dangerous.'

Isadora found herself torn between fury and an abrupt desire to laugh. 'I am n-not in the least dangerous.'

'You are, at a conservative estimate, more dangerous than a tigress. No wonder your poor family tremble in your presence. They must have viewed my arrival in the light of a saviour.'

This was so very close to the truth Isadora's quivering amusement was quenched. Was it possible that she, who was so strongly partisan when it came to the family's best interests — as she had thought — had less influence than this stranger? Roborough no longer felt a stranger; that she accepted. But that he should be regarded as a better judge than she of what must suit those she loved best was galling in the extreme.

Unknowingly, she had spurred Juliet on, heading towards home. Roborough automatically followed suit, wondering what he had said to give her so furiously to think. Her countenance gave her away so rapidly he was able to discern a trace of distress there. How had his teasing words brought that about? To be sure, she had made him — for a few hazardous moments — so blazingly angry he had found it hard to recover his usual self-control.

But upon reflection he might have known she would find him out somehow. Thornbury could not have betrayed him, he was persuaded. Which left only one solution. Isadora, the little devil, had been listening at the door.

Strange to say, he found himself more amused by this than angry. It really was so typical. She would not allow a little matter of delicacy to stand in her way. Though how she had concocted this mad idea he planned to marry her off to that boy he could not fathom.

Isadora, however, had lost all interest in that particular question. The matter of her family's view of her superseded all else. Even Harriet seemed to feel Roborough's capacity to assist them was greater than her own. Perhaps they were correct. She was the selfish one. Or so they saw it. Putting spokes in their wheels when all looked to be in a fair way to settling to their satisfaction. It did seem as if Roborough intended to see all right. Perhaps she had not given him enough credit.

Glancing sideways at him, she found his gaze was on her. She felt a flutter in her pulse as he met her eyes, a hint of a question in his.

But all he said, and that in a normal voice, was, 'Is there a way we may come at the house from the front from here?'

'Well, we're heading for the stables at the back. But if you wish we can take a line around there and come up the drive.'

She pointed as she spoke, and Roborough nodded. 'Yes, if you don't object to it.'

'Why should I?' she countered, and instantly regretted her tone. There was no occasion to bite his head off. Softening her voice, she added, 'I have no objection at all.'

'Lead on, then.'

As she urged Juliet towards the side, Isadora asked, 'Why do you wish particularly to see the house from the front? I should think you had already done so.'

'Yes, but I don't recall it being quite so hideous as it appeared from the top of the hill.'

Isadora giggled. 'It is hideous, isn't it? Papa was used to think his grandfather had been crazy to build it.'

'I believe it was the fashion of the day. Now, when we are so accustomed to Palladio's designs, and those of his imitators, it seems to us quite unattractive.'

'What is your house like?' Isadora asked with sudden interest.

'Oh, very stately and Italianate.' He grimaced. 'But for all its proportional beauty it lacks the homeliness of this one. That, however, has little to do with the house.'

'I know what you mean. A home reflects the people who live there.' She laughed. 'Ours shows how dreadfully untidy we all are.'

'But it is *warm*,' he said with an intensity that surprised her. 'That, believe me, Isadora, counts for a great deal.'

That odd note of bitterness had crept into his voice, and she glanced curiously at him. She would have liked to probe into this recurring aspect of Roborough's life, but she did not feel confident of receiving anything in reply — unless it be a comprehensive snub.

Before she could decide whether to pursue the opportunity, however, she saw, as they approached the driveway, that a carriage on its passage to the house had slowed to meet them. 'There is your friend,' she said, recognising Mr Syderstone.

She thought Roborough muttered something under his breath, but she did not catch what it was. The good humour faded from his face, confirming her earlier suspicions. This was no friend of his. Yet he behaved pleasantly enough when the other man hailed them.

'So there you are. What a wild-goose chase you have sent me on, Roborough.' Syderstone lifted his hat, smiling at Isadora as they brought their horses up to flank the carriage. 'Miss Alvescot, I protest I have been monstrously ill-used.'

'How is that, sir?' asked Isadora, wondering a little at the faint look of cynical amusement she spied on Roborough's countenance. What had he been about?

'This perfidious friend of mine,' said Syderstone, in a tone of mock-indignation, 'having invited me to sample the local ale, then left me — with an excuse that would not have fooled a two-year-old — in the company of cowherds and draymen in a noisome taproom, with the scantiest instructions on finding my way home anyone ever heard.'

'But you are here, nevertheless,' put in Roborough mildly, 'so they must have been adequate.'

'I have a very good mind to call you out, Roborough. They were not adequate at all. I have been obliged to enquire the way at least a dozen times.'

'But you found your way here before,' objected Isadora reasonably.

'Ah, but that was from the main thoroughfare, my dear Miss Alvescot, not from somewhere in the middle of an unknown countryside.'

'Yes, but Roborough does not know this country any better than you.'

'But he had your Mr Thornbury to aid him. I will not allow you to mitigate his offence, ma'am, for I see clearly why I was subjected to this unwarranted ordeal.'

Roborough thought it was probably true he did know why. For he must have realised his presence was unwelcome after their conversation yesterday. But he was ready to wager Syderstone would not admit to that.

Isadora was agog to know why Roborough should be playing such a trick on this man. It made it even clearer he had not come here in friendship. 'Well, why, then?'

Syderstone gave her the oddest look — positively roguish. What in the world —?

'Because, Miss Alvescot, he wanted to steal a march on me. And I see that is precisely what he has done.'

Mystified, Isadora blinked at him. 'Steal a march on you? What do you mean?'

'Come, come, ma'am, you must not be so modest.'

'He implies,' explained Roborough drily, 'that, having got rid of him by these devious means, I managed to persuade you to ride with me.'

Isadora looked at him frowningly. 'But what has that to do with Mr Syderstone?'

'Miss Alvescot, I protest,' cried Syderstone. 'Can it be possible you prefer Roborough's company to mine? I do not know whether I am more jealous of him or that other young fellow.'

Isadora's perplexity was abruptly replaced with astonishment. 'You cannot mean that you suppose Roborough —?' She broke off, realising to the full what was meant. Was she supposed to believe Syderstone wished to get up a flirtation with her? 'Fudge, sir,' she scoffed. 'And if by that other young fellow you mean Edmund —'

'Is that his name? I had supposed it to be something more romantic — such as Romeo. He certainly looks the part.'

Had Isadora not been so taken aback by this whole gambit, she might have laughed at the idea of Edmund playing Romeo to her Juliet. A more absurd notion she could not have invented. But that Syderstone chose to imagine a rivalry to be got up between himself and Roborough for her company she could barely comprehend. Unless — was it some ploy to use against him?

Her glance went from Syderstone to Roborough and back again. Roborough was looking amused, which was hardly surprising. He was bound to find it funny he could be accused of seeking her company for pleasure. Though it had, she recalled with an obscure sense of satisfaction, been his request that she come with him.

'Never mind it, Syderstone,' Roborough said in a cheerful tone. 'If you feel cheated, you may make up for it tonight. I have affairs to attend to and will be dining out, so you may monopolise Miss Alvescot to your heart's content.'

Oh, might he? Did Roborough suppose he could arrange her evening in this high-handed way? Isadora barely heard Syderstone's declaration of satisfaction with this state of affairs, nor took any notice of his making a play of deciding whether or not to forgive Roborough. She was convinced, in any event, all this was part of some scheme he had on hand.

She would deal with that later. For now, she was interested only in dealing with Roborough. She could only be thankful when Syderstone finally drove on towards the house. As the two horses moved off, she addressed herself wrathfully to Roborough. 'What do you mean by telling him he may monopolise me? You must know very well it is all nonsense.'

'Undoubtedly.'

'Then why did you not say so?'

'Because it suits me to have him think me complaisant in this particular matter.'

'Does it, indeed? And my feelings do not enter into it, I suppose?'

'On the contrary, I hope you will use them to the full.'

'What do you mean?'

He laughed. 'My dear Isadora, what better weapon could I have than to turn you loose upon the man?'

'I knew it. He is not a friend of yours at all, is he?'

'No, not at all,' he admitted.

'Then why is he here?'

Roborough regarded her enigmatically. 'Your curiosity is getting the better of you again, Isadora.'

She emitted an infuriated sound. 'Why can you never answer a simple question?'

'Why can you never keep your nose out of what does not concern you?' he countered.

'Don't talk to me as if I were a schoolgirl,' she flashed. 'And your selling the house is my concern.'

'I stand corrected.' He sighed. 'Very well, Isadora, let us compromise. If you will only refrain from interfering, I will tell you everything you wish to know.'

Isadora was silent. It was a fair offer. But to make such a commitment would be to shackle herself, and she was loath to do that. Especially when she did not yet know what might be in the wind. She looked round at him. 'How can I give you any such assurance? It is like making a commitment without knowing the terms of the contract.'

'Good God, girl, I don't know them myself! Do you think I am doing any of these things from choice?'

She regarded him steadily. 'Then why can I not know the reasons for your being obliged to do them?'

He shook his head, that bitter curl twisting his lips. He was aware what she asked was only just, but he could not expose the ugly truth. It had been bad enough telling Thornbury. But that had been unavoidable. There was no real reason for Isadora to know. Besides, one did not subject a female to that sort of tale, no matter how much she thought she wanted to hear it. 'Suffice to say there are reasons that would satisfy even you.' He looked at her then. 'Trust me, Isadora. I will not fail you, nor your family. But let me alone on this head, if you please.'

Isadora said nothing more. His air of sincerity touched her. All her instincts told her to believe him. But her native caution warned her to be wary. She did not know him.

All at once she realised that she wanted to — know him? Trust him? She could not tell. She only knew that something in her responded to his appeal, warming her to him quite against her will. It was almost persuasive enough. But not entirely. No, if he wanted her trust, let him earn it. And might she not with advantage pursue this game with Syderstone? It offered just the opportunity she had sought.

If Roborough was disappointed that she did not respond, he did not show it. His farewell was cheerful enough as he left her to go and change. Well, then. If he did not care at all, no more did she. She would concentrate on Syderstone.

CHAPTER SEVEN

Isadora's resolve suffered a set-back when she discovered what was afoot between the elder ladies that evening. Matilda began by bemoaning the absence of Roborough. 'Such a pity Cousin Roborough had to go out. It makes the house seem so empty. Do you not feel it so, Ellen?'

'Oh, dear me, yes,' fluttered Mrs Alvescot. Then she smiled at the visitor. 'But we have Mr Syderstone instead.'

'Yes, indeed,' agreed Matilda, casting a sly glance at Isadora. 'I am sure you, Dora, must be so happy to have dear Mr Syderstone's entertainment in your hands.'

Isadora gazed at her blankly. What in the world was this?

'You have not seen Dora act yet, Mr Syderstone,' put in Mrs Alvescot. 'Did you know how very talented she is?'

While Syderstone — elegantly attired for the evening in plum brocade and black silk breeches — was replying suitably to these comments, Isadora eyed her mama and Cousin Matty in some suspicion. If they had set their minds on this for a suitor, they would find themselves disappointed. Great heavens, she wondered they had not enquired of him whether he was single! All desire to play Syderstone's game left her.

'I look forward to seeing Miss Alvescot perform very much,' Syderstone was saying.

To Isadora's consternation, he rose from his chair by Mrs Alvescot as he spoke, moving towards the sofa set somewhat apart, where she had settled with a volume of Shakespeare. Now she only wanted to discourage him.

'I am glad they encouraged me a little,' he said, low-voiced. 'I could not think how I was to rescue myself without rudeness.'

'Why should you wish to?'

'Come, come, Miss Alvescot. You know very well, since we were seated apart at dinner, that I have as yet had no opportunity to obey Roborough's behest I monopolise you tonight.'

'I did not think it a behest,' Isadora said drily.

'That is because you do not rate your own attractions as high as you should.'

'I fail to follow your reasoning.'

He smiled in a rather superior way. 'Therein lies your charm. Roborough, you must know, is willing for me to have you all to myself only so that he may test his success.'

'Fudge.' Isadora almost snorted. 'I wish you will cease this absurdity. He has no such interest in me.'

Syderstone's gaze became a little more intense, his features taking on a serious look. 'That, Miss Alvescot, is to your advantage.'

There was an edge to his voice, and Isadora was conscious of a sudden shift in the atmosphere. Her heartbeat quickened slightly. What was this now? All the determined flirting had been a ruse, it seemed. 'Your meaning?'

He leaned a trifle closer. Isadora, aware of an inward shrinking, forced herself to remain still. There was a look of malevolence in the vivid eyes, although his voice was silk. 'Roborough, my dear, is scarcely suitable game for an innocent like you to be flying at.'

'Indeed?' Isadora tried to keep the coldness she felt out of her voice. Did he think she was setting her cap at Roborough? Inexplicably, whatever her suspicions of him, it was not at all to her taste, she found, to be told ill of him.

'You will not deny you are very little acquainted with him?'

'No, I will not deny that,' Isadora agreed, a touch of ice in her voice. 'But you, Mr Syderstone, have come here purporting to be his friend. How is it possible you can speak of him in this way?'

'I cannot bear to watch him acquire influence over you.'

'You are mistaken. Roborough has no influence over me.'

'We must hope not.'

She drew a breath. 'Mr Syderstone, you do not appear to like Roborough. Yet you followed him here. Why?'

'I had sufficient reason,' responded Syderstone, a smile on his lips that did not reach his eyes.

'You will have to be more specific if I am to believe anything you say of him. You are not his friend. He was not at all pleased to see you.'

The smile grew. 'What an observant child you are.'

'I am not a child, Mr Syderstone.' With a rustle of her black silk gown, Isadora made as if to rise. 'Do you intend to answer me? Because if not I have better things to do with my time.'

Syderstone put out a restraining hand. 'No, don't go.'

'Then stop prevaricating, if you please. Why did you come here?'

His eyes met and held hers. 'I came, Miss Alvescot, to redeem a debt.'

'A debt? You mean you owe him money?'

He laughed lightly. 'The boot, ma'am, is on the other leg.'

Isadora's heart dived abruptly. Roborough owed Syderstone money? No. Impossible. She could feel herself trembling somewhere inside. Why in the world this should upset her so much she could not for the life of her imagine. Somehow, that Roborough should be in debt to this creature filled her with dismay. And disgust. She could not believe it.

In a flash, she realised why. Gentlemen owed other gentlemen money for only one reason. Her lips felt cold and her voice seemed to scrape in her throat as she asked, forcing the words out, 'How can it be that Roborough owes you money?'

The smile on Syderstone's face was chilling. 'It is a debt of honour, Miss Alvescot. A gambling debt.'

Isadora slept badly. Indeed, she felt as if she did not sleep at all. For hours she tossed and turned on her pillows, by turns cursing Syderstone — the bringer of bad tidings — and Roborough, the subject of those ill words.

A gambling debt. Of all things she might have supposed to be the motivating force behind Roborough's actions, this was the last. It was not simply that he could have come here heartlessly to drive them out of their home for his own gain that horrified her so, but that he should have come looking for a solution to problems brought about by his own fell deeds.

She had heard of gamblers who played so high they lost everything, leaving their families destitute and at the mercy of compassionate relatives. But she had not expected to be tainted by such wicked irresponsibility in her own home. Indeed, in her own family, for he was related to her, however distantly. In the face of this monstrous evil, her own scheme to become an actress, damaging though it would be to her family's social position, seemed to her as nothing in comparison.

Worse yet was the realisation which came to her in the early hours that Roborough had very nearly succeeded in winning her over. Just as he had won over the rest: that pleasant, easy manner, the smiling reassurance, the teasing laughter, and the warmth. All false, a facade to screen the real intent — to use their home to save himself from ruin.

'Trust me,' he had said. And she very nearly had.

Here the image of his eyes, warmth radiating from the crinkling corners, and the burnished hair crowning the strong features, caused Isadora to groan and beat her pillows, fighting the melancholy truth. She had begun to like him. She would have given much to be able to trust him. But that was all at an end. She could never trust him after this.

A treacherous little voice in the back of her mind whispered that perhaps it was not true.

Isadora sat up in bed. Could it be that Syderstone, with some wish of blackening Roborough's name, had invented the story? But then, why was he here? That must be the reason. She was grasping at straws. Except that she knew nothing more than the bare fact. Of course she had enquired no further into the matter. How could she? So deeply shocked had she been by his revelation she had, as soon as she was able to move, excused herself abruptly and run to her room to sort out the chaos in her mind.

Hours later, heavy with lack of sleep and dulled into numbness with thinking, she had not sorted it out in the least. Worse, she felt quite ill. She could not possibly ride this morning. Hastily, she sent a message via her maid that Totteridge must make alternative arrangements for Juliet's exercise. If there was a sneaking suspicion in her mind that she was afraid of meeting Roborough, she banished it. She could not ride. She was not fit for it. One glance in her mirror confirmed this. There were shadows beneath her eyes and her skin was pale and drawn. She looked positively haggard.

Well, there was nothing she could do about it. Except that, at all costs, she must avoid comment. For she could not distress her family with this fresh piece of disastrous news.

Roborough might think her capable of that, but... The thought petered out. He had all but accused her of heartlessness towards her family. Such a surge of rage shook her she was obliged to grasp at the chest of drawers, where she was standing, to steady herself. Such duplicity! Such a mean spirit! To put her in the wrong when his own unspeakable fault ought to have been writhing his conscience. Oh, how she hated him.

It was a moment or two before she could compose herself sufficiently to appear normal before anyone she might meet. Not that she expected to find anyone, she was so late.

But a few minutes later, when she entered the breakfast parlour, she was disconcerted to see not only Syderstone, but Roborough too at the table. She halted in the doorway, aghast. Why had she not foreseen this? Somehow the knowledge of his perfidy had made his physical presence disappear. She had not expected ever to see him again.

Both gentlemen looked up. Both smiled in instant greeting, rising from their chairs.

'Ah, good-day to you, Miss Alvescot,' Syderstone greeted her.

'I missed you at the stables,' Roborough said, and then frowned as the expression on her face hit him.

It was almost like a physical blow. He had never experienced such a look. He did not know how to describe it — something between horror and hate. And although it vanished an instant later its imprint stayed indelibly in his mind — and heart. Good God, he felt hurt! What in the name of all the gods had he done to deserve a look like that from Isadora? After yesterday, too, when they had seemed to be going along with much greater ease.

She was responding to Syderstone's query about whether she had slept well as she took a seat. She did not look as if she had slept well, for all her inane and polite response.

'Very well indeed, I thank you, Mr Syderstone. And you?'

Roborough did not hear the answer. He brought his cup of coffee to his lips, regarding Isadora frowningly over the rim.

Aware of his scrutiny, Isadora kept her gaze firmly on her plate as Hampole served her. But the baked eggs brought her stomach up to choke her and she pushed the plate away, shaking her head at the butler. 'Not this morning, Hampole. Just coffee, and perhaps some bread and butter.'

Hampole withdrew the platter, but his perplexity was evident to Roborough. Clearly Isadora usually had a hearty appetite. What had caused her to lose it?

'You are sure you are well, Miss Alvescot?' Syderstone asked solicitously, apparently also having noticed the butler's puzzled look.

Conscious of Roborough's gaze, Isadora answered, 'I have the headache a little.'

'Ah, I thought as much. Too much sun, I dare say.'

'Too much of something, certainly,' muttered Roborough.

'I beg your pardon, my dear fellow?'

'Nothing.' He looked across the table at Syderstone. 'Do you intend to come out with me today?'

'I am afraid not, my dear fellow.' Syderstone added playfully, 'No, no, do not mistake me. No suspicion, I protest, of your serving me another such trick as you did yesterday has even crossed my mind. I have letters to write.' He smiled at Isadora. 'So you need not fear to leave Miss Alvescot alone with me.'

Isadora glanced up quickly. They were not back to that, were they? Great heavens, how could he suppose she might participate once more in his stupid pretence of flirtation after what he had told her? The man was as much a hypocrite as Roborough. And she was in no case to deal with this sort of thing.

Pushing back her chair, she rose quickly. 'If you will excuse me…'

Both gentlemen stood up at once, but although Syderstone bowed as Isadora hastily left the room, Roborough watched her in some perplexity. He turned instantly to Syderstone as the man resumed his seat. 'What has occurred between you?' he demanded abruptly, forgetting the presence of the servants.

Syderstone merely raised his brows in surprise. 'My dear fellow, I do not take your meaning. Miss Alvescot has the headache. No doubt she found she could not face food. I know how she feels. Often is the time —'

'Nonsense! Something has distressed her.' Roborough moved purposefully to the door. 'And I intend to find out what it is.'

Isadora was already halfway down the stairs when Roborough called her name. Oh no, she could not speak to him. Not now. Affecting not to have heard, she hurried on down, heading towards her little parlour.

It availed her nothing. Roborough caught her up in the passage just as she passed the library. 'Isadora, I must and will speak to you.'

She swung round. 'Well, I don't wish to speak to you. Leave me alone!'

'Not until you explain that look you gave me.'

'What look? I don't know what you are talking about.'

'Don't lie to me!'

'How dare you?' flashed Isadora. 'It is not I who am the liar here.'

Even in the dimness of the corridor she could see the light eyes take fire. His voice was dangerously calm. 'Just what is that supposed to mean?'

It was on the tip of Isadora's tongue to fling her accusation at his head. But something — she could not tell what — held her back. She tried to edge away.

Roborough grasped her arm. 'No, you don't.'

'Let me go!'

'Not until you answer me. What did you mean by that remark?'

'Nothing! I meant nothing. I have the headache. Leave me alone!'

He was silent for a moment, but she could hear his unsteady breathing and wondered at it. Why should he be so angry — it was anger, was it not? — when it was he who had done enough to set the whole family against him, let alone herself?

'Isadora,' he said, his rigid control evident, 'you are concealing something from me that has upset you very much. If it has something to do with me — and you need not waste your breath denying it — I have the right to hear it.'

Oh yes, and the right of denial too, Isadora thought. She must keep silent. For he would deny it, of course he would. And, she suddenly realised, with a lurch in her chest she did not comprehend at all, she did not want to hear him lying again.

'I do not wish to discuss the matter,' she said in a voice now suspiciously husky, and tried to pull her arm from his hold.

The grip tightened. 'You may not wish to but you are going to discuss it.'

The tone was peremptory and the odd desire to weep vanished in a surge of fury. 'Oh no, I am not! You may keep your secrets but I must divulge all my private thoughts? I do not think so, Roborough.'

Wrenching out of his hold, she darted to the door of her parlour. His hand slammed against it, holding it fast as she tried to turn the handle.

'*Will* you let me alone? This is my own parlour and I demand that you allow me to enter it.'

'Very well,' he said.

He released his hold on the door, but as she opened it he grabbed its edge, went into the room and, pulling her in after him, slammed it shut and leaned against it.

'You have entered your parlour.'

Isadora glared at him. 'How dare you do this? Leave this instant!'

In the brighter light that came in at the window she saw him shake his head. She almost stamped her foot. His iniquity was forgotten in sheer rage at his audacity in manhandling her into this situation. A sudden vision of Harriet barring the door the other day came to her. Why must people always be standing in her way? She was surrounded by barriers. Great heavens, all she wanted to do was to act!

Overwhelmed all at once by the tensions of the last hours, she sagged, sitting down abruptly in the nearest chair and sinking her head in her hands.

'That will avail you nothing,' came Roborough's cynical tones. 'You need not play-act with me.'

Isadora glanced up, her brow creased as if she was indeed suffering from the headache. She spoke wearily. 'I am not play-acting. If you knew me better, you would know that I never do so in life.'

There was a pause. Then Roborough said, in a softer tone, 'Then what is it that is troubling you?'

It was Isadora's turn to shake her head. It did not seem worthwhile reiterating that she did not wish to discuss it. She had almost forgotten the whole matter anyway. She certainly no longer felt the rage and disgust that had plagued her all night. She must just be too tired and numb to feel any longer. 'I do not know why I have allowed myself to be so moved,' she said, almost to herself. 'At the end of it all, what difference will it make to me?'

'You are talking in riddles,' Roborough told her snappily. 'Make sense, do.'

Isadora reared her head up as a spark of life lit inside her again. How this man had the power to rouse her — in every way. 'It was not I who sought this interview. You may take me as you find me or not at all.'

To her annoyance, he gave a light laugh. 'I don't appear to have much choice. Short of throttling you — which I don't mind telling you has more than once occurred to me — there is little I can do about you, Isadora.'

She was up at once, confronting him. 'No one has asked you to do anything about me. Nor do I wish you to do anything. I would not accept anything you did for me. And what is more—'

'As if that were not enough!'

'— I do not need anything you might do for me,' she finished, riding over him as if he had not spoken. 'I don't need anyone. I am going to fend for myself.'

Roborough eyed her with interest. 'Oh, indeed? How?'

'By becoming an actress, of course,' said Isadora without thinking.

He blinked. 'I beg your pardon?'

Abruptly realising what she had said, Isadora froze. Oh dear heaven, it was out. She had not meant him to know. Now he might find a way to prevent her. He would almost certainly forbid her. Not that she cared for that. Especially now she knew the truth — the kind of man he really was. But she must brace herself for argument. She was certainly not going to back down.

'I said,' she repeated defiantly, 'I am going to be an actress. A real actress. On the boards. Like Mrs Siddons.'

'I see,' Roborough said calmly.

There was a long pause. Isadora, waiting for an explosion that did not come, began to frown, in a good deal of perplexity. Nothing was to be read behind Roborough's steady gaze. He appeared to be studying her face intently.

'Well?' she prompted at last, goaded. 'Have you nothing else to say?'

Roborough looked away from her, glancing about the room. His eye alighted on the outside door. 'Ah. Shall we go outside? It is remarkably close in here, don't you find?'

He was at the door in a moment, undoing the bolts and dragging it open. Stepping outside, he paused, holding the door and gesturing for Isadora to come through.

A trifle dazed at this extraordinary reaction, she obediently walked past him on to the grass and watched him shut the parlour door behind them. As he began to walk across the lawn, he spoke in the most natural way in the world.

'Do you suppose you could keep yourself on the money you would make as an actress?'

Isadora, quite taken aback, fell in beside him. 'I — don't know.'

'Do you know how much an actress is paid?'

'No,' replied Isadora, not without a touch of defiance.

'Nor do I,' Roborough said calmly. 'I imagine it would cap a governess, though, don't you? Of course, you would be obliged to pay for your lodgings and food. But then I dare say when you were famous enough you might merit a benefit night.'

Never having considered this aspect of the matter, except in a vague way that merely assumed vast sums accruing to the latest tragedienne who would naturally be feted and rewarded by Society, Isadora found this prosaic prospect daunting. And extremely irritating. If it was not just like Roborough to try to spoil her dream.

'I should not care what I earned,' she snapped.

'Of course not. You will be suffering for your art — is not that the correct term?'

'I have no idea. Why are you taking up this attitude?'

'My dear Isadora, I am merely trying to enter into your sentiments. Believe me, I have every sympathy with your ambitions. Indeed, I dare say I might be able to do something to help you on your way. I am, after all, a viscount. I imagine if I gave you a letter of introduction to present to one of the Kembles it would not be ignored.'

Isadora hardly knew whether to believe him serious. She had never looked at the practicalities of achieving her aim. But one thing she did not want was a letter of patronage from Roborough. 'I thank you, but you cannot possibly recommend me. I will not become an actress under my own name.'

'Oh, you've thought of that?' he said, turning to her with a look of surprise.

'Of course I have thought of it. I am not entirely stupid. I know I would have to be incognito.'

'It is a pity, then, that Syderstone has met you. For he would be bound to recognise you, and if he should speak of it you would be quite undone.'

They had reached, Isadora saw, the rose garden, which was enclosed by a brick wall with several openings, leading either back to the front lawns or on around them to the flowering gardens. She had been walking aimlessly, but she paused now, hardly hearing what he said as she took in that Roborough, while he spoke, was behaving rather oddly.

'The shame of it is,' he was saying, touching a rose with one finger, 'that you cannot use your own name.' He crossed the path and grasped the stem of another rose with his full hand. He grimaced. 'A thorn — yes.' The hand came away and he examined it closely as he continued, 'Isadora Alvescot is an excellent name for an actress. I do not think you could better it.' Taking another bloom in hand, he let it rest in his palm, gazing at it in frowning silence.

'What in the world are you doing, Roborough?'

He looked round. 'What am I doing?'

'With the roses.'

'Oh, that.' In a confidential sort of voice, he said, 'I am just making certain I am here.'

Isadora stared. 'What do you mean?'

'This is the rose garden, isn't it? We are in Pusay?'

'Well, of course.'

'Thank God for that,' he said, relieved. 'I was convinced I had died and gone to a topsy-turvy sort of Limbo.'

For the space of several seconds, Isadora simply gazed at him, quite unable to comprehend him. Then it dawned on her. 'You are humouring me!' The wretch. She did not know whether to laugh or scream. Despite herself, she began to giggle. 'I thought you would rant and rave at me when you knew my plans.'

Roborough grinned. 'I know you did.'

'So instead you pretend to take an interest, and —'

'Expose the utter impossibility of your doing anything of the kind,' he finished.

Her amusement died abruptly. 'So that is it.'

'Yes, that is it. You cannot, I regret to say, Isadora, become an actress.'

'But —'

'Don't argue! No power on earth would serve to make me permit you to drag my family name in the mud.'

She gasped. 'That is all you care about? I might have guessed it, indeed.'

'You might, if you ever in your life took the trouble to think about anything other than your own gratification.'

'This from you?' gasped Isadora in accents of disbelief.

'Why not from me? There seems to be no one else with the power to curb you and your whims.'

'You think you have power over me? You are mistaken. Merely because you are related to me —'

'If I were not,' he interrupted coolly, 'be sure you might have become an actress with my good will.'

Isadora barely knew how to contain her spleen. 'You are the most selfish man I have ever met in my life! I hate and loathe you. More than that, I utterly despise you!'

Turning on her heel, she fled away, leaving Roborough with some uncomfortable reflections on his handling of her. He had, he flattered himself, been on the point of recovery with her. His method of dealing with that actress nonsense had amused her. What in the name of all the gods had possessed him to carp at her like that?

He had not intended to accuse her of selfishness — and what she supposed he had done to become the most selfish man she had met he could not begin to fathom — but something in him had seemed to rise up against her. It was almost as if he wanted to punish her for that killing look in the breakfast parlour.

But that was ridiculous. Why should he be so upset by Isadora's disapprobation? It was not as if she meant anything to him. Her tantrums merely amused him. Or did they? Yes, when they were not directed with such venom. God, she did hate him!

The thought was so unpalatable he pushed it away. She had spoken in anger. She would recover in a few hours. She could not have meant it. She did not know him well enough to hate him. Unless... Just what had occurred last night? They had parted on reasonably good terms.

Syderstone! It had to be. What in the name of all the gods had the man said to her?

Isadora, meanwhile, escaping she knew not where, but only running to get away from the disturbing presence of the man, had come slap upon Harriet walking around from the stables.

'Good gracious, Dora, what in the world is the matter?' called Harriet, catching sight of the distraught running figure.

Isadora skidded to a halt. 'Harriet! How came you here?'

'In the carriage, of course,' answered Harriet. 'What has happened?'

'Everything!' declared Isadora comprehensively.

Next moment, Harriet was hustling her into the little parlour and pushing her into a chair. 'You look dreadful, Dora. I hope this has nothing to do with Edmund's visit here yesterday, because —'

'Edmund?' echoed Isadora. 'No, indeed.'

'What did occur? He told me he had behaved badly, but —'

'Oh, it is not worth talking of,' said Isadora dismissively, too full of recent events to care. Edmund! She had all but forgotten the episode.

'But what did he do?' Harriet persisted.

'He offered, and when I refused him he tried to kiss me, that is all.'

'All!'

'It was truly nothing to fret over, Harriet. Even Roborough made nothing of it.'

'Roborough saw it?' shrieked Harriet, horrified.

'I don't know exactly what he saw, but he made it possible for Edmund to retire with dignity, and —'

'It does not appear to me his conduct was in the least dignified. And to think Roborough should have witnessed it!'

'Great heavens, Harriet, what does it matter? I do not give a fig for anything that wretched man may think about the affair.'

'Oh, Dora, you are impossible. Of course it matters. If he is to see you kissing other men, you will stand no chance of attaching him.'

Isadora jumped up. 'Not that again. Let me tell you, Harriet, that if Lord Roborough were the last man in the world nothing would induce me to attempt to attach him. And if you knew as much about him as I do you would say the same, believe me.'

'I don't believe you. You have taken one of your nonsensical notions into your head, and —'

'Nonsensical notions? Oh, indeed, it is utterly nonsensical of me to refuse to put out lures to a man who is nothing but a hardened gamester.'

Arrested, Harriet stared at her. 'What?'

Not without a touch of satisfaction, Isadora reiterated the statement. 'He is a gamester. He owes Mr Syderstone money for a gambling debt. That is why Mr Syderstone is here.'

'Mr Syderstone? Oh, you mean the friend who came the other day.'

'He is not a friend. I told you so at the time and I was right.'

'But how can you know this is true?'

'Because Mr Syderstone himself told me of it only last night.' Isadora glared into space, reminded once more of the iniquitous nature of Roborough's unmitigated selfishness. 'Now you see what sort of a man you advocate for my husband.'

Harriet frowned. 'Have you asked Lord Roborough whether it is the case that he owes this man money?'

'Of course I have not. You don't suppose he would admit it, do you?' Isadora gave a mirthless laugh. 'He is so far from being conscious of his wrongs he dares to call me selfish.'

'But you are, Dora. You know you are.'

'I would not sell my inheritance and deprive my entire family of their home only to pay off a gambling debt,' Isadora said scathingly. 'I may be selfish, Harriet, but I am not wickedly so.'

Harriet stared at her for a moment or two, a heavy frown marring her prettiness. At length she said slowly, 'I don't believe it. There must be some mistake. Ten to one you have misunderstood the matter. You usually do.'

'I thank you.'

'Well, you do, Dora. I dare say this Mr Syderstone has some reason for putting you against the viscount.'

Isadora looked struck. Was it possible? She felt her pulse begin to quicken. Could she be mistaken? 'What reason?'

'Perhaps he thinks Roborough has an interest in you, and is jealous.'

This was so close to the conversation of yesterday Isadora almost accepted it for a moment. But had not Syderstone more or less abandoned that line of talk just before he had revealed his little snippet of poison last night? She drew a breath. It had indeed been a poisonous thing to say. Why had she not thought of that before? Gentlemen did not traduce one another's characters to a lady — except for some fell purpose. What motive could he have? Had she not herself suspected him of some ploy against Roborough?

'I wonder if you can be right,' Isadora said slowly.

'That Mr Syderstone is jealous, you mean?'

'No, he is not that. But he has something against Roborough. If he was lying…' Isadora moved purposefully towards the door. 'There is one way to find out.'

'You are going to ask Lord Roborough?' Harriet asked, following her out into the corridor.

'Certainly not. I am going to seek out Mr Syderstone and question him more closely.'

CHAPTER EIGHT

When Isadora discovered Mr Syderstone he was found not to be writing letters as he had claimed he intended, but chatting to Mrs Alvescot and Matilda in the drawing-room.

'Ah, there you are, Dora,' exclaimed Matilda, the instant Isadora and Harriet walked into the room. 'How do you do, Harriet? Here we had been wondering where Dora had got to and she has been with you all the time.'

'Dora, my love,' uttered Mrs Alvescot plaintively, 'we have been neglectful of poor Mr Syderstone, just as Matty says, and we do think you might consent to perform for him.'

Syderstone had risen at the entrance of the young ladies, and he bowed as he added his entreaties. He was urbanity itself. One would suppose he had no notion of having so shocked Isadora last night.

'My dear Miss Alvescot, you will make me the happiest of men. I protest I have been held spellbound with the tale of your skills. I beg you will demonstrate them to me. Be warned I shall not take no for an answer.'

'Oh dear,' fluttered Mrs Alvescot, dismayed, plainly unaware this sort of expression was merely social banter.

'There is no occasion to concern yourself, Ellen,' said Matilda. 'I have no doubt at all Dora will be only too happy to oblige Mr Syderstone.'

Harriet, apparently unable to take so sanguine a view, glanced apprehensively at Isadora's face. 'Now, Dora…'

'Make yourself easy, Harriet,' Isadora said. 'I am content to perform for Mr Syderstone, if he wishes it so very much.'

Amid the clamour of praise and pleasure that greeted this decision, Isadora wondered what Syderstone's motive was in seeking company with her mama and Cousin Matty. How had he come upon them at this hour in the first place? Her mama was usually only to be found in her own sitting-room until luncheon, and Cousin Matty ought to have been attending to Rowland and Fanny's lessons.

'Have you given the children a holiday, Cousin Matty?' Isadora asked, and thought she saw a tinge of pink enter her cousin's cheeks.

'Oh — no, indeed,' said Matilda airily, but a trifle self-consciously, Isadora thought. 'I have set them some reading. One cannot be forever tutoring, you know. And — and your dear mama and I have also to see to the housekeeping, so that we had our discussions on hand today.'

Isadora blinked at her. Discussions? What discussions? Cousin Matty ran the house, discussing domestic matters only with Hampole or the cook. Did Cousin Matty look meaningfully at her mama just then? A moment later, she was sure of it.

'Oh, dear me, yes,' said Mrs Alvescot in a conscience-stricken way. 'Yes, that is quite right, Dora. We have been discussing all about the — the —'

'Dinner,' Matilda said firmly. 'With two gentlemen in the house, you know, one is anxious to set before them an adequate repast.'

Syderstone instantly disclaimed any thought that the hospitality he had been offered had been deficient in any way. While Matilda and Mrs Alvescot enjoyed an absurd but light discussion on the subject, disclaimer following disclaimer, Isadora looked frowningly across at Harriet. Yes, there was enlightenment in her friend's face. She would demand an explanation immediately.

On the pretext of asking advice about which piece she should perform for Mr Syderstone, she drew Harriet away from the vicinity of the chattering elder ladies to the other end of the drawing-room. At least they were too occupied with the man to notice her own drawn looks. But if their occupation was what she feared…

'What in the world have they been at?' Isadora demanded of Harriet in an under voice. 'Mama has not the slightest interest in what is served for dinner.'

'I know it,' Harriet said, and put out a tentative hand. 'You will not get up on your high ropes, will you, Dora?'

'Not if you tell me what is in the wind.'

Harriet bit her lip, fidgeting with her sprigged muslin gown. 'It seems to me they are hedging their bets.'

Isadora frowned. 'On what?'

'On which of the two gentlemen may show more of a disposition to wish to marry you.'

'I knew it!'

'Now, Dora, you promised.'

Isadora drew a breath. 'Yes, very well. But this is the outside of enough. As it chances, I thought of this last night by their manner to Mr Syderstone, but I had forgot it after what he said about Roborough.'

'They are certainly assiduous in their attentions,' Harriet mused. 'For my part, I believe they would do much better to concentrate on the viscount.'

'Harriet!'

'But I suspect,' Harriet went on, paying no attention to the interjection, 'since you have shown yourself to be so against

140

him, they are hoping you might prove more amenable to Syderstone.'

'Well, I shan't. Great heavens, what is the matter with them? What is the matter with all of you? Does no one hear me when I speak?'

'Hush! But if you are so against it, why did you agree to perform for the man?'

'What would you have me do? I cannot drag him from the room and demand he give me the information I seek. Better that he believes me complaisant. I may find an opportunity to question him the more readily.'

But the moment Isadora set her mind to going over her various pieces to decide which of them she might display to advantage everything else went out of her head. Not least because over luncheon — for which Harriet accepted an invitation to remain — the family insisted on involving themselves in the decision once it had been settled Isadora should prepare herself to perform after dinner that evening.

'You are not going to drag us into it, I hope,' Fanny said with misgiving.

'Can I be the headsman again?' asked Rowland excitedly, which was productive of an outbreak of groaning protest.

'Rowland, be quiet!'

'Not Lady Jane!'

'Oh no, Dora, pray —'

'But, my love, it is you Mr Syderstone wishes to see,' Mrs Alvescot said, coming in under the hubbub. 'Lady Jane is very enjoyable, but —'

'Have I said anything at all about Lady Jane?' demanded Isadora, justly annoyed. 'It was Fanny who mentioned it, not I. But,' she added, with a minatory look at Fanny, 'it may be I shall need you to read in lines for me.'

'Oh, Dora,' moaned Fanny. 'Why can you not do one of your monologues?'

'Do Juliet,' suggested Harriet.

'Juliet?' After the way Roborough had criticised it? 'No, indeed. I cannot possibly perform Juliet in public at the present time.'

'For my part, any of your Shakespearian pieces will give uniform satisfaction,' said Matilda pacifically.

But Isadora had a sudden recollection of what Roborough had said to her this morning. At the time, she had not really taken it in. She had been too much moved by her emotions. But now it came back to her like a warning bell. Syderstone would remember her performing. Great heavens, she must not let him see her in action! But she had agreed. If she cried off now, the whole family would make an issue of the matter, and how could she explain? An idea occurred to her, and she rushed impulsively into speech. 'I am not in the mood for tragedy,' she announced. 'I shall do Sheridan. I have quite made up my mind.'

Only Fanny groaned on hearing that she had chosen *The School for Scandal,* for it meant that she must read in the words of Sir Peter Teazle. Everyone else was perfectly satisfied, Harriet in particular saying as she left, 'An excellent choice, Dora. I wish I might remain only to see Roborough's reaction to it.'

'For heaven's sake, Dora, I am not performing for him. In any event, I dare say he will dine out again.'

She was mistaken. Roborough was not only present at dinner, but he had brought Mr Thornbury with him. As the youngsters had been permitted to dine with the adults, Fanny insisting it was the least reward she might expect for helping Isadora with her performance, it was a lively assembly who met that evening in the drawing-room. If it had not been for the black silk evening gowns, their mourning state might have been forgotten.

Roborough, on hearing earlier of the proposed entertainment, had maintained all his usual outward calm and pleasantness in the face of the most unexpected shaft of envy. Because Syderstone, meeting him in his way to his chamber to change, had playfully rallied him on the matter.

'Now, my dear fellow, I think you must admit you are amply repaid for your perfidy of yesterday. Miss Alvescot is to render a performance purely for my benefit. Is that not a triumph?'

For a moment Roborough had been unable to speak. Isadora was to act for Syderstone? A rush of emotion had very nearly choked him and he had felt as if his chest must burst. Thoughts had chased one another through his head. Good God, he was feeling precisely as Syderstone's raillery was meant to make him feel. Except that it should have been a mock-sensation. Why should he care? The little monster had probably done it just to score off him. Perform for Syderstone? What a petty revenge. But, he was obliged to admit it had worked.

'Oh yes?' he had managed coolly. 'A triumph indeed. I wonder what arts you employed to achieve it?'

Syderstone had laughed. 'To say truth, none at all. I am bound to confess the whole suggestion came from her mama and the effusive cousin.'

The relief had been stupendous. Yet Isadora had agreed to it. Had she been forced by politeness? No, that would not weigh with Isadora. Had she so easily dismissed what he had to say about her acting career — that idiotic ambition she had? Chasing moonbeams, silly little devil. Or was it some form of revenge for his refusal to entertain the notion, a determination to show him she meant it?

He sighed inwardly. Who could hope to fathom Isadora's mind? Not he, certainly.

But she had seriously ruffled his sensibilities, he discovered. For he found himself childishly ignoring her throughout the meal, giving his attention rather to Fanny and Rowland, whom he kept in a ripple of amusement with a series of joking remarks. He could not have said whether Isadora even noticed. Or cared. Why should she? Had she not specifically stated her feelings towards him?

But when they were all settled in the drawing-room, and Fanny and Isadora began the little scene — an amusing pastiche of early married life he had seen performed by far more experienced players — Roborough found himself riveted.

She was superb. He had been taken enough by that unofficial sight of her Juliet. Now, seeing her tackle comedy, with a sureness of touch, a lightness that had nothing to do with her ability to call forth the depths of her emotions, he was quite lost in admiration. She did live in her parts, just as she had tried to explain. She *was* Lady Teazle — the young wife running rings around her elderly husband. And what was so astonishing was the character could not have been further from Isadora's own personality.

Something swelled in his chest. A sensation he could not recall experiencing before. Pride? No, something more than that. Then, as Isadora turned to deliver a line, her brown eyes bright with the mischief of it, the feeling swamped his very attempt to identify it. She was enchanting!

An insinuating voice interrupted his pleasure, destroying it at a blow.

'Yes, she is enchanting when she is acting,' said Matilda soulfully, her tone low enough that only he might hear. 'If only we could find her a husband...'

Roborough started, jerking round. The woman had changed her seat for one next to him on the small sofa, and she was looking at him with expectancy in her face under the black velvet turban. It threw him off balance. Had he spoken aloud? She must have seen his reaction in his countenance and made something of it. Or was he mistaken?

'She is very good, isn't she?' Matilda said innocently.

'Very,' he agreed quietly. 'But hush!'

Obediently, Matilda waited for the end of the little piece, much to his relief. Perhaps he had imagined the insinuation. Nevertheless, he found himself unable to concentrate on the performance, too much aware of the female at his side and what she might say.

He hoped, as the piece ended, she would move on. But under cover of the general applause, and Syderstone's extravagant congratulations, she resumed her remarks.

'You do think she looks attractive when she is acting, Cousin Roborough?'

He smiled, but his eyes were wary as he turned to her. He was ready for her now. He kept his tone polite, but distant. 'Or at any time.'

'I knew you must think so,' said Matilda in a smug voice, apparently unaware of his reserve. 'You must know, Cousin Roborough, we have all been wondering what you intend to do for poor Dora.'

His raised his brows. 'Have you?' Poor Dora? She was more capable than the rest of them put together.

'Dear Ellen is most concerned for her,' pursued Matilda. 'You know she is nearly one and twenty, and that she has no dowry at all?'

'Yes, I am quite aware of that.'

'You must be, such care as you have taken to discover all our needs,' simpered Matilda. 'And you will have taken especial notice of her circumstances, being yourself unwed.'

Roborough froze. Then he had not been mistaken. Had they all of them some idea he might marry Isadora? Good God, what next? And had they put this fantastic notion to Isadora herself? What in the name of all the gods had she said to that? He dared swear he might guess. But this must be nipped in the bud. He was going to be manoeuvred neither into promise nor compromise. Yes, he was unwed, thanks to his expert depression of the pretensions of matchmaking mamas. Or, if it came to that, matchmaking cousins.

'Naturally that has been a consideration,' he agreed smilingly. 'A bachelor guardian always gives rise to comment. But as Mrs Alvescot — or my own mother — will always be present in any house where I might find myself in company with Isadora, I cannot think we need fear any daunting consequences.' Seeing the expectancy fading into disappointment on the lady's countenance, he lost no time in driving home the message, adding cheerfully, 'Of course, it is my belief we need not concern ourselves unduly. It is unlikely Isadora will remain single for very long.'

'Oh, do you think so?' said Matilda, hope creeping back into her features.

This one was not easy to snub. He would have to hit harder. He waved a hand to where Syderstone was still engaged in expressing his enjoyment of Isadora's performance. 'You have only to use your eyes, Mrs Dotterell. My friend had not been inside the house for more than a day or so before his attentions became decidedly marked.'

'Is he eligible?'

'Eminently,' said Roborough, conscious of a touch of malice in his tone. Well, good God, she had asked for it. 'And if not him, then some other. We are not all of us hardened bachelors.'

Matilda's gaze flicked back to his face, questions all over her own. 'Hardened? But Cousin Roborough, you will have to beget an heir.'

His lip curled. 'I have one. My father had a brother, you know. The succession is in no danger.'

He saw by the crushed look in her eyes he had succeeded in convincing her of his utter lack of interest in Isadora. Would he might as easily convince himself. Not that he was precisely interested in her in that way. Heaven forbid! She would drive insane any fellow who was fool enough to take her to wife. She was a fascinating female in some ways, but the last he should think of in terms of marriage. Besides, she hated him.

Ignoring the hollow feeling this thought opened up in his chest, he made an excuse to leave Matilda and went over to engage in a low-toned conversation with Thornbury.

Had he but known it, Isadora was far more conscious of his presence than she either expected or wished to be. Discovering him to be of the party had thrown her into confusion. Why was she doing this performance? Only so that she might get Syderstone to discuss further his situation with Roborough. But how could she do so when the subject himself was present?

It was typical of him to behave in this contrary fashion. Moreover, with him in the room, she was on her mettle. Not that there was any reason in the world why she should be. Why should she care what he thought of her performance?

Nevertheless, she felt a good deal put out. In the first place, Roborough was so rude as to have addressed not one syllable to her all evening. And in the second, he apparently had not a word to say of her Lady Teazle. True, she was forced to recollect, after their acrimonious discussion that morning, it was not surprising he should be reluctant to talk to her. But he ought to have known she had not meant that she hated him.

She caught herself up. What was this absurdity? She *did* hate him. Was he not the selfish brute who schemed to sell her home only so that he might settle his gambling debt with Syderstone? Mind, that was not quite decided. Not that she had much doubt it would prove to be true. Only, she thought, with a yearning she barely acknowledged, she did not wish to prove Roborough's character in so base a light.

In the event, the party did not break up until late, and she had no opportunity to converse in any privacy with Syderstone. She was so tired by the time she got to bed — the previous night's deprivations now taking their toll — she fell asleep almost immediately and did not wake until morning.

Reaching the stables, she discovered Roborough had already ridden out on Titian. A bleak depression fell over her spirits. Not that she wished to ride with him, of course, but it was impolite of him not to have waited for her. It was clear enough how little he wished to attempt to make up their differences — if such differences as they'd had could be made up. Which, of course, they could not, if it should prove he was in debt to Syderstone.

These thoughts did nothing to lighten her mood. The ride helped. But if she had half hoped to come upon Roborough she was disappointed. By the time she came in to breakfast, he had already eaten and gone, as had Syderstone. She ate a solitary meal, therefore, and experienced a perverse satisfaction when she discovered it was raining. That would teach him to spend the day gallivanting all over the estate.

She knew she ought to rehearse, but she had no heart for it. Instead she wandered restlessly into the drawing-room just as Matilda was coming in through the door that led to Mrs Alvescot's sitting-room.

'Is Mama already up?' Isadora asked, and then perceived her mother entering behind.

'Dora, there you are,' cried Mrs Alvescot. 'My love, you must listen to what Cousin Matty has told me. Everything is changed and we must remake all our plans.'

'What plans, Mama?'

'Dora, my love, there is no depending upon Roborough, it seems,' said Mrs Alvescot, catching at her daughter's hands and squeezing them.

A cold wind seemed to shiver through Isadora. Don't say Syderstone had been repeating his dire tidings to her mama, of all people. Or was she merely talking of the family's future? 'If you mean he will not help us,' she began, 'I am by no means sure that —'

'We cannot talk here,' interrupted Matilda urgently. 'Let us go back into your sitting-room, Ellen. It would not do for either of the gentlemen to come upon us discussing these matters.'

'Oh dear, that is very true, Matty,' fluttered Mrs Alvescot, allowing herself to be ushered back the way they had come.

'Cousin Matty, what is all this?' demanded Isadora as she followed them both into the little room, unmistakably still exuding a gentlemanly air, with its wood framings and comfortable leather chairs, apart from the pretty striped sofa brought in for Mrs Alvescot, which stood out so oddly, along with the higgledy-piggledy bits and pieces dropped here and there that inevitably accompanied the lady of the house in her daily perambulations.

Dragging Isadora down to sit with her on the sofa, and barely waiting for Mrs Alvescot to be seated in a chair opposite, Matilda launched into her explanation.

'Dora, I had occasion to speak to Cousin Roborough last night, and it pains me to tell you there is no hope from that quarter.'

'None at all,' agreed Mrs Alvescot, shaking her head sadly. 'Such a pity. For when we heard he was still single, you know, my love —'

Wrath swept through Isadora. 'So that is it. Really, Mama, I would have thought my sentiments towards Roborough had been sufficiently well advertised. How could you suppose —?'

'It is not your sentiments that have settled the matter,' interrupted Matilda, 'but the viscount's.'

Isadora's eyes came round to her. She was conscious of a most uncomfortable sensation as her anger gave way to some unnamed emotion. 'What do you mean?'

'I do hope you will not mind too much, Dora, my love,' said Mrs Alvescot anxiously. 'But after all you have said of him I do think we were in any event hoping for too much.'

'What has he said?' Isadora demanded, the feeling in her breast intensifying so that she experienced some difficulty in controlling her breathing.

'I only hinted at the matter,' Matilda told her, a touch defensively, 'and he immediately quashed the possibility outright.'

Isadora drew one or two painful breaths. 'Are you telling me you put it to Roborough that — that he should marry me?'

'Not in so many words,' Matilda said hastily. 'I only suggested vaguely, you know, the interesting circumstance of your both being single.'

'Only!'

'But he is determined to remain a bachelor, Matty says,' Mrs Alvescot disclosed sadly. 'He says he already has an heir in his uncle.'

'But what did he say about me?'

It was Matilda who took up this point. 'Although he made it abundantly clear he had no interest in marrying you —'

'Well, I could have told you that,' put in Isadora, 'but how dared he say so?'

'He did not precisely say it,' said Matilda conscientiously, 'but I could not mistake his meaning. Nevertheless, he seemed to feel you would very soon be married, and gave the strongest encouragement for you to look to Syderstone.'

Isadora stared at her. The strange discomfort vanished. She had no difficulty in recognising the surge of emotion that took its place. 'He did what?'

The two elder ladies exchanged glances of dismay. Then together they rushed into speech.

'Now, Dora —'

'My love, pray —'

'— there is no occasion to —'

'— do not get upon your high ropes!'

'Cousin Matty,' Isadora broke in with careful restraint, 'do you tell me Roborough had the audacity — the vulgarity — the — the —?'

'I do not know why you should take on so, Dora,' said Matilda reprovingly. 'No doubt Lord Roborough considers himself to be acting in your best interests.'

'*My* best interests!'

'Dora, my love —'

'Mama, do not speak to me, for I cannot at this moment be trusted not to say what I shall afterwards be sorry for,' Isadora begged in a barely controlled tone, rising hastily to her feet.

'Dora, you shall not conduct yourself in this way,' said Matilda, getting to her feet also and seizing Isadora's arm.

'Matty, pray,' pleaded Mrs Alvescot uneasily.

'No, Ellen. It is a great deal too bad of Dora to take up this attitude. Lord Roborough has shown her no sort of harm, and when he proves himself to be interested only in the security of her future — for he said himself Syderstone is eminently eligible; those were his very words —'

'Eminently eligible. I see,' Isadora said flatly. She had listened with barely suppressed impatience to Cousin Matty's speech, thinking only that if she had known what Isadora knew she would have spoken very differently. But her quarrel was not with Cousin Matty. She withdrew her arm from that lady's hold and strode to the passage door. 'Then let him repeat those words to me — if he dares!'

She marched from the room and straight up to the stair head, pausing there a moment to catch her breath. She was so angry she could barely contain herself. She wanted to scream and rant and rave. She wanted to rip her nails across Roborough's face. How could he? Oh, but she would kill him for this! Now she saw all the ramifications of his plot. She had been a fool ever to suppose Syderstone spoke anything but the truth. This despicable scheme confirmed it all.

Rushing down the stairs, she was making for her parlour, intent only upon finding some measure of calm so she might confront Roborough when he returned in a controlled fashion — for he would only get the best of it if she attacked him in her present mood — when voices caught her ear as she passed the library. He was already back, was he?

Without pausing for thought, she threw caution to the winds and, seizing the handle, flung open the library door. It crashed back upon its hinges, startling the occupants of the room.

Roborough, seated at the desk by the window, and facing the door, watched in stunned silence as Isadora strode into the room, her brown eyes blazing. He had started as the door banged open, dropping the quill pen with which he had been putting his signature to papers Thornbury had brought and splattering ink across the sheet and blotter.

'Damnation!' Roborough muttered, noticing the mess as he rose automatically to his feet. He had time for no more than a brief look at Thornbury, who was staring blankly at Isadora — as well he might.

'Lord Roborough,' Isadora uttered in a voice of suppressed passion, 'would it be too much to ask if you might spare me a few moments of your valuable time?'

Good God, what on earth was the matter now? The sarcasm was lost in the volcano of her fury. He doubted whether she realised she had used it. Signing to Thornbury — whose astonished gaze had come around to him in mute question — to leave them alone, he bowed slightly. 'Certainly, Isadora.' Waiting only until the door closed-quietly, thank God! — behind Thornbury, he said briskly, 'What have I done this time?'

'What do you mean by telling Cousin Matty that you wish me to marry Syderstone?' Isadora demanded without preamble.

His brows rose. 'I was not aware I had done so.'

'Oh, don't try those tactics on me!'

'What tactics? You will have to be more explicit, Isadora, if I am to understand you.'

'I think you understand me very well indeed,' Isadora said dangerously. 'Syderstone is *eminently eligible*, is he not? No doubt that is why you have determinedly thrown me in his way.'

'Thrown you in his way? Are you mad?'

'And pretended to participate in this stupid game of rivalry, in which you know perfectly well you had no serious intent whatsoever.'

Roborough drew a breath. 'Isadora, either you have completely taken leave of your senses or —'

'Do you deny that you said I should very likely be married soon?'

'I may well have said so, but if that is all your reason for this ridiculous accusation —'

'Oh, I have scarcely begun, Roborough, when it comes to accusations.'

His eyes narrowed as anger burgeoned in his own breast. Now what had she in mind to throw at him? Was there no end to the crimes he was supposed to have committed? 'Indeed?' he said icily. 'Perhaps you would care to be more specific.'

His tone gave Isadora pause. She eyed him, a little of her ability to think coming through again now she had discharged some of her spleen. She wanted to move him. She had come here precisely for this. But the sight of those light eyes, the sound of that easy voice — both hardening against her — cut at something so deep within her it sliced right through her anger, leaving her open to … oh, God, was it pain?

'Well?' he prompted as she hesitated. 'You have vilified me so much already that one more item to my discredit is hardly likely to concern me.'

'Vilified…' Isadora turned away from him, striding restlessly to one of the big bookcases and running aimless fingers across the glass that sheltered her papa's leather-bound tomes. *Vilified.*

An ugly word. Had she spoken only ill of him? She was confused, her brain cloudy. She had come in here to take him to task — how was it she could not remain furious with him? 'If I have done so,' she said, low-toned, not looking at him, 'have I not had cause?'

'Real or imagined?' came Roborough's dry tones.

She spun instantly, the unsettling confusion flying into fury again. 'Oh, and did I imagine what I heard you speak to Thornbury in this very room? Was I dreaming when I was forced to comprehend Syderstone's words to me the other night?'

Roborough's mood darkened. Had he not known it? What mischief had the man brewed? 'What did he say to you?'

Isadora advanced towards the desk, something between anger and entreaty in her face. Distress gave her voice a husky quality. 'If I tell you, are you going to swear it isn't true? Or will you take your usual method and thrust the matter aside? After all, what business is it of mine?'

'Isadora, I cannot answer you if you will persist in talking in riddles.'

'I don't wish you to answer,' she cried, 'for I know what you will say and I cannot bear it!'

There was silence for a moment. Roborough found his anger melting away. Isadora was leaning her hands on the desk, confronting him across the top of it. But her eyes were luminous with unshed tears, and something — compassion, what else? — caused his heart to contract.

Without quite realising what he did, he came around the desk. She straightened up as he reached her, staring him defiantly in the eye, although she blinked the wetness away.

His nearness seemed to menace her, although he made no attempt to touch her. But Isadora felt as if a heat radiated from him — a heat that raced like quicksilver down through her limbs and about her loins, and up through her bosom to spread over her face.

Roborough saw her lips quiver and the words that had been hovering on the tip of his tongue slid away from him. He grasped at them, tried to recall them. But all he could think about was her features gazing up at him, something in her eyes that seemed compound of alarm and bewilderment. Then what came out of his mouth was not what he had meant to say at all. 'What cannot you bear?' he asked softly.

'The knowledge,' Isadora answered out of the extraordinary closeness that had appeared from nowhere, 'that you are a reckless and irresponsible gamester.'

Watching him, for an instant Isadora thought her words had not registered. But then his face changed. The line of his jaw tightened, the light eyes hardened, and the whole cast of his countenance took on that bitter look. He curled his lip as he spoke. 'Syderstone's work, I collect?'

Isadora, painfully conscious of his freezing-up, wished she could recall the words. But they were out, and she had no choice but to say it all. 'He told me you owe him money for a gambling debt.'

The bitter twist to his lip became more pronounced. His voice was harsh. 'Which of course makes me a reckless and irresponsible gamester.'

Isadora bit her lip. 'Are you saying it is not true?'

'Why should I? Would you believe me if I did?'

Slowly she shook her head, aware of a huge weight descending upon her. He was right. She had expected him to deny it. That he did not, she found, was not sufficient to allay her ill belief of him. But it should make a difference. It should.

Or he should at least, if he was innocent of the charge, plead it so. 'You don't deny it, then?'

'The debt?' he said, and laughed shortly, without mirth. 'No.'

Isadora felt her heart contract. 'Then it's true.'

Roborough had not moved from where he stood. But his close proximity now only served to heighten the dreadful sensation of alienation Isadora was experiencing. It was a hateful feeling. She wanted to scream at him, *Deny it! Tell me it isn't true!* But there was no scream left in her. 'Roborough,' she said in a forlorn sort of voice, 'this is not some hideous notion you have of punishing me for daring to accuse you? For if it is, I beg you will not continue with it. If Syderstone was lying —'

'He was not lying,' he said in the hardest voice she had ever heard him use. 'I owe him money. The money is for a gambling debt.' Then he turned, moving away, as if he could not bear to be near her. If he had been asked to describe his emotions he could not have done so. He did not understand them himself. He had never experienced so flat a feeling of finality, such deadly sickness within himself. He knew that beneath it all there was a hard core of intense and vibrant fury. But it was directed at Isadora, and some small vestige of what he had enjoyed in her company — it seemed all at once a very long time ago — prevented him from allowing himself to unleash it.

Perhaps, too, some vague recognition of justice. Syderstone must shoulder part of the blame — that part he did not attribute to Isadora. The rest — well, that had long been brought home to its source.

He looked back at Isadora's still questioning features. The bitter hurt that underlay the anger thrust itself through. Was there nothing in his conduct, in his manner, in his very speech to distinguish him from the real perpetrator of the evils? But it was not that. It was, pure and simple, her lack of faith. There was no reason in the world, he acknowledged, why she should trust him any more than she would trust any man. But her failure to do so was as devastating as if she had actively betrayed him.

Isadora felt his thought like a scourging whiplash although she did not understand it. It had the effect, however, of rousing her ire once more.

'Well, do not glare at me as if I am in the wrong,' she protested fiercely, pinning his feeling down with uncanny accuracy. She moved away, putting distance between them.

'As if it would make any difference to you if you were,' he threw at her across the room.

'Oh, so now we have it, do we? You have done wrong, but I must pay the price, is that it? Well, I promise you, Roborough, if you have the idea to pay off your gambling debt with me, you may think again.'

For an astounded moment, his anger was suspended. 'What nonsense is this?'

'Is that not what this has been all about? You will marry me to Syderstone and thus cancel the debt?'

He answered out of the turmoil within him, with neither thought nor intent. 'That, if it were only possible, is the most tempting solution you have yet saddled me with. But frankly, Isadora, I doubt if he would consider you worth it. For my part, I would not blame him.' With which, he turned swiftly away and walked out of the library.

CHAPTER NINE

Disconsolate, Isadora stared through the outer door of her little parlour, watching the unending drizzle that had misted down from a brooding sky day after dreary day for the last — how long? It felt like a lifetime, although it could only have been a few days. But time had submerged into one single whole since the precipitate departure of the gentlemen last week.

She could not deceive herself that her mood was caused merely by the dismal weather. The whole household was dull; tempers were peevish and she herself was at outs with everyone. Not that there was anything unusual about that. Except that they all blamed her for Roborough's sudden decision to leave for Barton Stacey. Even Thornbury had tried to convince Cousin Matty he had taken the step on receipt of a letter from home, which just happened to coincide with the outbreak of hostilities in the library.

'But we heard you, Dora,' Fanny had insisted. 'Rowland and I both heard you and Cousin Roborough shouting at each other.'

'Then you should not have been listening,' Isadora had told her furiously.

But it would not do. Fanny had made out enough of the words to report to her mother that the two of them had been quarrelling over his decision to marry her to Syderstone, and since Cousin Matty herself disclosed these tidings only moments before to Isadora there could be no doubt she had so much infuriated Roborough he could no longer bear to stay in the house. Thus determined the family.

Moreover, with his departure — the very next morning, to make matters worse — Syderstone had felt himself unable to remain. So it was that the family were deprived of the enjoyment of their company, and Isadora lost two potential suitors at one blow. In vain did she remind Cousin Matty of her own understanding of Roborough's determination not to marry — least of all herself — for both elder ladies felt he might have changed his mind if she had only conducted herself suitably.

Just as if she had never announced her own feelings on the subject. After informing her accusers in no uncertain terms that she could not care tuppence for the loss of two such suitors, either one of whom she would have married only at gunpoint, she had flounced off to her parlour to brood on the fact that Roborough had proved himself as black as she had painted him.

This thought she could not readily shrug aside. Why she did not know. Had she not determined his character at the outset? Oh, he was ready enough with his tongue — a quip at every turn to charm unwary ears. But the outward show of warmth and friendliness, his very determination to make everyone like him — had she not known from the very first? — was all sham and artifice. Stripped of his mask, had he proved equal to the challenge of beguiling her into believing in his integrity? Had he denied the offence, called her doubts into question and laid them all to rest? No, he had not. Oh, but how much she yearned for it that he had. But instead he had admitted the offence.

And, not content with blackening his own character, he had turned the accusation around and flung it in her face. He could not think her worth the price of the debt — that was what he had meant. How dared he? What had she done to him that he should belittle her so? True, she had not curbed her temper, or kowtowed to his authority. But nothing she had said or done could in any way match the heinous crime of which he had admitted his guilt.

She must conclude his real character had shown through at the last. He would not bother to don that playful act again — how alluring had been the facade! — now she knew him for what he was. Though he had resumed it for the family. Her discomfort in his presence that evening at dinner had been acute. Such charm; such wit and laughter! But for herself not a look, not a smile, not the slightest vestige of acknowledgement she even existed.

Though it killed her to admit it, this omission had afflicted her to no little extent. He must have known how distressed she was by the outcome of their confrontation. He *had* known. For had there not been that one soft moment, just before she had loosed the shaft that changed the tide? But so callous was he that all he had been concerned about was consolidating his position within the family — presumably so that anything she might choose to say against him would not be believed.

Well, if he cared so little, she, let him be assured, cared not at all. But she sighed on the thought, drawing her black shawl more closely around her shoulders, for it was chilly in spite of the small fire the butler had caused to be lit for her in her private parlour.

If only the rain would cease. It must be that which weighed so heavily on her spirits. How long had it been since she had even opened a volume of Shakespeare? Let the sun but come out again, and she could find once more the joy in her acting that had illuminated her life prior to the entry into it of a certain gentleman on whom she no longer wished to spend a single thought. He was not worth it.

But this immediately reminded her of the lowering value he had placed on her own worth, and for the hundredth time she replayed that dreadful scene in her mind. She was rescued at length by a light knock at the door and Hampole entered on her invitation.

'Mr Witheridge is here, Miss Dora, and begging the favour of a word.'

Edmund? What did he want? She had not seen either of the Witheridges since Roborough's departure, for Harriet had sent a note to say she had caught a cold that rainy day of Isadora's quarrel with Roborough, and would be abed for a day or so. Perhaps Edmund came in the guise of a messenger to tell her how Harriet did?

'Very well, Hampole, I will see him in here.'

She had not been used to see anyone but Harriet in her little parlour. But things had changed so much, and they were inevitably now to leave this place, so there seemed no point in maintaining her undisputed rights over it.

It was evident, when Edmund entered the room, that he had ridden over. He had shed his greatcoat and hat, but his fair locks were damp at the ends and his boots showed evidence of recent wiping. Moreover, he was rubbing his un-gloved hands as he eyed Isadora a trifle self-consciously.

Taking in these signs of cold, Isadora straight away forgot their previous meeting and came up to pull him towards the fire. 'Great heavens, Edmund, do you wish to catch a cold like poor Harriet? Sit down here at once.'

Pushing him on to the stool before the fire that she had just vacated, she drew up one of the chairs for herself and sat down as he held his hands towards the small blaze.

'My thanks, Dora,' he said, adding shyly as he cast a deprecating glance at her, 'though I would not have expected you to behave so kindly towards me.'

'Not have expected —?' echoed Isadora, widening her eyes at him. Then she remembered. 'Oh, I see.'

Edmund turned on the stool. 'Dora, forgive me! I behaved badly, I know.'

'Do not give the matter a thought,' Isadora said, smiling kindly at him. 'I have not held it against you, be sure.'

He frowned a little. 'But are you not angry with me?'

Isadora laughed. 'My dear Edmund, I have had so much since to plague me I had quite forgot the matter.'

This did not appear to find great favour with her young suitor. His frown deepened, and he sounded a good deal put out. 'I had not realised it was of so little account to you.'

'Edmund, pray don't take an affront into your head. Anyone would suppose you wished me to harbour a grudge against you.'

'Not that, no, but I should have expected you at least to understand the serious nature of my feelings.'

Isadora perceived, with an inward groan, it must now be her task to pacify him because she had not taken his offence seriously. Were it not for the long-standing affection she had always felt for him, in spite of this absurd *tendre* he had lately conceived, she would certainly not have wasted her time. But Edmund was Harriet's brother. And Harriet was her friend. She had to have some regard for his wounded feelings.

'Edmund, I was extremely angry,' she offered, and saw that he brightened at once. 'You behaved very badly. But since there was no possibility of my accepting your offer I could make allowances for —'

'But why is there no possibility of your accepting it?' he interrupted. He reached out and grasped her hands tightly. 'Dora, I could make you happy. I know I could.'

'What do you expect me to say to that, Edmund?' she asked, trying to pull her hands away. 'How could either of us be happy when there is no mutual regard?'

'But there is! At least, I love you. And your situation here is now so uncertain I would think you must welcome the chance to be rescued.'

Isadora got up, wrenching her hands out of his as she spoke. 'Once and for all, Edmund, I am not in need of rescue. How many times are we to go through this absurdity?'

'But it's not absurd,' Edmund protested, rising also and putting out a hand as if he would catch at her shoulder.

Isadora evaded him, uttering warningly, 'Edmund!'

'Marry me, Dora! I swear I will do everything in my power to make you happy!'

'I am sure you think you mean it, but —'

'I do mean it. Why should you not marry me, Dora?'

'Because I don't choose to.' She saw argument in his eye. Driven to the last ditch, she added quickly, 'And even if I did, you may take it Roborough would never permit me to marry you.'

He was silenced. Frowning deeply, he said in an accusing sort of voice, 'He is your guardian, I suppose.'

He was nothing of the sort. But it was evidently going to prove useful for Edmund to believe he was. She had flung the excuse out in sheer desperation. Clearly, though, Edmund was far more inclined to accept prohibition from Roborough *in loco parentis* than her own disinclination. But she could not quite bring herself to acknowledge him as her guardian. 'He will not allow me to marry you,' she repeated.

It was not quite a lie, for had he not said he would have her placed under restraint if she showed any disposition to wish to marry Edmund? He had been joking, of course. A pang smote her but she thrust it away. Must she now acknowledge a loss to herself in the withdrawal of Roborough's stupid jokes? Fudge!

Edmund was chewing his lower lip, apparently turning over in his mind this introduction of a new element into the debate. Before he could speak again, the door opened and his sister Harriet walked in.

'I knew it!' she said crossly. 'Dora, I beg your pardon. I told him not to come, and if I had not been abed these many days —'

'Harriet, what are you doing driving over in this rain?' demanded Isadora, sweeping over to her friend and seizing her by the hands. 'Edmund got wet enough. Great heavens, Harriet, you must be mad!'

'Don't fuss, Dora,' Harriet said impatiently, and Isadora noted she was in fact warmly clad in a woollen cloak over a pink seersucker gown made high to the throat. There was only a trace of her cold remaining in her slightly thickened voice. 'I am very well now, and I had the intention of coming over in any event.' She eyed her brother suspiciously. 'Have you been importuning Dora again, Edmund?'

'If by that you mean have I offered again —'

'Never mind it, Harriet.'

'I do mind it. Edmund, stop making a cake of yourself and go home!'

Her brother drew himself up. 'I shall do so,' he said with an attempt at dignity. 'I know when I am not wanted.'

'Good,' was all Harriet had to say to this.

But Isadora, feeling quite sorry for the poor boy, gave him her hand and urged him to hurry before the drizzle turned into a real downpour. He appeared a little mollified and, although he cast his sister a glance of dislike, said nothing further to disturb either female.

Shutting the door behind him, Isadora came across to Harriet, murmuring, low-toned, 'As it chances, I think I have convinced him that it will not do.'

Harriet tutted, throwing off her cloak. 'Have no fear, Dora. I have arranged with Joseph that he will take him off with him when he goes back home in a few days. On the pretext of getting in a little shooting on his estates, you understand. Edmund will not be able to resist that. And it will take his mind off you.'

Isadora smiled. 'That is thoughtful of you, Harriet. Much more and I should certainly have been driven demented.'

'You don't think I was going to allow my silly brother to drive a spoke in your wheel, do you? I have quite made up my mind that you *will* marry Roborough, Dora.'

To her own astonishment as much as her friend's, Isadora burst into tears.

'Dora! What in the world is the matter?' cried Harriet, rushing to put a comforting arm around her.

'Don't talk to me of R-Roborough,' Isadora managed between gasping sobs. 'I cannot *bear* R-Roborough!'

Harriet promptly pushed her into the one little sofa the room contained and, taking her place beside Isadora, drew her into a close embrace.

'Dearest Dora, what has happened? I know you said Roborough had left here, but —'

'Oh, Harriet, we had the most dreadful quarrel,' Isadora confessed, raising her head and groping in her sleeve for a pocket handkerchief.

Harriet patted her soothingly as she blew her nose, tutting and fussing. But as soon as Isadora was a little recovered she demanded instant enlightenment.

'It was all on account of Syderstone,' Isadora told her, drying her eyes. 'Because Cousin Matty twitted Roborough on thinking of me for a wife, and —'

'She didn't!'

'— of course he told her he would die rather. At least, not that, but it is what he meant. For when,' she went on, dissolving into tears again, 'I t-tackled him on the subject of his wishing me to marry Syderstone, he s-said he would not blame him if he thought I was not even worth that wretched debt.'

Harriet patted her again as she gulped on the rising sobs, but said in a bewildered tone, 'I don't think I quite understand, Dora. What has Syderstone to do with it?'

Isadora turned to her, her brown eyes brimming. 'Harriet, he *does* owe Syderstone that money. And it *is* a g-gambling debt. Oh, my God, I hate him so much.'

'But how do you know? I thought you said —'

'He told me,' Isadora wailed. 'He said it was all true.'

'Roborough said it was true? He admitted it?'

'Yes, I tell you,' Isadora said, once more applying the damp handkerchief to her ravaged features.

Harriet gazed at her, looking quite appalled. Faintly, she muttered, 'There must be some mistake.'

'There is no mistake,' Isadora said in a stronger voice, sniffing at the residue of her tears. 'He is as heartless and selfish as I had at first supposed and there is n-nothing to be d-done about it.'

But this time she managed to control the threatening sobs. Why she should be behaving like a watering-pot all for the sake of Roborough's wretched debt she had not the least idea in the world. It must be relief at finally sharing with someone else the truth of what she had discovered. Certainly, the bout of tears had done something to release the tensions of the past few days.

As if she read her thoughts, Harriet said in a tone of interest, 'How is it that you are so cast down about the affair, Dora?'

Isadora sniffed again, and thrust the sodden handkerchief back into her sleeve. 'I am not cast down at all, but only furious. If I am cast down, it is only natural I should be so to find my family at the mercy of one who is clearly an inveterate gambler, and in all probability a libertine to boot.'

'For shame, Dora. You have no evidence of any kind to support a supposition the poor man might be a libertine.'

'Well, the two usually go hand in hand,' Isadora said defiantly. All she needed was to discover Roborough had a string of mistresses in his train. That would set the seal on her total condemnation.

But Harriet would have none of it. 'Nonsense. You are just trying to find more ammunition to fuel your dislike of Roborough. A dislike which, I strongly suspect, you are manufacturing at this very moment.'

Isadora jumped up off the sofa. 'Of all the stupid things you have ever said, Harriet, that takes precedence. Great heavens, is it not manifestly apparent that I utterly despise and loathe and — and —? Oh, I cannot talk to you!'

Harriet regarded her as she swished up and down the little parlour. 'In any event, you will concede he has had the grace not to compound his fault by lying to you when you accused him of it.'

Isadora halted, turning on Harriet. 'No, because he does not consider it worth his while to attempt to beguile me any further. Why should he, when he must know it is clear to me why he intends to sell this house?'

'You mean to pay the debt to Syderstone?'

'Yes, to pay the debt. And also, I don't doubt, to replenish his pockets so he may gamble it all away again. The best we have to hope for is that he will find no one willing to purchase this horribly ugly house, which I warned him would be found to be the case.'

But when Harriet and she at length went up to the drawing-room — for Isadora would by no means allow her to brave the elements again without being fortified by a luncheon — they discovered Mr Thornbury to have arrived, with extremely unwelcome tidings.

Mrs Alvescot surged out of her chair at the sight of her daughter and almost fell upon her neck. 'Dora, my love, I had not believed it could happen, but it is all too true.'

'Mama, dearest, what is it? What has happened?'

Matilda, who, along with her two children, was looking stunned and shocked, came forward. Isadora's erstwhile unpopularity was apparently forgotten in the face of a fresh disaster. 'Dora,' she said gravely, 'we must all confront the future bravely. Mr Thornbury tells us that there are purchasers coming to look at the house.'

It was evident no one in the family besides Isadora had ever seriously considered it would come to this. Clearly they had so lost their common sense in admiration of Roborough that they had supposed he would somehow take care of them all without resorting to this extreme. But if Mr Thornbury's attempts to allay their alarm succeeded, Isadora thought cynically, Roborough would very quickly recover his lost prestige.

'He cannot mean to desert us,' Matilda said, appealing to Thornbury.

'My dear ma'am,' Thornbury returned, 'there is no occasion for all this distress. While I appreciate it comes in some sort as a shock to you that his lordship intends to sell this estate, I believe there was an intimation of this from Miss Alvescot.'

'They did not believe me,' Isadora said.

The family broke out at her words, all four demanding how they were supposed to believe anything that came from Isadora. By the time Thornbury managed to get a word in again, it was clear to her the shock was starting to wear off. No doubt they would very soon come around to the notion, and, thanks to Thornbury's efforts, feel all their old trust in the perfidious viscount.

'I can heartily assure you all that Lord Roborough has no intention of deserting you. He has pledged himself to make sure none of you suffers by this necessary sale.'

All too necessary, no doubt, if the wretch was to line his pockets again. As for pledging himself to see none of them suffered, what price that from a man who thought nothing of selling the roof from over their unsuspecting heads merely to pay off his gambling debts? But, seeing her mama's distress, Isadora had not had the heart to add to it by disabusing her of her new-found comfortable conviction all would be well in the end.

'My advice to you,' Thornbury was saying, 'is to go out for the day to spare yourselves the pain of seeing these people walking around your home.'

'You mean you want us out of the way,' interpreted Fanny shrewdly.

Thornbury laughed. 'In a word, Miss Fanny, yes. But I do think it would be to your advantage to remain aloof.'

Harriet clinched the matter. 'You are right, Mr Thornbury, and here I may be of service. Why do you not all come to our house for the day? I know Mama will be delighted.'

The suggestion found instant favour, and as the family exclaimed their pleasure Isadora found herself standing by Thornbury.

'I dare say you will be obliged to meet these horrid people here and show them over the house?'

'Unfortunately, no,' he responded. 'I have an engagement elsewhere on the appointed day which I cannot break.' He smiled. 'But although they are coming from a distance I trust they may not be too *horrid* for Hampole.'

'Hampole? You cannot be serious. Why, the poor man can barely walk.'

He laughed. 'I expect he will manage. It is only for a couple of hours.'

The idea hit Isadora like a thunderbolt. Great heavens, dared she? No, no, Roborough would kill her. But why should he find out? Hampole would never betray her. And Thornbury would not be there. In any event, it would serve Roborough out. She would show him she fully intended to fight him every inch of the way. Yes, she would do it.

CHAPTER TEN

When the day of the prospective purchasers' visit dawned, Isadora surprised the family with an announcement. 'I cannot think it fair to poor Hampole, Mama. You know how unsteady are his legs. I shall remain and help him to show these people over the house.'

Only Fanny saw anything odd in this decision. 'What are you about, Dora?' she demanded, getting her cousin on one side.

'Never you mind. And if you so much as breathe a syllable to anyone, Fanny, I shall put horrid creatures in your bed.'

Fanny was silenced, but she continued suspicious. Isadora could only trust that losing herself in the squire's maze would divert her from dangerous speculation. No sooner had the family departed in the open carriage than Isadora dashed upstairs to her bedchamber. She emerged some half an hour later, just as the front door bell clanged. Racing, she flew down the stairs, arriving in the hall at the same moment that Hampole came doddering out from the green baize door at the back.

'I will answer it, Hampole,' she called. 'Do you return to your pantry.'

The butler, however, came on his dignified way, merely casting a reproving glance in her direction. His gaze froze as he came close enough to take her in, and he came to a swaying halt, his jaw dropping wide.

Isadora giggled. 'There is no need to look like that, Hampole. You see before you the housekeeper.'

She pirouetted, showing off the old-fashioned low-waisted gown of dark stuff she had borrowed from her own maid's winter wardrobe. She had about it a stiff leather belt with dangling keys, and over her dark curls she had placed a white cap with frills and lappets. But although the costume was startling enough she was perfectly aware that Hampole's eyes, having run up and down her person, were now fixed in widening horror on her countenance.

'Miss — Dora!' he gasped, evidently taking in the ageing shadows and lines she had added to her features with the assistance of some burnt cork. 'I've never seen the like, not in all my puff! You look fifty if you look a day.'

'I know, but I have my reasons.'

'Aye, and I've my wits and all. Old I may be, Miss Dora, but senile I'm not.'

'No one is suggesting you are, Hampole —' began Isadora in a placating tone, but another clanging at the door interrupted her. 'There, we have no time to argue. Go away, do, there's a good fellow.'

The butler drew himself up. 'That's the door bell, that is,' he said with dignity, 'and it's my place to answer it.'

Isadora seized his arm as he tried to proceed on his way towards the door. 'No, no! At least, you may remain if you wish, but don't try to stop me. Remember, I am the housekeeper and I conduct these people around the property.'

Before Hampole could gather himself for a response, she darted to the door and flung it open. Outside stood only a footman, but in the driveway a lady's face poked out of the window of a chaise that stood there.

'Is this the Alvescot house?' demanded the footman.

'It is indeed,' Isadora confirmed, glancing at the carriage. 'Your — er — employers have come to look at it, I collect?'

'That's right. I'll tell them to get down, shall I?'

'Pray do,' Isadora said cordially, noting with satisfaction from the easy manner in which the man addressed her that he took her for what she purported to be.

As the footman went up to open the door of the carriage, she found Hampole at her elbow. Turning, ready for battle, she was both touched and surprised by what he said.

'I'll send the servants round the back so that Cook can give them ale, Miss Dora. You ask what the quality would like and I'll fetch it to the dining-room. You can start the visit in there.'

'Hampole, you're an old darling,' she told him gratefully.

The butler grunted, but said in a tone of disgust, as he saw the lady and gentleman descending, 'They'll get the Madeira, they will. They're not quality, Miss Dora. Trade, that's what they are.'

Looking the couple over, Isadora swiftly came to the same conclusion. They were overdressed for the occasion, the lady highly fashionable in a satin-trimmed pelisse over a high-waisted gown, topped by a rich bonnet of velvet, feathers and jewelled clasps, the gentleman clearly uncomfortably hot in full town rig, his breeches and coat tightly moulded to his form, his short black boots shiny with polish, and unhandily trying to manage a beaver hat, a cane and leather gloves. They were of middle years, and as soon as the woman spoke, her polite accents overlaying rougher tones, her origins were obvious. Yes, they were definitely trade. Trust Hampole to know it at a glance.

'I am Mrs Haltwhistle,' announced the woman importantly, and, waving an airy hand in the direction of the man, added, 'And this is my husband. We are come to see if this house is suitable to our purposes.'

Isadora dropped a curtsy, wishing very much for a brief moment she had not adopted a housekeeper's character, so that she might tell Mrs Haltwhistle to get straight back in her carriage. How dared Roborough sell their home to such people? It was of a piece with everything else that he should not care what sort of persons inhabited the place after they had been forced to leave it.

'I am the housekeeper, ma'am,' she said in as servile a tone as she could summon up. For she was now determined her plan should succeed.

'Your name?' demanded Mrs Haltwhistle.

For an instant, Isadora panicked. How could she have forgotten to provide herself with a name? She ought to be Mrs somebody. What on earth was she to do?

'My daughter, Miss Hampole, ma'am,' came the butler's voice beside her. 'I am Hampole, the butler.'

Isadora threw him a grateful look, mentally blessing his loyalty. She hoped very much that her papa was not turning in his grave. No, he was more likely to be laughing. He had ever a sense of the ridiculous.

It transpired, when she offered refreshment and the use of the facilities of the house, that Mrs Haltwhistle had attended to all that at the village inn, and they desired nothing more than to proceed at once with their tour of the property. This put Isadora in mind of the whole purpose of her housekeeper act, and she at once threw herself into the role.

'Ah, yes, ma'am,' she said, sighing, 'I am sure you will be pleased, for although it is a trifle untidy there is nothing, I am persuaded, actually wrong with the house itself.'

'Wrong?' repeated Mrs Haltwhistle at once. 'What is wrong with it?'

'Now, m'dear,' came mildly from the man, who appeared, from his accented speech, to have fewer pretensions than his wife, 'miss didn't say as how there were anything wrong with the house. Quite otherwise, as I heard.'

'Exactly so,' said Isadora, smiling warmly at him, though she wanted to scowl. He was not going to be of much help to her. 'Nothing is wrong, beyond the few little items any house of this age might expect.'

'And what might they be?' demanded Mrs Haltwhistle.

'Why do you not have a look for yourself, ma'am?' suggested Isadora sweetly. 'And if there is any little particular problem I have encountered in my work, I shall certainly let you know of it.'

Mrs Haltwhistle grunted, but, urged on by her spouse, she consented to begin with the downstairs rooms. Isadora led them into the good saloon, which was fortunately so rarely used no one bothered to open the windows to air it. Consequently, it smelled of must, offering Isadora an instant opportunity to implement her scheme.

'The family rarely use this room,' she offered, drawing the drapes so that light fell on the Chippendale sofas and chairs, all gilt and brocade, the green of which was repeated on the walls. She sniffed delicately, holding the back of her hand against her nostrils. 'I am not obliged to have the maids work too hard in this saloon.' Then she muttered, in an aside loud enough to be heard, 'Merciful heavens, I hope the damp has not got in here too.'

The implication was not lost on Mrs Haltwhistle. Her ears pricked up. 'What's that? Damp? Did you speak of damp, miss?'

'Damp?' echoed Isadora innocently. 'Dear me, no, ma'am. Damp? No, no, no. Nothing of that sort is to be found in this house, I am sure.'

Mr Haltwhistle frowned a little as his wife snorted her disbelief, his eyes on Isadora's countenance shrewd and assessing. She prayed he would not divine the tell-tale lines on her face. She made haste to remove the visitors from the saloon, with which Mrs Haltwhistle was professing herself satisfied, and continue on to the library.

Hampole re-joined them as they filed through the door, tottering in behind Mr Haltwhistle and throwing Isadora a questioning glance. She hoped he would not interfere when he heard her in action.

In the library the evidence of Roborough's recent tenure was still present in the half-filled inkpot, the used pens and the stained blotter, none of which anyone had troubled to clean or replace since his departure. But Mrs Haltwhistle's care was to slide a finger across the glass cabinets for dust. Isadora plunged recklessly in, refusing to look at Hampole.

'Oh, I do hope you will not find any dust, ma'am. But there, for all the maids will try and keep the place spick and span, it is so very difficult when every breeze from an open window carries the dust from the farm fields. And then, you know, there are not enough of us to care for such a crumbling old — I mean, such a *large* establishment.'

Once more Isadora came under scrutiny from those businessman's eyes in the silent features of Mr Haltwhistle. But his helpmeet, catching the slip just as she had been intended to, immediately demanded enlightenment.

'What do you mean, miss? Crumbling, you said?'

'Did I? No, I think you must be mistaken, ma'am. Old, perhaps.'

Without allowing her any further opportunity to open her mouth, Isadora turned for the door. Encountering Hampole's eye as she passed him, she had the grace to blush a little, but with a little defiant toss of her head she led the way out. In spite of the butler, she chattered all the time as she showed them over the dining-room and the two parlours, dismissing her own private domain with barely a glance.

'It is always the same in these old houses, ma'am. You must prepare for a good deal of polishing, for there is so much panelling to be taken care of, and one must needs guard against an infestation of the sort of beetle that destroys wood, although I am happy to say there has been no sign of that.'

'How do you know?' asked Mrs Haltwhistle, pausing to stare at a patch of panelling in the hall, as if she might see the beetle actually eating away there.

Hampole's face was a study. Controlling a strong desire to giggle, Isadora made haste to respond. 'Oh, I am quite sure of it, ma'am, although I must admit one does not quite know until the wood falls away from the walls. But tap it how you will —' she laughed jovially — 'none of our walls have yet fallen down.' She saw Hampole's expressionless eyes had veered to her face again, and, passing close so he might clearly see the look that positively dared him to intervene, added, 'You will as readily see ghosts appearing through the panelling.'

The butler put out a hand to steady himself against the wall, but he did not speak.

'Ghosts?'

'Pshaw!' came from Mr Haltwhistle, giving his first comment of the morning. 'Don't ye allow this woman to alarm you, m'dear. There's as little chance of ghosts here as there is of this wood beetle she speaks about.'

'I should think not,' Isadora said instantly, laughing. 'Ghosts, indeed! Though to be sure there *is* that dreadful creaking in the basement whenever I am obliged to go down there to fetch up supplies. My poor dear father will not go down at all, will you?'

Receiving nothing other than a blank stare in response to this from the butler, who no longer hobbled down to the basement only because his legs would not permit him, she went on, 'But there. All old houses creak a little, don't they?'

'That they do,' Mr Haltwhistle said sternly, and he added with an unseemly cackle, 'And even were there ghosts, m'dear, they'd be afear'd o'coming out with you on the premises, they would.'

His wife gave him a minatory glare, but said nothing until they had climbed the stairs to the upper floor where Isadora led them into the big drawing-room.

'Now, this is nice,' she cried on a satisfied note, marching into the middle of it and looking about with interest. 'I like a big room.'

'And you'll likely have the furnishings to make it look good, too,' suggested Isadora, fetching a sigh. 'My mistress has never had the means, you see, to do it up as she would like.'

'Well, I don't have the furnishings, as it happens,' said Mrs Haltwhistle, looking out of the windows. 'Look at this view, Matt. But I can see as how a matching set would smarten the place up no end. Yes, I could see myself entertaining on a grand scale in here.'

Isadora was dismayed. This would not do. She went up to Hampole, who had chugged up the stairs some way behind and was now standing just inside the door, looking more like a wax effigy than a butler. Isadora signalled a frantic question with her eyes. His only response was to cast a brief glance of despair to the heavens. There was no help to be got from that quarter. She must think fast.

'Yes, indeed,' she said, crossing the room to join the lady by the windows. 'A good view, isn't it? If only my mistress could afford the upkeep of such grounds. It takes an army of gardeners to keep the lawns down, and you can see how overgrown they are with all this sun and rain. Still, that won't weigh with you, ma'am. You'll no doubt be able to restore the flower gardens to their former glory, and improve the roses no end, I should think, if you mean to make a large investment in it.'

'How large?' asked Mr Haltwhistle suspiciously.

'Well, I'm no expert, but I dare say it may cost as much as the keeping of indoor servants. But there. A pity the house itself could never match the splendour of the gardens.'

Mrs Haltwhistle turned on her. 'And why not? It seems to me a very good house, miss.'

'Oh, it is,' said Isadora, with an excess of sincerity. 'An excellent house. Only…'

'Only?' prompted the lady, bending a frown upon her.

Isadora sighed. 'Ma'am, I beg you will not ask me. I should be failing in my duty to my mistress, ma'am, if I should tell about the rot in the rafters, and —' She broke off artistically, throwing a hand to her mouth and looking with horror-filled eyes over the top of it.

'Rot?' said Mr Haltwhistle in an ominous voice.

'Forget I said it,' Isadora pleaded quickly.

'Forget it?' reiterated Mr Haltwhistle. 'Not I!'

'You've done it now,' sighed Mrs Haltwhistle in a disappointed voice, forgetting her pretensions. 'He won't buy it. Not if the house was ever so beautiful — and that it ain't.'

'Oh, sir,' mourned Isadora, turning to the man. 'It really is not such a serious problem as you might think. The rot is only very little advanced as yet, and —'

'That's enough. I thought when you came in with your wood beetle and ghosts, miss, you was trying to put us off the place. I don't hold with ghosts, and wood beetle you can treat if you catch it early. But if there's one thing I won't risk it's rot. Once let rot in and the place is done for.' With which, much to Isadora's relief, he made for the drawing-room door, followed by his reluctant spouse, who was trying to persuade him to check for the presence of rot before he made up his mind.

Isadora, exchanging at the door a triumphant glance with Hampole, followed them out and down the stairs. In the hall, she made a last attempt — in her character of housekeeper — to avert disaster. 'Would you not like to see more of the house, sir? I know so little of these matters, and I am sure if there is rot Mr Thornbury would know of it and would have warned you.'

'Thornbury? Don't talk to me of that fellow,' said Mr Haltwhistle. 'I'll have a word or two to say to him. He has no business trying to sell a pig in a poke to a man of my experience, and so I shall tell him.'

'That he will, be sure,' put in his wife.

'Rot, is it?' muttered her spouse, bearing out this pronouncement.

'Speaks his mind, does Matt. Why, who's this?'

Isadora saw the woman's attention was caught by someone at the front door, and realised, to her horror, that Roborough was standing just within it, the handle of the open door still within his hand.

Great heavens, what in the world was he doing back? And why must he come now? But this was no time to question or think. She must act. 'My lord!' she said, moving forward swiftly to mask the astonished look on Roborough's face. 'We did not expect you so soon. You must be famished. I shall have Cook prepare something for you on the instant.'

Without giving him an opportunity to reply, she went quickly back towards the visitors, saying in a lowered tone, 'Mrs

Haltwhistle, this is Lord Roborough — the owner of the property, you must know. His lordship has taken us a little by surprise. We will not keep you, for I know he does not wish to be involved in these negotiations.'

'Oh, aye,' said Mr Haltwhistle, giving an embarrassed cough and glancing briefly across at Roborough who had moved into the hall. 'No need to tell him until we're gone, eh?'

'But won't we meet —?' began Mrs Haltwhistle in a disappointed way.

'No, no,' Isadora insisted in a lively and quite genuine apprehension. 'Not to be thought of. His lordship will be so disappointed that you do not wish to buy the place. Indeed, he may make every effort to change your minds.'

'Well, he won't do that,' came from the determined Mr Haltwhistle, who ushered his wife out before him. 'Come along, m'dear. We won't disturb his lordship. I don't know about you, but I'd be mighty disconcerted to have to tell him as I don't like his house.'

This view of the matter seemed to affect his wife powerfully, for she abandoned any idea of getting the introduction she craved and allowed herself to be pulled towards the waiting chaise, to which the servants had fortunately already returned. The footman jumped down at once and opened the door for the Haltwhistles to enter.

Isadora waved them off with a sigh of relief, and turned back to the house to find that Roborough had come out of it again and was watching her, wearing — to her secret dismay — his enigmatic face. He had removed his hat and gloves and was standing with folded arms, looking her over calmly. She had quite forgotten the circumstances of their last meeting, this fresh disastrous arrival throwing them quite out of her mind — which now froze on her. What was she to say?

Then, as his gaze travelled slowly over her person and came to rest on her face, she recalled her disguise. In spite of all, she was obliged to muffle a giggle, turning it unconvincingly into a cough.

Fortunately, Hampole chose this moment to come out of the house too. His short-sighted gaze peered from Roborough to his young mistress, and thence to the chaise which was just rumbling off down the drive.

Roborough's glance left Isadora and went, in frowning question, to the butler. Isadora instantly intervened. 'Pray don't blame Hampole. I made him support me. It was all my own doing.'

Roborough's eyes came back to her. 'I am well aware of that.' He looked at the butler again. 'I was merely going to ask you, Hampole, if you would be good enough to arrange for me to join the company at luncheon.'

'You may join Miss Dora, my lord,' Hampole said very correctly. 'The rest of the family are at Witheridge.' Then he bowed, and, with a glance at Isadora that might have been of commiseration, he went back into the house.

Roborough strolled forward. 'Do you wish to go and remove that perfectly ridiculous costume immediately, or shall we walk a little?'

'Oh no,' Isadora said instantly. 'If you mean to scold me, by all means let us get it over with directly.'

She turned towards the lawns and began to walk, steadfastly regarding the grass beneath her feet. For his presence had awakened all sorts of odd reactions in her. She was dreading what he might say — evidenced by the leaping of her heart in her breast — and yet she was conscious of a sense of satisfaction at his being here again.

That could only be because she was glad to have him find her out in her fight against what he would do. But it did not account for the chills that ran up and down her spine, or the fluttering in her stomach, both of which had attacked her almost instantly once her initial horror had died away. She supposed that must be due to fear of his reaction. Why she should be so afraid of anything he might say she had no idea in the world. Great heavens, she could match him angry word for angry word if she chose! It did not make sense.

She was not left wondering about such matters for long, for Roborough spoke once they were out of earshot of the house.

'This is far enough, I think,' he said, halting in the middle of the wide lawns and turning to confront her.

Only now did Isadora notice he had relaxed the strictness of his costume, for under the black coat his waistcoat was grey and he had reverted to white linen at neck and wrists. It lightened his look so much that her tension eased a trifle. Not that she anticipated that they would shout at one another, as they had at their last meeting...

It all came back to her in a flash. The unkind words that had been hurled back and forth across the library. Abruptly, she wondered how she could have said such things to him. Forgetting the evidence, the fact he had himself admitted to the debt, she saw only the warm friendliness of his strong features. For — why she could not imagine — there was no burgeoning anger in his face. He looked bland, yes, but his features were relaxed and there was even a trace of the old warmth in the back of his eyes.

'Perhaps, Isadora,' he said in the mild tone he was wont to use with her, 'you will be kind enough to explain the meaning of that exhibition I have just witnessed.'

'You must know very well what it means,' she told him, goaded.

'And,' he pursued, with a gesture that encompassed her costume, 'the peculiar circumstance of your choosing to wear a servant's gown, and mud all over your face.'

'It is not mud,' Isadora said indignantly. 'It is burnt cork, for the purpose of making me look older.'

He affected to examine her features more closely, frowning. 'Yes, I suppose there is something in that. Why must you look older?'

'Because I am the housekeeper, of course. Great heavens, Roborough, cannot you see what I am about? I have been making sure those people did not buy the house.'

'Yes, that much I had understood. I presume you succeeded?'

'Yes, I did. And now you may ring your peal over me as much as you wish, but it will change nothing.'

He regarded her silently for a moment or two. Then he said calmly, 'I suppose you think you have been very clever.'

'I do, as it chances,' Isadora responded unthinkingly, and unable to help a ripple of amusement escaping. 'I pretended, you see, there was nothing amiss, and only let fall hints of such matters as might serve to put them off.' She giggled. 'Poor Hampole nearly had an apoplexy when I talked of ghosts coming through the panelling.'

'Ghosts?'

'Yes, but that was after my invention of wood beetles had failed to rouse Mr Haltwhistle.'

'Oh, my God,' gasped Roborough, and burst into laughter.

For a few moments he was quite incapable of speech. For not only did this escapade appear to him to be exquisitely humorous, in spite of its devilish intent, but Isadora's blank amazement at his reaction only added to his amusement.

She could not know it, but the very fact of her having chosen to thwart him in this ridiculous fashion just today, when he had returned in a spirit of the utmost humility, ready to do whatever he must to patch up the hideous misunderstanding between them, was in itself extremely funny. It was so typical to discover her in mischief such as this. He ought to be angry. But his capacity to be angry with Isadora was, for the present moment, exhausted. He was far too anxious to make his peace with her after that dreadful day in the library.

He had left here in a mood of such violent resentment he had doubted of ever returning while Isadora remained on the premises. But that ridiculous notion had melted, along with every vestige of fury, when realisation had hit him on the journey. He had wanted to turn back there and then. But he had recognised that would be both impractical and foolish. For Isadora needed time to calm down too — if there was ever to be anything between them that did not gnaw his conscience and drive him into a state of mental anguish.

He was glad, at any rate, to find she did not instantly return to her theme begun in the library. He could only hope that, like his, her anger had cooled over time. Although he would not put it past her to hark back to that business any time she lost her temper. Which might be at any moment, if he did not control his amusement.

'Don't — don't look at me like that,' he managed to say, hiccupping on his mirth.

'Like what?'

'As if I am quite mad for laughing.'

'Well, you are. After all, I have stopped the sale of the house.'

'I know you have,' he agreed, grinning, 'and if you had your deserts for such a prank there is no saying what I might not do to you. But I can't help but be amused by it.'

'It is not really a prank, Roborough,' she objected. 'You could not seriously expect me to stand by and see my family ruined all for your sake. Though I see how it must appear to you.'

'I seriously doubt that,' he said drily, for she had no idea how it appeared to him. In fact, seeing what she believed of him, he did not blame her in the least. It only added to her manifold attractions, if the truth be told. 'However, I have to admit that buyers who would be frightened off by such nonsense would very likely have ended by not purchasing the property in any event.'

Isadora gurgled. 'Well, that was not quite all, you know.'

He raised his brows. 'Oh?'

'Indeed,' she went on with relish, unexpectedly delighted by the thought he was sharing her enjoyment, 'it seemed as if neither ghosts nor wood beetles had the power to frighten Mr Haltwhistle off, although his wife would have been, I believe. Only then she chose to become enamoured of the drawing-room, and I thought I was quite undone. I could think of nothing at first to counteract it, although indeed I made much of the army of gardeners they would need to keep up the grounds. Then, by very good fortune, I chanced upon the one thing that appears to be Mr Haltwhistle's *bête noire*.'

'And what was that?' asked Roborough, the warmth of laughter in his eyes.

'Rot.'

He blinked. 'Rot?'

'Yes. Rot in the rafters, was what I said, if I remember rightly. I could not have hit upon anything better.'

'Indeed?'

'No, for he immediately called off any idea of buying the place, and Mrs Haltwhistle assured me there was no chance of him altering his mind. Which, as you may suppose, I was very glad to hear.'

'I imagine you were, 'Roborough said drily. 'I, on the other hand —'

'Oh, fudge,' uttered Isadora in a conscience-stricken way, remembering to whom she was speaking. 'Here it comes. I might have known you were only teasing me, pretending to be amused, and humouring me again. Now I suppose you will rail at me, and I shall scream back at you, and everything will be as horrid as ever.'

He eyed her in silence for a moment or two. Then he asked quietly, 'Is that how you believe it must be between us?'

Isadora did not answer. She was conscious of the strongest desire it should not be like that between them. But how could it be otherwise, with what she knew of him — with what he thought of her, added to what he must now feel about what she had done this day? What chance was there of setting up any better understanding? Not that she wished to. Only — why had he to be the villain of the piece? Why could it not have been Syderstone who had lied?

'Isadora?' he said softly, recalling her attention.

She looked at him. 'Roborough, can you not find some other way to pay Syderstone? Does it have to be this house? There must be other means at your disposal.'

He was so disappointed she had ignored his question he found himself retaliating bitterly, 'Give you to him in marriage, perhaps?'

She did not flash back at him, much to his surprise. He had thrown her own accusation back at her, and it would not have astonished him if she had even hit him, as he had once seen her hit Edmund Witheridge.

But instead her features softened, her eyes beseeched him and her lips trembled.

'I would even be prepared to do that, if it will help Mama,' she said in accents that would have moved Pontius Pilate, he thought. What was she doing? Suddenly he understood. The cunning little devil!

'I am not quite the fool you take me for, Isadora,' he said calmly. 'You may play-act for all you are worth — and I may say that today your assertion that you never do so in life seems strangely misleading — but the house is going to be sold, and in spite of this fiasco you will not stop it.'

Her face changed instantly. Yes, that was more like the Isadora he had grown to know. He could deal with this, with ease. Yet it brought him no nearer to what he wanted. Better, however, than a shouting match.

'If it is sold,' Isadora threw at him crossly, annoyed he had seen through her act, 'it will be over my dead body.'

'That,' retorted Roborough thoughtfully, 'is not such a bad idea. At least it will save me having to provide for you.'

'Oh! Abominable!'

Roborough bowed. 'Back to normal, I see.'

'You *will* see, I promise you.' With which, she turned from him and walked swiftly back to the house. Really, he was impossible. Here she had been unconsciously warming to him again, and what happened? He began with his stupid teasing remarks to drive her into hating him once more. Well, she was positively glad of it. She needed this reminder of his real character to stop allowing herself to be ensnared by his wiles.

Having removed her costume, and thanked her maid for the use of it, she washed off the burnt cork, and had herself dressed once more in her muslin mourning gown. She must meet Roborough for luncheon, she supposed, but there was no reason why she should speak to him.

In the event, however, he was not there. He had eaten swiftly of the cold collation, Hampole told her, and left the house; with a brief parting word that he should be expected for dinner.

Isadora was conscious of disappointment out of all proportion to the circumstances. It was not as if she had been looking forward to a tête-à-tête with the man. She had not been going to say a word. But somehow, when he was not even there not to have that word said to him, she was infuriated. How foolish. What in the world did it matter to her? She wished he had not come back.

A new thought struck her. She would wish it even more when the family got wind of her escapade. That would not matter, if Roborough was not there to hear the inevitable recriminations, for they would be twice as bad for his presence.

But when she came down to dinner, having hidden in her parlour to avoid meeting the family as they returned beforehand, she was astonished to be received, if not with delight, then at least with enthusiasm. Not for her, to be sure. But every one of the family was plainly in alt.

'Dora, isn't it wonderful?' said Fanny ecstatically.

'Isn't what wonderful?'

'Barton Stacey!' yelled Rowland, grinning widely.

'Dear me, yes, my love,' chimed in Mrs Alvescot, beaming, 'it is true, and we are all to go.'

'Could anything be more fortunate, just now when more buyers will likely come around to see the place?' said Matilda.

Mystified, Isadora looked frowningly from one to the other, while the family gazed at her in perplexity.

'I am afraid,' put in Roborough gently, 'that you are all before Isadora with the news. I have not seen her since I put the arrangements in hand.'

A sense of extreme foreboding entered Isadora's breast. What had he done? 'What arrangements?'

Roborough smiled blandly. 'Why, to take you all on an immediate visit to my home at Barton Stacey.'

Isadora gazed at him. 'Visit?'

'An indefinite visit,' he said smoothly. 'While the house is being looked over by potential purchasers.'

Isadora's bosom swelled indignantly. The unmitigated, unscrupulous wretch! And she thought *she* had been clever. She had reckoned without her host. She had been neatly out-generalled.

CHAPTER ELEVEN

It was an uneasy meeting. The two families gathered, at Roborough's request, in the lesser of the two receiving saloons at the mansion in Barton Stacey. If, as he had told Isadora last night when pointing the room out, it was the more informal, she dreaded to think what effect the main saloon might have on her family.

Isadora's poor mama was looking quite crushed. But that might well be due to Lady Roborough's languid and melancholy demeanour. As well perhaps their arrival had been so late that only the upper servants had still been awake to welcome them.

'Forgive my not receiving you last evening,' said her ladyship as her son presented Mrs Alvescot, not even troubling herself to rise from her chair, 'but I trust Stratton saw all right?'

'I think you mean Roborough, Mama,' piped up one of the two young Stratton girls in gently chiding tones.

'What, Bettina?'

'Titus is not Stratton any longer.'

A great sigh escaped the lady's lips. 'How right of you to remind me.' She gazed sorrowfully up at her son where he stood to one side of her chair, still engaged in the presentations. 'Dear boy, forgive me. So difficult to remember you have the title now.'

'Think nothing of it, ma'am,' Roborough said unsmilingly, and continued with his introductions. Even Roborough's spirits appeared to be damped by his mother's woebegone attitude, Isadora decided, recalling the way he had contrasted the warmth of her own home so favourably with the atmosphere of this one. There could be no doubt that the extreme formality — everything in its place, all furnishings precisely matched — and the sophistication of the surroundings were oppressive. It was certainly having its effect on Matilda and her children. Isadora had never known them so quiet.

She foresaw a trying time ahead. Could any of them ever feel at home here? They had no other home, once the house was sold. She dared swear the family would all become homesick, and undoubtedly turn their frustrations upon her again.

For it had not been long before the real reason for Roborough's inviting them to Barton Stacey had leaked out. Fanny again, of course. She had — very conveniently — overheard Roborough telling Thornbury about the housekeeper act, and saying he was packing Isadora off to Barton Stacey where she could do no further harm.

'I knew you were up to something, Dora,' Fanny had stated smugly as she had repeated the gist of the overheard conversation to her elders.

Isadora had been obliged to endure the family's loud expressions of annoyance at having to share in her disgrace, and had found herself unexpectedly in debt to Roborough. For no sooner had he understood she had been found out than he had made haste to pour oil on the troubled waters.

'You must not blame Isadora,' he had said to the room at large when Fanny's indiscreet tongue had let the matter out, 'for it would have come to this in any event. Perhaps we should rather all be grateful Isadora's little masquerade has precipitated the inevitable.'

Isadora had been grateful for that small mercy — for naturally, she had cynically noted, everyone obeyed Roborough's instruction — and for the sudden activity provoked by the necessary sorting and packing, which had left none of them time to think, and generated a universal current of excitement for more than a week.

The only jarring note had been introduced by Harriet, who wept to think that Isadora would not be at her imminent wedding. 'But I shall console myself with the thought that I must soon receive an invitation to yours, my dearest Dora,' she said brokenly.

'Harriet, will you never give up?'

'But you told me Roborough had been so kind to you, Dora. He must have forgiven you.'

'Forgiven me? And what of my forgiveness, or is that of no importance? Anyone would suppose I was the gambler.'

Harriet pleaded that she had rather been forgetting that aspect of the matter. But, despite her protestations, in secret Isadora caught herself wondering if she might not overlook Roborough's iniquities, should he show any disposition to wish to marry her. Shocked at her own thoughts, she banished them hastily, trying to recall her dislike of him and doing her best to rekindle her determination to become an actress.

Oddly, this ambition seemed to have lost its lustre as a prospective future. This, she also set down to Roborough's account. Had it not been he who had ruthlessly opened her eyes to facts about that profession which she had never even troubled herself to contemplate?

She would not allow herself to soften towards him. Fortunately the preparations had occupied so much of her time she saw very little of the man — a fact of which she tried to persuade herself she was very glad indeed.

But now, she pondered, coming back to a present which promised little in the way of distractions, she could not imagine how she was going to occupy her time, or indeed how they were any of them to go on in such a household, presided over by the extraordinary Lady Roborough.

Glancing across at her, enthroned in an easy chair, a footstool supporting her weary legs, Isadora was seized by an idiotic desire to giggle. Her ladyship appeared exhausted, which, together with the deep shadows about her eyes and cheeks, lent credence to her assertion she slept but fitfully at night, and she exuded such an air of gloom and despondency as affected all who came into contact with her — her son in particular. Isadora had never seen him so little at his usual friendly ease. She was conscious of feeling almost sorry for him.

The two Misses Stratton were plainly equally uncomfortable in their mama's presence. Bettina, at fifteen already displaying the accepted decorum of a debutante, and Corinne, a year younger and quite as politely behaved if a little more fidgety, both bade fair to rival their brother's attractions. The chestnut hair had in them a brighter sheen, and both displayed the friendly warmth of Roborough in their smiles.

They plainly held their brother in great affection, casting him unmistakable looks of admiration now and then, and laughing immoderately at his sallies — until called to order by a governess who looked to be strictness itself.

Or perhaps, thought Isadora, noting how that female glanced apprehensively at her mistress each time the girls burst out, that was a mask for Lady Roborough's benefit. It certainly did not appear as if the daughters of the house feared their preceptress.

'Oh, Cally,' cried out Corinne suddenly, and then swiftly added as the governess frowned her down, 'Oh, drat. I mean, *Miss Callowell*, how shall you bear it having another pupil quartered on you —?'

'Oh no, no,' broke in Matilda. 'I should not dream of imposing —'

'But Fanny must join us,' Bettina interjected. She turned eagerly to her brother. 'Must she not, Titus?'

'Oh, Cousin Roborough, I pray you will not trouble Miss — Miss —'

'It will be no trouble, Mrs Dotterell,' put in the governess in a kindly tone, leaning forward to smile at Fanny. 'That is, if Miss Dotterell — Fanny — will care to partake of her cousins' lessons.'

There could be no doubt of this. Fanny began to look more cheerful.

Miss Callowell, evidently noting Rowland's apprehensive face, smiled at him. 'There is no occasion for you to look glum, young man. I am sure his lordship has quite other plans for you.'

Roborough grinned. 'School, I'm afraid.'

'I knew it,' muttered Rowland in a disgusted under voice, only to receive a dig in the ribs from his sister beside him.

'Never mind, Rowland,' laughed Roborough. 'I survived it.' He looked at Matilda. 'I have already requested my agent Dalbury to make the necessary arrangements.'

'There now, Matty,' fluttered Mrs Alvescot, 'I knew we might be comfortable at the last.'

Overcome, Matilda quite lost herself in a morass of half-sentences, from which it emerged she would do all in her power to repay such kindness.

'Nonsense,' said Roborough dismissively. 'There will be time enough for thanks when we have settled everyone to our mutual satisfaction.'

His glance encompassed Isadora as he spoke and, not much to his surprise, he encountered a suspicious glare. What underhand schemes did she suppose him to be hatching this time? She had borne little part so far in this meeting. He rather suspected her mind had been largely otherwhere.

Isadora's mind snapped to attention a moment later, for Lady Roborough suddenly entered the lists.

'I am glad,' she said, in anything but satisfied accents, 'you have settled one matter at least, Stratton.'

'Roborough,' corrected Bettina automatically, in a guarded whisper.

'Never mind it, Bettina,' intervened Roborough. He added briefly to his mother, 'You will become accustomed in time, ma'am.'

'No one can tell me about becoming accustomed,' said her ladyship, roused to plaintive protest. 'My whole life has been dedicated to accustoming myself to circumstances over which I have no control.'

'Yes, very well, ma'am,' said Roborough repressively. 'But we were talking of the needs of our guests.'

Casting him only a reproachful glance, his mother eyed the now silent company. Her wandering gaze found Isadora and halted. 'Ah, poor child. What shall we do for you?'

'Me, ma'am?' said Isadora, startled.

A lugubrious sigh left Lady Roborough's lips. 'Stratton tells me you are twenty already. Twenty, and not even out.'

Surprisingly, it was Mrs Alvescot, bristling in defence of her young, who took up this point. 'It was not Dora's fault, ma'am. My poor dear husband was so ill, and though Lady Witheridge offered to bring her out, Dora would not think of leaving her papa.'

'Of course not, Mama,' agreed Isadora bracingly. 'I beg you will not distress yourself. I have no regrets, Lady Roborough, I assure you.'

'But unwed,' mourned her ladyship. 'At twenty.'

'Yes, yes, ma'am,' put in Roborough hastily. 'You may believe, however, that Isadora has not yet felt the want of a husband.'

'I can speak for myself, I thank you, Roborough.'

At that, the entire family — with the exception of Rowland, still brooding darkly over his immediate future — broke brightly into speech.

'Oh, Lady Roborough, what a fine house you have!'

'Oh dear, I don't think I have caught quite all the names. Bettina, was it, and —?'

'I do hope I may be able to keep up with Corinne and Bettina, Miss Callowell.'

The significance of these interventions was not lost on Isadora and, casting Roborough a look that promised vengeance presently, she settled back again in her seat, firmly closing her mouth. Seeing it, the family breathed a collective sigh of relief and subsided. Roborough, amused, took the lead again, addressing his mother.

'What you do not know of Isadora, ma'am, is that she is a remarkably fine actress.'

This brought Isadora instantly under the scrutiny of all eyes again. But she noticed it only peripherally, for her attention was on Roborough. Now what was he at? The glance he threw her was full of teasing warmth and she felt her resentment melting away, quite against her will.

'You did not appear to think so when I did Lady Teazle,' she said, forgetting the company.

'On the contrary.'

'Oh, now, he did like your Lady Teazle, Dora,' put in Matilda pacifically. 'I can vouch for that.'

But Isadora, recalling how Roborough had outwitted her, determined to have her revenge. Turning to his mother, she spoke in her sweetest tones. 'It is so kind in you to invite us, ma'am, but you cannot wish to have us all quartered on you forever. Do you not wonder what his lordship intends to do about us?'

'There is time enough to be thinking of that,' Roborough intervened before his mother could respond. 'We are all of us still in mourning, and nothing can be finally decided until that period is over.'

Isadora, glancing ruefully about the room, began to wish it were well over. It had been bad enough at Pusay. How were any of them to be anything but miserable decked out like so many crows? She was relieved when it seemed Roborough had had enough of this gathering.

'Bettina,' he said, looking over at his sister, 'why do not you and Corinne take Fanny and Rowland on a tour of the grounds? I am sure Miss Callowell will not object.'

The governess was far from objecting to what amounted to an order from the master of the house. The youngsters were obviously only too delighted to be free of the restraining atmosphere, jumping up eagerly. Matilda, deferring to Miss Callowell's judgement, asked if she might be of the party. A gracious consent being forthcoming, she too rose.

Lady Roborough, much to Isadora's astonishment, offered to show Mrs Alvescot to a sitting-room which she might regard as peculiarly her own, and actually dragged herself to her feet. The effort this cost her was evident, and she was glad to lean on Mrs Alvescot's proffered arm, on which she floated out behind the rest, leaving Isadora alone with Roborough.

There was silence for a moment as the chattering in the corridors died away. Isadora, unable to help herself, looked up to encounter Roborough's eyes on her.

'Perhaps you would also like to see the grounds, Isadora?' he asked in a tone of unmatched politeness.

'Thank you,' Isadora said sweetly, 'but you need not concern yourself over me. You must have business on hand — you always do — and I am content to be left to my own devices.'

'Yes, but it seems to me that you are at your most dangerous when you are left to your own devices,' Roborough complained.

Isadora rose swiftly to her feet to face him. 'What are you going to do, then, put me under lock and key?'

'I wish I might.'

She emitted an infuriated sound. 'You are a hateful man. What do you suppose I can do from here to stop you selling the house?'

'I don't know, but I feel sure you will think of something.'

'I shall think of murdering you, that much is certain! I wish very much I had taken on the character of Lady Macbeth instead of Lady Teazle. You would see then how dangerous I could be — if I were as horrid as you seem to think.'

He laughed. 'Where did you come by the notion I think you horrid?'

'Well, you will keep on saying I am dangerous,' said Isadora defensively, 'just as if I had done something really wicked, like —' She broke off, appalled at hearing herself almost fling her accusation at him again.

The good humour left his face, and Isadora was conscious of the most uncomfortable sensation in her chest. Guilt. And dread. Oh, God, let him not be angry with her again. Not like that hideous day in the library at Pusay.

'Like me, you mean,' he said curtly.

'No,' she cried despairingly. 'I didn't mean that. At least, I did, but I did not mean to carp at you, I swear it. There is — there is nothing to be done about — I mean, I know I cannot change anything by railing about it, only — oh, fudge, I wish I had never met you!'

The warmth was back at the corners of Roborough's eyes as they crinkled in amusement again. 'Extremely lucid, Isadora. Perhaps you would care to join Fanny in the schoolroom so that you may learn to express yourself with more coherence?'

Isadora cried out and raised clenched fists to heaven, but her sense of humour betrayed her and a giggle escaped her lips. 'Abominable! I hate you.'

He grinned. 'I know it, alas. Never mind. Let us agree to defer our differences for the moment, shall we? I have something of some moment to ask you.'

She was diverted at once. 'Indeed? What is it?'

'Just this. If you would not care to be shown over the grounds, perhaps you would instead like to come with me to the stables and choose a horse to ride until Juliet arrives.'

Isadora stared at him. Her heart swelled with warmth for his kindness. 'You are having Juliet brought here for me?'

'Is it so strange I should do so? Totteridge will bring both her and Titian. I left him to make all the necessary arrangements.'

'But I thought you would sell her,' said Isadora unthinkingly. 'I thought you would sell all the horses.'

A shadow crossed his face. His voice was harshly bitter. 'Did you?' He uttered a short, mirthless laugh. 'Of course you did. What else were you to think?'

Isadora gazed at him, realising abruptly that he was hurt. Her heart plummeted. How could she have done that? Without pause for thought, she crossed the space between them, holding out her hands. 'Don't look like that, Roborough! Curse me for a shrew, if you will, but pray don't look at me so. That was too unjust of me. I know you are not that cruel.'

He received her hands in his, clasping them strongly. His countenance relaxed, and he said in the gentlest of tones, 'Damn you for a shrew, Isadora Alvescot.'

Isadora smiled at him. Roborough, hardly conscious of what he was doing, released her hands and cradled her face between his own.

'You are extraordinary, Isadora. I think, if I had to select the side of you that maddens me the most, it must be this volatile tendency to sweep from one extreme to another without any warning at all.' Isadora watched the warmth radiate at the corners of his eyes and felt his thumb lightly caressing her cheek where he held it. His voice was almost tender. 'It is very unsettling.'

Unsettling? What was Isadora to say of the sensations churning inside her? She was frozen to stillness by his touch, but heat was sweeping through her in waves. Her bones seemed to go weak and a quivering began in her limbs.

Roborough's brows drew together. 'You're trembling.'

His hands left her face, moving down to grasp her shoulders. The urge to drag her closer was almost irresistible.

Isadora read it in his face. Remembrance threw her into panic. What was she doing? And with this man! Abruptly she thrust him away, wrenching back.

His countenance altered, the frown descending so rapidly she was conscious of dreadful discomfort once more. But her own treacherous emotions were too all-consuming to allow it to weigh with her. Her thoughts tumbled from her mouth unchecked. 'You nearly did it. Oh, God, but you nearly had me softening again, cozening wretch that you are! What do you hope to gain by it? I must have taken leave of my senses indeed. I have not forgotten, if you have, what you truly are under this mask you wear. I will not forget it!'

Roborough said nothing. What was the point? For a moment he had thought there was a faint hope. He could, of course, reveal it all now. Why, though? It was all so disheartening. In spite of all, he hankered for that elusive, impossible trust. She had almost softened. Somewhere beneath the suspicion and doubt there was a measure of belief, only her hostility was so hurtful all desire to disabuse her of her misconceptions left him totally. 'This time you are clear enough,' he said coldly. 'I shall leave you to amuse yourself. Pray consider the place your own.'

He left her on the words. Isadora watched him go, and, discovering that she was still trembling, sat down again, clenching her hands in her lap.

CHAPTER TWELVE

The sitting-room given over to Mrs Alvescot's use was a quiet parlour which, thankfully, had none of the grandeur of the receiving-rooms. After a light luncheon attended by everyone except Roborough — a fact which afforded Isadora a bagful of mixed emotions, for she had only seen him at meals these two days — the family congregated in this apartment at the request of Matilda.

'We have discovered something which you all should know,' she began impressively.

Isadora, espying on her young cousin's countenance the smug look she knew well, uttered drily, 'You mean Fanny has discovered it.'

'Well, yes,' admitted Matilda, 'but you may be sure I sought the truth of the matter from Miss Callowell before troubling you with it, and it seems there is no mistake.'

'Oh, dear me,' sighed Mrs Alvescot apprehensively. 'Is it something dreadful, Matty?'

'Dear Ellen, I am afraid you will be seriously shocked. I have been so myself.'

A pulse began to throb in Isadora's temple. No! Oh no. Cousin Matty had discovered the truth about Roborough. Now they would all despise him. Hate him perhaps, just as she did herself. She could not endure the thought of it. It was one thing for her to know him for what he was, quite another to have the family — who had, God knew, taken him to their collective heart — so shamefully disabused.

'Oh, Matty,' her mother was saying, 'you are raising the most fearful apprehensions in my mind. Tell me the worst at once!'

'I'll tell, shall I, Mama?' pleaded Fanny, obviously dying to do so.

'Why you?' demanded Rowland jealously. 'I could tell them just as well as you.'

'Be quiet, both of you,' snapped Matilda, in a manner so out of character that both her children subsided at once.

Isadora held her breath. It had to be that. Why else would Cousin Matty be so distressed? She wanted to cry out that she knew the truth already, but her tongue would not utter the words.

'Matty, speak,' cried Mrs Alvescot.

'It is about Lord Roborough,' pronounced Matilda solemnly. Then her countenance collapsed piteously. 'That poor woman! Oh, Ellen, I confess I had thought her demeanour quite odiously affected and silly. But if I had been obliged to endure what she has endured —'

'Matty, what do you mean? Are you speaking of Lady Roborough?'

'Yes, poor soul. You see, Ellen, he lost *everything*. And all through his own wretched folly.'

'He was a gambler,' said Fanny with relish, determined to shove in her oar. 'He gambled away all their money.'

Isadora saw her mother's eyes widen in horror, and her heart contracted. She wanted to cry out that it was not true. Roborough was not that kind of man. But how could she defend him against what she already knew to be the truth, for had he not condemned himself out of his own mouth?

'Fanny, do be quiet,' begged Matilda, far less strict now the news was out. 'They are desperately poor, Ellen. Isn't it terrible?'

'Oh, terrible,' said Mrs Alvescot faintly, looking quite bewildered. 'From what we have seen, one would never have supposed such a thing.'

'No, but I must confess I had wondered, as we passed through the halls — such elegant sweeping arches — how it came about the carpeting was so threadbare in places.'

'The drapes are faded and worn, too,' put in Fanny irrepressibly. 'Corinne says it is only in the big saloons where they receive their guests that they have managed to replace the furnishings.'

'How do they live?' asked Mrs Alvescot. 'To be sure, we have ourselves been obliged to make retrenchments, but —'

'Oh, it is far worse than our situation,' said Matilda earnestly. 'Only consider the size of this house. Do you recall, Ellen, Lady Roborough saying she has been obliged to accustom herself all her life to things over which she has no control?'

'Yes, for she repeated the words to me only yesterday.'

'For my part, I thought I was unfortunate when I became widowed at so early an age,' pursued Matilda, 'but, though it pains me to say it, I had rather be a widow than discover my husband to be addicted to gaming. Why, one would never know a moment's peace of mind.'

Isadora, who had been grappling with what she was trying to convince herself was quite unwarranted distress, here blanked completely. Husband? She gazed at Cousin Matty, hearing nothing of what either she or her mama was saying. Lady Roborough's *husband* was a gambler? 'Cousin Matty,' she interrupted imperatively. 'Are you saying that the *late* viscount was a gambling man?'

Her cousin looked round at her, raising her brows. 'You don't suppose I meant Cousin Roborough, do you, Dora?'

The sarcastic inflexion went right over Isadora's head. Yes, that was precisely what she had supposed. A hollowness opened up in her chest. Could it be — was it possible that —? 'Are you sure?'

'What is the matter with you, Dora?' demanded Fanny. 'Of course she is sure. Why, Bettina and Corinne told us all about it because we commiserated with them on losing their papa.'

'What did they say?' asked Isadora, painfully conscious of a weight of remorse threatening to descend upon her at any moment, with the realisation Roborough was innocent.

'Bettina said we must not mind it if they seemed not to be grieving unduly,' Fanny recounted, 'because the truth of it was their papa ruined their mama's life with his gambling, and they were all of them more relieved than sorry at his death — especially since it meant their brother Titus would now be in command.'

'Yes, for their portions had been all swallowed up and they could not get a husband,' added Rowland. 'Only they suppose Cousin Roborough will mend everything in time.'

Isadora heard the rest of what Corinne and Bettina had said only through a haze. She thought she was going to swoon. Roborough was not the gamester. It was his father who had brought them to this pass. Then Syderstone's debt must have been —

Oh, of course. Syderstone was a much older man. He had never said, had he, that the debt had been incurred by Roborough himself? He had called it a debt of honour — gentlemen stupidly believing they might readily neglect to pay their tradesmen only so long as they paid their friends. Her papa had explained it all to her once, those peculiar standards of honour obtaining among the stronger sex. Naturally, Roborough would consider himself to be under an obligation

207

to pay his father's gambling debt. The debt of honour would have devolved upon him.

A sudden gust of rage shook her. Iniquitous! That the late viscount had ruined his son's inheritance was bad enough, but that his son should also be obliged to pay for the precise thing which had ruined it — oh, she wished she had the deceased Lord Roborough before her. She would tell him a thing or two to make his ears burn. Instead, she had said all those things to his son.

Her heart lurched. How unjustly she had treated him! How cruelly she had lashed him — as if he had not enough to endure without her added spite. But it had not been spite. She had spoken in good faith, indeed she had. And Roborough —

Her fury veered suddenly. Why in the world had he not told her the truth? Great heavens, he had allowed her to believe it of him! How dared he let her make such an out-and-out fool of herself? He must have guessed she would discover the truth within days of stepping within his doors. Oh, the unmitigated, hateful wretch!

She was up on the thought, heading for the door, only vaguely conscious of the family's eyes suddenly fixed upon her, and the abrupt silence that had fallen.

'Dora, what is it?' her mother quavered.

'Where are you going, Dora?' said Matilda sharply.

Isadora paused at the door, gazing at them almost unseeingly. 'There is something I must do.'

She was gone on the words, closing the door behind her on the family's babble of comment. She neither heard nor cared what they might say. She must see Roborough immediately.

Almost running along the corridor, away from the sitting-room that was situated in one of the back rooms on the first floor, she headed towards the front of the great mansion, intent only upon finding *his lordship* — venomously thought — that she might tell him precisely what she thought of him.

Crossing the gallery that ran along the upper storey above the main stairwell to the arched hallway below, she made for the study she had discovered housed Mr Dalbury, Roborough's agent. Lady Roborough had complained that her son spent all his time in there and neglected his family.

At the study, she rapped smartly on the door. The voice that called her to come in was not Roborough's, but she recognised the dapper little man behind the desk as the agent, who had been introduced to the family the other evening.

He rose at once. 'Miss Alvescot? What can I do for you?'

By this time Isadora's temper had begun to cool. She could not have identified the emotions in her breast if she had wanted to, they were so confused, but she was aware of disappointment at discovering only Dalbury.

'I was looking for his lordship,' she said rather lamely.

'He has gone down to the stables, ma'am.'

Isadora stood at the door, biting her lip in a good deal of uncertainty. What should she do? All her instincts told her to seek Roborough out at once — whether he was at the stables or on the moon. But the threatening remorse had superseded the subsiding anger, and now she did not know what she was going to say to him.

The little man coughed. 'Is there anything I can do to assist you, ma'am?'

'No,' Isadora sighed. 'No, thank you.'

She turned to leave, and hesitated. She must find a way. She could not meet Roborough at dinner unless she had first spoken to him. On the other hand, she needed time to collect her thoughts. It would be better perhaps if she did not attend dinner. She would plead a headache and ask for a tray in her room. Looking back into the study, she spoke again.

'Please you will give his lordship a message?'

'Certainly, ma'am. What shall I say?'

Isadora smiled suddenly. 'Present to him my compliments, if you please, and say that if he will be so kind as to select a horse for me, I shall be delighted to accept his invitation to ride with him tomorrow before breakfast.'

Let Roborough make what he might of that. He had not invited her to ride, but she thought she knew him well enough to guess he would be both amused and intrigued by her message. Particularly when she did not come down to dinner. He would meet her at the appointed time, she was sure of that.

Nor was she mistaken. When she arrived, suitably garbed in her dark blue habit and guided by one of the servants, for she had not yet been to the stables, she discovered Roborough waiting with two horses at the ready. He was looking forbidding rather than amused, and Isadora felt her pulses begin to race. Ignoring that, she turned her gaze on the magnificent black horse that awaited him.

'Good morning,' she said brightly. 'That is Othello, I collect?'

'It is,' he agreed, his countenance relaxing a trifle. 'I trust you slept well? Has your headache gone?'

Isadora glanced at him. 'Oh yes, thank you.'

In fact it was astonishing she did not really have the headache, she had slept so badly, unable to relax for the thoughts that would persist in plaguing her. She had still not determined on what she would say, but determined she was to say *something*. He might be content to allow her to go on believing ill of him but she would not rest until she had cleared the matter up. And if he supposed the re-establishment of his character in itself was enough to placate her he would very soon learn his mistake.

They had barely settled in the saddle and trotted away towards a wide expanse of rolling land that bordered the immediate grounds around the house when Roborough turned to her, speaking in a level tone.

'To what am I indebted for this particular honour?'

Isadora glanced across at him. 'I wish to talk to you.'

'Ah, I see. I rather suspected you had not sought a ride for the sheer pleasure of enjoying my company.'

Isadora said nothing. The faint bitterness in his voice affected her to no little extent. She recalled those many occasions on which just that note had betrayed his inner disquiet. She had wondered at it, she remembered. Now she understood it. She would very much have liked to dispense with all the preliminaries and tell him instantly how sorry she was for his evident distress of mind. But it could not be done. There was so much to say — and so much to unsay.

'Is there somewhere we may dismount?' she asked abruptly. 'I must be private with you, Roborough.'

His frowning gaze came about and he eyed her in a puzzled sort of way. What did she mean by this? It was the last thing he had expected after that first morning. But then, he reminded himself, that was Isadora all over — unpredictable.

The revulsion she had displayed towards him, however, was too painful to allow him any room for amusement at her present antics. He had deliberately kept out of her way, and had believed, on learning of her lame excuse of a headache for her non-appearance at the dinner-table last night, that she was avoiding him equally. Then, while he had been drinking his port after the ladies had retired, a note had been brought to him from Dalbury, containing that idiotic message.

Now here they were, riding silently across the park-lands of his estates — in a very different humour from that which he had allowed himself to imagine might be the case when they did so ride together — and he was none the wiser as to what Isadora wanted of him.

He led the way up a gentle hill to the edge of a small copse on its summit. Here, two fallen tree-trunks, lying almost end to end, provided a neat spot for the proposed tête-á-tête. Reining in, he swung out of the saddle and tethered Othello. Turning, he found that Isadora had already kicked her foot from the stirrup and was preparing to dismount.

'For pity's sake,' he exclaimed, moving quickly to the horse's side. 'Do you wish to break an ankle?'

Reaching up, he caught Isadora by the waist as she slithered from the horse's back, holding her strongly to steady her as she reached the ground.

Isadora looked up into his face, her hands automatically coming up to grasp his arms for support. 'You need not scold. I am quite capable of dismounting without falling.'

For a moment or two he was incapable of speech. Her nearness disturbed him so much he had to exercise tremendous self-control not to repeat the fiasco of the other day, when she had divined she had cause to wrench herself out of his hold.

But Isadora did not move. She could not have done so if she had tried. Acutely conscious of his hands at her waist, of the warmth that radiated from him to whisk down her limbs, she was barely capable of standing on her own two legs.

He let her go abruptly, and she all but staggered, moving quickly to the fallen branches and grasping one of them for support. By the time she was able to turn, she found Roborough had taken her mount and tethered it with his own.

He came back towards her, halting a few feet away, mute question in his face. Here at Barton Stacey, perhaps in deference to his mother, he wore dark, sober garments even to ride, which added to the impression of aloofness.

Yet this was it. There was nothing else for it. She must speak now. Isadora drew a breath and met his eyes boldly. 'Why did you not tell me the truth about your father?'

He frowned. Then she saw enlightenment in his eyes. 'Damnation,' he said softly.

'Yes, that is all very well, but it does not answer my question.'

Roborough moved a little away from her, looking out over the valleys that led back to the estate. He did not pretend to misunderstand her. It was too late for that. He supposed he had known she must find it out at length. 'The opportunity never seemed to arise,' he offered.

'That will not do. If I had no difficulty in creating opportunities to say what I had to say to you, then you could easily have done the same.'

He was silent. He had no defence. She was right. But he could not have told her the truth. Not then. What would she say if he confessed he had desired her trust?

'You let me believe the worst of you,' Isadora said forthrightly, 'when a little word of explanation would have cleared everything.'

He did not look at her. 'It was easier to allow you to believe what you did of me than to confess my father's folly. You must understand it is not something I readily discuss — with anyone.'

'Oh, that is quite unreasonable. You might say so at first, yes. But afterwards, when I was driven to accuse you — there can be no excuse for your silence then.'

He turned a narrowed gaze upon her. 'Can there not? Why in the name of all the gods should I have sued to you for understanding? You had no doubts at all. You knew I was a reckless and irresponsible gamester. Your very words, Isadora.'

She caught her breath. 'I know. Do you suppose I have not suffered agonies of remorse? And I did not want to believe it. You must have realised I wanted you to deny it. Yet you persisted in allowing the mistake to continue. I was in the wrong, yes, but I cannot absolve you, Roborough.'

'I can't imagine there ever being a time when you would,' he said involuntarily.

A stifled giggle left Isadora's lips. 'Probably not, but — oh, I do beg your pardon for my wrong, in any event.'

He blinked. 'What?'

Her lips quivered. 'You heard me.'

'Yes, but I don't think I believe it. Of course I realise all that ranting and recrimination is your notion of an apology, but actually to beg my pardon? Are you sure you are well, Isadora?'

Isadora burst into laughter. 'You, Roborough, are —'

'Abominable,' he finished. 'Yes, I know.'

Her gaze caught by his, Isadora became conscious of spreading warmth in her veins, a tingle that seemed to signal — something. She did not pretend to understand it. The light eyes, crinkling at the corners in that endearing manner, appeared to be running over her face. She felt — how could she express it? — different. Yes, free. It was as if she might enjoy the sensations aroused in Roborough's presence, for she need no longer be suspicious of him.

Abruptly, everything fell into place. All the things he had done that had seemed to her so needlessly cruel — trying to think how to dispose of her, the plan to sell their home — and the friendly warmth that had seemed so contradictory, that she had taken for a false front cultivated for the purpose of bending them all to his will.

'Oh, great heavens,' she exclaimed impulsively, 'I have been so wrong about everything! You are selling our house because you must, not for your own selfish gain. And of course you must wish to get rid of me suitably, for —'

'You are mistaken,' he interrupted. 'I have no wish to get rid of you. Quite otherwise.'

Isadora stared at him, her heart beating rather fast. What did he mean? Sudden shyness attacked her. It could not be that, in spite of all, he liked her — could it? Enough to wish to —? No, of what was she thinking? After the way she had treated him? She rushed into speech.

'Well, of course you feel you must provide me with some sort of dowry, but I assure you —'

'Let us not discuss your dowry at this precise moment.'

Dared he speak now? If her sentiments were not what he hoped, then anything he said would surely alienate her totally. Then it would be impossible even to remain upon terms with her. And that, now, would be unendurable.

'I was only going to say that you need not concern yourself about it,' Isadora pursued. 'I could not bear to be the cause of involving you in any more expense at the present time. You must have enough on your hands as it is.'

He was touched. Though he might have guessed Isadora would be as generous an ally as she had been implacable an enemy. Was she not a creature of extremes?

'Isadora, that is a generous thought. But what concerns me the most is that no one should suffer for my father's depredations upon the estate. Besides, in a way I owe your family more than my own. The inheritance of your father's property must be counted a godsend. I am heartily glad of it, but only insofar as it will enable me, by raising capital, to provide for us all eventually.'

'Then you don't intend to pay Syderstone with the proceeds?'

'Heaven forbid! Though his purpose in seeking me out was to persuade me so to do.'

'For my part, I think you should refuse to pay him at all.'

Roborough gave a short laugh. 'Unhappily that is not a solution open to me.'

Isadora frowned deeply. 'Do you suppose he would release you from the obligation if I married him?'

'Since you are going to do no such thing, we shall never know.'

'Well, but —'

'Loath as I am to reopen hostilities, Isadora, I warn you that if I hear any more on this head I shall be obliged to take strict measures of prevention.'

Isadora was conscious of the oddest sensation as she stared at him — a glow that seemed to spread right down to her toes, and a feeling of intense satisfaction. 'You don't wish me to marry him?'

'I don't wish you to marry anyone,' Roborough retorted in a harassed sort of way.

God, but in a moment he would be saying precisely those things he had determined not to say. Not yet. Why she was not cutting at him for daring to dictate to her on such matters he could not fathom. He drew a steadying breath, trying for a measure of calm.

'All I am trying to say is there is no necessity for you — or anyone, for that matter — to be thinking of personal sacrifices. We are not out of the woods by any means, but once the Pusay house is sold we may at least look to a promising future.'

Isadora was silent. If she had hoped for a declaration she had been deservedly set down. Not that she had. She could not imagine why she was even thinking of such a thing. It was not as if she wished to marry Roborough. Why, if Harriet had not persisted in holding him up as the ideal, it would never have occurred to her. Yet she was conscious of disappointment out of all proportion to the event. With an inward sigh, she turned her attention to the matter in hand. 'All very well to be thinking of the future,' she said slowly, 'but what of the immediate present? Is the situation very bad?'

'I have told you, Isadora. There is no need for you to worry your head over it.'

Her temper flared. 'Don't treat me like a child!'

'Did I do so? I beg your pardon. I just don't want you to become involved.'

'That is absurd. I am involved. Why in the world should you not trust me with the truth?'

A short laugh escaped him. 'That is rich, coming from you.'

'You mean because I would not trust you? Whose fault is that, I should like to know?'

Roborough raised his eyes heavenwards. 'I might have known. It is my fault, of course, that you could not find it in yourself to trust me — despite the fact you discovered me not to be my father, who had given you cause for offence, despite the fact you were the one listening at doors, not I — and making what you chose out of everything you overheard.'

'All of which you could readily have avoided,' returned Isadora, 'had you been honest enough at the outset to tell me the truth. But of course I am merely a stupid female who cannot begin to understand matters of business.'

'Nothing of the sort, but —'

'Roborough, you are conducting yourself precisely in the same way as you have done all along. And that, let me tell you, is certain to end in my quarrelling with you all over again.'

He grinned. 'I am scarcely fool enough to suppose you are done quarrelling with me merely because you have choked yourself over an apology.'

She laughed but, reaching out her hands towards him, she said earnestly, 'Pray tell me the true situation. I want to understand it all, truly I do.'

He automatically grasped her hands, holding them hard. 'You compel me to answer you. Perhaps I did contribute to your mistrust.'

Her fingers clung to his, although she scarcely noticed, so important did it seem to her she should gain his confidence. 'You did, and you continue so to do every moment that you deny me access to your thoughts. How can you expect trust and — and faith, if you will not be open with me?'

For a moment he was tempted — to be utterly open. But the thought of seeing that mercurial temperament turn once more against him — no, he could not endure it. Too dangerous. By comparison, the prospect of relaying to her the details of his sorry situation seemed ridiculously simple. He could not fathom now why he had not done so before. 'You are right. I have been too cautious. Let us sit down a little.'

Leading her to the fallen tree-trunks, he obliged her to take a rather precarious seat there, himself perching beside her. Supporting his hands on the tree beneath him, he looked over to where the two horses were quietly cropping at the grass.

'The situation is extremely serious. There is no ready cash, and nothing with which to realise any. Not here, in any event. About the only thing my father did not do — and only because he could not — was mortgage the house. The rents have been raised beyond what is either fair or acceptable, and many of our tenants have moved away as a result. No repairs have been effected for several years. In a word, we are cleaned out.'

'But did not your father ever win?'

'Of course he won. But your true gambler loses as much as he wins — and more.'

His voice was so full of bitterness Isadora ached to comfort him. She spoke the thought in her mind. 'I see what it is. You feel cheated.'

Roborough turned to look at her. 'Yes, I'm afraid I do.'

'There is every reason why you should. Why, in your place, I should be livid.'

'I don't doubt it. But I am not proud of such a feeling. I wish I might take it all in my stride. After all, I have known for years what I was likely to find.'

'Knowing something will happen does not necessarily arm one against the shock of it, or lessen the feelings involved,' Isadora offered. 'Papa's death —' She hardly noticed she used the dread word with unaccustomed ease — 'is a case in point. We knew he was dying. He was even glad of it, for he told me so. But we were devastated when it happened none the less.'

'Yes, I think I see. My mother, who had as I thought been soured forever, was thrown into deepest gloom when my father died.'

'She must have cared for him, in spite of all.'

Isadora scarcely realised what she had said. It was as if a key had turned suddenly, opening her mind to her own inspection. She had cared — in spite of all.

She stared at Roborough's profile, for he was no longer looking at her, but gazing at the horses. Was it possible? Had he insinuated himself so thoroughly into her affections she had been fighting against the feeling — all this time — because of what she had thought she knew to his discredit?

'What is it?'

The question came softly, and she realised he had turned, was meeting her eyes, a concerned frown in his own. What could she say? Heat — the unpleasant heat of embarrassment — swept through her. 'N-nothing,' she stammered, quickly rising from the trunk of the tree and moving away.

He was up at once, following her. He grasped her shoulders and turned her to face him. 'Isadora, don't you shut me out now.'

Involuntarily she looked up, meeting his anxious gaze. It was not in her to prevaricate. Yet her tongue would not utter the words she wanted so desperately to say. 'I am ... confused,' she managed.

'What confuses you?'

'You do. You confuse me. I thought I knew — understood at least, but...'

She meant she had understood her own emotions, only to find them overturning in a manner that both shocked and appalled her. She could not be feeling this.

But Roborough took her words quite differently. 'You are having doubts of my character again? Why, what have I said?'

'Nothing. I don't mean that.'

'Then what do you mean?'

'If I knew, I would not be confused, would I?' she threw at him, overwhelmed by the bewildering sensations in her breast.

He laughed and released her. 'Now I am confused. I'm damned — if you will forgive the expression — if I know what to make of you, Isadora Alvescot.' He made a move towards the horses. 'But come. We shall be missed.'

On the whole, Isadora was rather relieved as she settled herself after Roborough helped her into the saddle. She needed time to sort all this out. There was no need to converse as they cantered back towards the mansion and her confusion began to subside. She was rather inclined to suppose she must temporarily have taken leave of her senses. For a few perilous moments she had actually believed she had come to care for Roborough.

Now they were riding companionably side by side, however, the odd sensations had left her — fortunately. God knew she did not wish to feel like that about him. He might not be the villain she had taken him for, but one did not, all in a minute, alter one's mind about someone to that degree. Great heavens, she had been mad! Or perhaps she had imagined it. Moved, no doubt, by compassion, she had mistaken that feeling for something warmer. Her attention was recalled by Roborough as they came within sight of the stables.

'Good God, who is this turning up at such an hour?'

Glancing in the direction of his gaze, Isadora perceived that a travelling carriage stood beside the stables. It had evidently only just arrived for the grooms were still releasing the team of horses from the shafts. A dreadful thought struck her.

'Don't say it is Syderstone come to plague you again.'

'No, no. He always drives himself in his curricle.' Then Roborough's tone altered, something of pleasurable excitement entering it. 'I fancy I know those horses. Ursula, by all that's wonderful!'

He spurred his horse as he spoke, cantering quickly up to the vehicle. Automatically, Isadora urged her own mount to a faster pace. But before she could catch up she saw Roborough raise a hand in salute, calling out a jovial greeting.

'I knew it was you, you rogue!'

All at once, Isadora caught sight of a female figure moving out of the shadow of the house towards the stables. Bringing her horse to a standstill, she watched Roborough leap from the saddle and stride towards the woman.

A feminine laugh rang out, and the female, an elegant vision in a black pelisse with a fashionable feathered bonnet perched on a riot of golden locks, held out welcoming hands. 'Titus, my dearest!'

'Ursula, my love!' came the glad cry in response as Roborough seized the proffered hands.

Isadora sat as if turned to stone. Blank emptiness stifled every thought but one. Roborough was hugging this female as if his life depended upon it. Her pulse started up again, her heart hammering painfully in her breast. Who was she? Did it matter who she was? All that mattered was what Roborough had called her. His love?

Something stabbed in her chest. Nausea came up from her stomach to choke her. Then an alien voice penetrated.

'Miss? Can I assist you to alight?'

One of the grooms was standing at her horse's head.

'Oh yes, th-thank you,' she managed to say through lips numb and stiff.

Her limbs felt as if they did not belong to her as she made ready to dismount, sliding to the ground with the groom's assistance. She was amazed her legs did not buckle under her. Thank heaven they did not, for she must get away. Go inside. Escape. On what pretext? Her brain did not seem to wish to operate. But yes, she must change. It was breakfast-time, was it not? She could not breakfast in her riding dress.

As she began to move towards the house, she could hear the buzz of voices. His — and hers. But the words were meaningless, until — Oh no, Roborough was leading the female towards her. She could not meet her. But she must. Where was the actress in her when it was so sorely needed?

'Ursula, I want you to meet Miss Alvescot.'

From somewhere, Isadora summoned a smile.

'Isadora, this is Lady Ursula Stivichall, a very great friend of mine — of the family.'

Registering the hasty correction at the back of her mind, Isadora extended a hand and found herself looking down — for the female was half a head shorter than she was herself — into a countenance somewhat older than she had expected.

Surprise caused the dreadful inner turmoil to dull slightly. Why, the woman was thirty if she was a day. Nor was she beautiful. Pleasing, yes, but not as lovely as Harriet, for example. And, like all of them, Isadora suddenly realised, she was in mourning. The costume, for all its elegance, was unmistakably significant.

Lady Ursula smiled — more warmly than Isadora cared for. 'I am delighted to meet you. I have heard of you all, of course. Titus wrote about you.'

'Did he indeed?' responded Isadora in a fair approximation of her usual tone, albeit somewhat dry. 'He mentioned nothing, on the other hand, of *you*.'

She had not meant to place that undue emphasis on the word. A swift glance at Roborough showed her he had taken instant notice of it, for a quick frown creased his brow. What did he expect? She must pull herself together. After all, what right had she to behave so? She forced another smile. 'I am happy to make your acquaintance. We appear to share a common state.'

'The mourning, you mean,' said Lady Ursula calmly. 'My husband. But my year is almost up.' She cast a mischievous glance at Roborough. 'Though it seems to me a lifetime, which is why I am here. You, Titus, are to entertain me before I go out of my mind with boredom.'

'With the greatest of pleasure,' he responded, 'only I trust it will not greatly inconvenience you if I breakfast first?'

Lady Ursula went into a peal of mirth. 'That is just what I mean.' She turned laughing eyes on Isadora. 'Isn't he the most outrageous jokesmith? I vow he keeps me in a ripple of amusement — which of course is why I have come.'

Privately Isadora doubted this was her only reason. She was tempted to say Roborough kept her rather in a fever of fury, but she was conscious just at this moment of a welling of something decidedly not fury. It threatened to spill over if she did not get away immediately. 'Excuse me, if you please,' she said as calmly as she could, 'but I must change.'

'Oh yes, off you go, Miss Alvescot.' Lady Ursula tucked her hand in Roborough's arm. 'I shall detain Titus but a moment, and then he shall change too.'

'I thank you. Perhaps you would care to organise the rest of my morning also?'

Isadora escaped into the house, hearing the ripple of Lady Ursula's laughter break out again behind her. Lifting the long skirts of her riding habit, she sped as swiftly as she could up the back stairs and through the corridors of the great mansion. It was not until she had gained the safety of her bedchamber, and closed the door behind her, that she allowed her burgeoning emotions rein.

Her heart was palpitating so unevenly she was breathless. She ought to ring for her maid, but instead she moved to the end of the bed and sank down, grasping one of the posts for support.

She needed some few moments alone to grapple with the dreadful truth. For there was no use in deceiving herself any longer. She could not mistake the significance of the violent feelings that had attacked her, and were still causing the most unpleasant sensations of nausea and, she conceded, with tears welling at her eyes, of grief. She was jealous! Uselessly, stupidly jealous, of the female who had just arrived.

The thought caused such a bursting within her bosom she pushed herself to her feet, tearing at the buttons of the bodice, which had become suddenly too restrictive to be borne. The tightness at her chest eased a little as the bodice came loose. She left it hanging open over her silk chemise, drawing a few steadying breaths. Then she moved to the window which overlooked the walled gardens at the side of the house.

Roses bloomed below. An image flashed into her mind. Roborough, touching the roses to satisfy himself, as he had said, that he was really there. A little laugh escaped her, choking off into a sob.

When had it happened? How had it happened? All the time, while she had been hating him so fervently, fighting him at every hand, the wretch had been stealing away her heart. And for what? Because the female — Ursula, had he called her? — already had his. That much was obvious. Or was it?

In her mind's eye she saw again his softened features, heard his voice gently — oh, so gently — asking in concern about her distresses. Could he behave thus to Isadora, if his heart was in the possession of another?

And the morning after they arrived had he not almost kissed her? Great heavens, now she was more confused than ever! Except for one thing, of which she was now more certain than she had been of anything in her life. The thing she had determined would not happen. Only it had.

This was all Harriet's fault. Had her friend not put the idea into her head, she was sure she would never have fallen in love with Roborough.

There, she had admitted it. Oh, but she hated him for making her love him so. She was the most miserable creature alive. For of course he did not feel about her the way he had made her feel about him. No, he was head over ears for that Ursula. And even had he not been — which she could not doubt he was — what hope had she of attaching him, after everything she had said and done, after doing all in her power to alienate him forever?

Well, let it be so. Isadora flung herself away from the window and bracingly tugged at the bell pull to summon her maid. She was not going to sue for Roborough's affections. She would die rather. And nothing would induce her to allow the Ursula female to suspect for one moment that she envied her such a conquest. She would face her brazenly — and act. She had enough talent to fool her and Roborough both.

CHAPTER THIRTEEN

It was amazing the difference a single person made to the atmosphere of the house. Isadora was obliged to admit the presence of Lady Ursula Stivichall had considerably lightened the general mood. Even her costume contrasted with the unrelieved black of that of the residents, for white twisted bugling adorned the black satin evening gown and her turban was ornamented with a white satin bandeau.

She was clearly a favourite even with Lady Roborough. Bettina and Corinne had fallen upon her in glee, and were now — having been permitted, at the guest's earnest entreaty, to join the adults for dinner — hanging upon her every utterance and clinging one to each arm where they sat beside her on one of the elegant sofas in the receiving saloon.

Fanny seemed less enthusiastic. Or perhaps, Isadora decided fairly, she was feeling left out. In the absence of her brother — Rowland having been packed off to school — she was dependent upon the Stratton girls for company. Matilda was very obviously disapproving, which Isadora tried hard not to be glad of, although Mrs Alvescot was pleasant enough to the lady.

But then her mama was ever ready to take people on trust. She would not recognise in Lady Ursula the snake who had caused her daughter's heart to be broken — unless Cousin Matty drew her attention to matters she might not otherwise notice. Not that even her mama could have failed to notice the way Lady Ursula monopolised Roborough. No sooner did he come in from his solitary port than she left his young sisters flat and rose at once to curl possessive hands about his arm.

'Titus, at last! I thought you would be at that wine of yours forever. Come and sit by me.'

'Temptress,' he said, laughing. 'Nothing would give me greater pleasure, but I must tear myself away upon this occasion. I came in only to ask you all to excuse me. Dalbury has set me some business and I must write letters tonight, without fail.'

'But I protest,' objected Lady Ursula gaily. 'This is merely an excuse, for you have been obliged to entertain me all day and you are tired of me.'

'Alas, you have seen through my subterfuge,' mourned Roborough.

That trill of laughter came, setting Isadora's teeth on edge. The mock-chiding tone was sickening.

'Wicked, wicked man. For that I shall force you to accept my escort to the study.'

'Must you? It is all due to you these letters have remained unwritten all day.'

'Then you have no time to waste,' said Lady Ursula, pushing him out of the door. She laughed back at the company. 'I shall return when I have suitably punished him.'

As she whisked from the room, Miss Callowell, who was present in company with her young charges, immediately called upon the girls to retire.

'You will not wish to outstay your welcome,' she said firmly when they protested. 'Come along.'

Fanny, urged perforce by her mother, also left the room, leaving the field clear for Matilda to pump Lady Roborough for information.

'Lady Ursula is charming, is she not?' she said unctuously, switching her seat for one nearer to the lady of the house.

'She is attentive to the girls,' offered her ladyship wearily.

And to Roborough, Isadora might have said. But there was no need for her to say it, for Matilda was on to the item like a foxhound. 'Cousin Roborough appears to be uncommonly attached to her.'

Her ladyship sighed. 'Ah yes. So suitable, now Stivichall has passed on. Whether Stratton will choose to marry her is another matter.'

Isadora felt her heart skip a beat. What could that mean?

'But if he is so fond of her...' suggested Matilda.

'Fond? Oh, they are fond, I make no doubt of that. Yet Stratton has ever set his face against matrimony. Although Stivichall left her very comfortably circumstanced, and if Stratton had any sense of what is due to the family —' Lady Roborough broke off, sighing again. 'But it is always the same. One meets everywhere with nothing but selfishness.' She dragged herself to her feet. 'You will forgive me if I retire. These late hours are so injurious, and I am never in the best of health.'

Matilda solicitously aided her to the door and carefully shut it only after she had made sure Lady Roborough had drifted off down the corridor. Then she turned to survey Mrs Alverscot and Isadora. 'Well!' she exclaimed in a shocked under voice.

'Oh, what is it, Matty?' Mrs Alvescot quavered.

Matilda came over to settle beside her once more. 'Ellen, it is just as I suspected, I am quite convinced of it.'

Mrs Alvescot threw a hand to her mouth. 'Oh! You don't mean —'

'She is Roborough's mistress.'

Isadora jumped violently. What? Such a thing had never occurred to her. Convinced her relative was mistaken, she broke into speech. 'Cousin Matty, have you run mad?'

Eagerly, the elder woman turned to her. 'Only consider, Dora. Here is Lady Roborough debating that Cousin Roborough will not marry her, even though they are fond. I ask you, what else is one to make of that?'

At this inopportune moment, much to the general confusion, Lady Ursula herself slipped back into the room. 'I have left him to his letters. I do believe he did have them to write.' She looked about. 'Oh, has Albinia gone to bed?'

'I don't think —' began Mrs Alvescot doubtfully.

'Oh, silly me. I mean Lady Roborough, of course. Poor dear, she has been quite broken by her wretched marriage. We are not all fortunate in our husbands, sadly.'

'Very true,' Matilda agreed, recovering her poise. 'I trust you were happily wed?'

'Ecstatically.' And the tinkling laugh rang out. Then, to Isadora's secret dismay, Lady Ursula came over towards her chair, leaving Matilda and Mrs Alvescot whispering together. 'How about you, Miss Alvescot? Oh, may I call you Isadora? I do so hate formality.'

'Certainly, ma'am,' Isadora said, with an assumption of ease she was far from feeling. All she could think about was whether it might be true. Was she Roborough's mistress? The very notion caused a distressing stabbing pain in her chest. She did her best to banish the thought, but another swiftly succeeded it. Had Lady Ursula indeed been ecstatically happy in her marriage? For if she had, then she would not wish to —

'I have been telling Titus,' said the lady herself, breaking into Isadora's thoughts, 'that he must, at all costs, make sure he marries you to someone both sensible and kind.'

Oh, had she? Sensible and kind? Mentally, Isadora wondered what in the world Roborough might have had to say to that. Aloud, she said acidly, 'As far as I know, he is not planning to marry me to anyone at all. What is more, I do not require his assistance in the matter.'

Lady Ursula went into her peal of laughter. 'He told me you would say so.'

'Did he indeed?' Just what else had the wretch been saying about her — discussing her freely, no doubt, with his 'love'?

'Yes, for I asked him all about you,' said Lady Ursula with artless candour. 'Is it really true you are as good an actress as Mrs Siddons?'

'Better,' Isadora said before she could stop her tongue. Then, ashamed of herself, she added, 'At least, I am told my knack with tragedy rivals hers.'

'I can't wait to see you perform, then. But it is doubly important for Titus to discover the right husband for you. It must, of course, be someone who appreciates your talent. Now, can you think of anyone you know who fits this description?'

'Lady Ursula,' Isadora said, an edge to her voice, 'I cannot think the subject of my possible marriage can be of interest to anyone other than myself.'

To her intense astonishment, far from being properly snubbed, Lady Ursula's eyes began to dance. 'Can you not? Dear me, I rather thought I detected a great deal of interest from someone other than yourself.'

Isadora frowned. What in the world was the woman at now? 'I do not take your meaning.'

The lady laughed. 'Never mind. I dare say it will astonish you to hear that even I — a comparative stranger — take an interest in your prospective husband, Isadora.'

It did. In fact it astonished Isadora so much she refused to believe it. What game the woman was playing she was unable to imagine. The only possible interest she might have had — if she had been able to see into Isadora's heart — would have been in the knowledge she coveted Lady Ursula's own prospective marriage partner. If indeed she did plan on marrying Roborough. And that tidbit she could not know, for Isadora flattered herself she hid the state of her emotions very well.

It cost her an effort of will to do so, but she discovered the very next morning — after another of those painfully sleepless nights with rather more shedding of useless tears than she thought either acceptable or deserved by the unnamed subject of them — that her will had barely been tested in the presence of the Ursula female. The sensations that attacked her when she realised Roborough meant to ride with her — despite Lady Ursula's more urgent claims to his attention — were far less susceptible of control.

Great heavens, why was he waiting for her? She had come to the stables with no such expectation. Indeed, she had refused to contemplate it, determining in the long night hours to ask one of the grooms to escort her. She knew she ought not to ride after such a night, but had convinced herself that if she did not get away from the mansion she would go mad. The very last thing she had expected was to be obliged to get away from the mansion with Roborough.

What was she to say to him? How was she to conduct herself? She could not — who could expect it of her? — behave towards him in her normal fashion. Already her betraying pulses were leaping in her veins, making speech well-nigh impossible.

As a result, she greeted him with a good deal of cool reserve — a shield hastily raised to guard her lacerated emotions — and watched, in dismay, the frown descend upon his brow.

Now he would demand an explanation. And she did not have one, heaven help her.

Her instincts proved true. No sooner had they ridden the pair of horses out of earshot of the stables than Roborough immediately referred to her mood.

'What is the matter with you, Isadora? Don't you wish to ride … with me?'

The little addition drew her head round with a jerk. 'Oh yes,' she cried involuntarily. Then she quickly drew the shutter down again, for she must not reveal her feelings.

His frown deepened and she looked away.

'I slept badly,' she offered stiffly. 'A headache.'

'Again?'

'What do you mean?'

'My dear Isadora, you must not expect me to be completely gullible. On each occasion you have complained of a headache you have looked as if you tossed on your pillows all night. Every such occasion has, by some extraordinary coincidence, been followed by your picking a quarrel with me. Am I supposed to believe this is an exception?'

Isadora bit her lip. She could not look at him, for the teasing quality in his voice was productive of a strong desire to burst into tears. She must not. That would be fatal. She tried for a light note, unaware of the husky quality in her own voice. 'You are imagining things, Roborough. There is no reason in the world for me to pick a quarrel with you today.'

Roborough brought his mount up close and leaned across to catch her bridle. The two horses came to a halt. Isadora turned frowning eyes upon him, the desire to weep receding as surprise took its place.

'What are you doing?'

He eyed her. 'You, my girl, are a lying little devil.'

'I am no such thing,' she flashed, firing up.

'Don't argue with me. If you think I am going to endure another stupid misunderstanding only because you will not tell me what is troubling you, you are very much mistaken.'

Isadora pulled at her rein. 'Let go of my bridle! I don't know what you're talking about.'

'Oh yes, you do. We are going back up to that little clearing by the fallen trees and you are going to tell me what is in your mind. Do you understand?'

'How dare you? By what right do you take this tone with me?'

His features broke into an abrupt grin. 'That's the Isadora I know. I had rather have you on your high ropes any day than moping in that uncharacteristic fashion.'

Isadora fought for control. 'Do you —?' She stopped, drew a firmer breath, and started again. 'Do you mean to tell me you deliberately provoked me? You — you — and don't dare to put words in my mouth merely because I cannot think of anything at the moment!'

'Certainly not,' agreed Roborough cheerfully. 'I shall wait until you have searched your mind for the exact adjective — failing, of course, your favourite one.'

'You abominable man!'

'Oh yes, that one. How could I have forgotten?'

Isadora's fury faded rapidly and she erupted into giggles. 'I hate you!'

'Thank God for that! I had begun to fear you were altogether indifferent towards me, and that would never do.'

He released her bridle as he spoke and urged his mount onward, knowing she would automatically follow suit. There was something troubling her. He might have distracted her for the moment, but he could read her countenance so well now he simply knew. She was unhappy. He could feel it. He could no more stand by and let it alone than he could purposely give her cause for unhappiness.

Leading the way to the fallen tree-trunk, he reined in again. Looking around, he found that although Isadora had readily accompanied him to the spot she was looking extremely apprehensive. No matter. She might not wish to confide in him but he was determined she should. He swung out of the saddle and tethered his horse.

Then he came up to her and held up his arms. 'Come.'

Isadora looked down at him. Was there any way out of this? God knew she would give anything to enjoy his company thus alone. But it was not safe. In his presence, she did not know if she could conceal anything.

'Come, Isadora,' he repeated, a command in his voice.

She was in no condition to resist him. Making ready, she allowed him to help her down, pushing instantly away in a manner he found highly suggestive.

'It is to do with me, isn't it?' he asked, unable to help a harsh note from creeping into his voice.

Oddly, Isadora derived strength from it. An ungentle Roborough she could deal with. She rushed into speech. 'It is nothing of the sort. If you must know, it has nothing whatsoever to do with anyone except myself. I am — I am bored. Yes — bored.' She had hit upon a theme she might with advantage use. She pursued it ruthlessly. 'I have nothing to do, you see.'

Roborough frowned. She was fluent enough with this excuse, but he thought it was just that. An excuse. Still, he supposed there might be something in it. 'What were you used to do at Pusay?'

'Oh, practise my speeches.'

'There is nothing to stop you doing so here. In fact, it would be an excellent plan if you were to get up a play for Ursula's benefit. She has been expressing a wish you would perform.'

Get up a play for Lady Ursula's benefit? That was to add insult to injury. Only he naturally would not realise that. She saw him frown again and knew her face was giving her away.

'I see that the idea does not find favour with you.'

Thinking fast, she turned this instantly to her advantage. 'Of course it does not find favour with me. I do not wish to perform here, but on the stage. The real stage.'

Roborough's frown deepened and his voice was dry. 'You hold by that scheme, do you?'

'I have never wavered from it,' Isadora lied in a defiant tone, tossing her head. 'Why should you suppose I have changed my mind? I am still determined on becoming an actress, and you will find you can do nothing to stop me.'

'Perhaps you are right,' he said slowly. His gaze raked her from her head to her heels and back again. In a voice of soft menace, he said, 'But if you do I am afraid there will be nothing for it but for me to follow you and set up as your protector.'

Shock held Isadora silent. She gazed at him blankly. That could mean only one thing. Was he mad? 'My — my protector? You mean — you mean you would make me your mistress?'

Roborough held her eyes. 'In the circumstances, no other liaison would be possible.'

'No other liaison?'

He glanced about in a puzzled way. 'There seems to be an echo hereabouts.'

Unheeding, Isadora burst out, 'That is utterly absurd. I could not possibly become your mistress.'

'Why not?' he demanded, his gaze coming back to hers. 'Would you dislike it?'

Isadora's pulse began to thrum in her veins. Dislike it? No, indeed. Quite otherwise. Only she could not say so. All thought of any other mistress had gone quite out of her head. The only thing she was aware of was the disturbing sensation of her blood pumping passionately in areas of which she had never previously been aware. 'That is a — a stupid question,' she managed to say, though her lips quivered on the words.

Roborough's gaze became riveted on her mouth. He could not fathom what had possessed him. He had spoken out of the ardour he had been damping down for so long. She protested it was a stupid question, but he would give his life for the answer. No, that was ridiculous. But this was ridiculous. He must stop at once.

But his gaze came up a little, and Isadora's brown eyes were regarding him with something in their depths he intuitively recognised. Acting on the knowledge, without intention, without thought, he kissed her.

Isadora, taken completely by surprise, responded instinctively. She kissed him back.

His arms crept round her, pulling her close. Driven by the movement of her lips under his, he pressed more firmly.

A wash of heat engulfed Isadora, and her mouth opened, allowing a velvet touch of softness to meet a welcome within. Fire rushed to the seat of desire and her body shrank involuntarily into the hardness of his limbs. Roborough dragged her roughly against him and Isadora moaned softly as his mouth left hers, tracing a path of burning flame into the hollows of her neck. Isadora arched back in response, and, without will reached up her hands to his head, tugging him down that she might seek his mouth again.

As she did so, her eyes fluttered open, letting in a sliver of sky and trees and daylight, incongruous against the dark passion she was experiencing. It flung her back to reality.

Her eyes flew fully open. Even as she took in the enormity of what she was doing, she was pulling back, thrusting away, turning, retreating — oh, God help her, what in the world had she done? — to the fallen tree-trunks where she dropped down, panting and hanging on for dear life to one of the jutting dead branches.

It was a moment or two before she was able to get her breath, even longer before the quivering in her limbs began to subside and the pounding of her heart eased a little. She almost jumped when Roborough's voice came from behind her. She turned her head. He had not come close. He was looking grimmer than she had ever seen him. But his voice was ragged with some emotion she could not have identified if she had tried.

'I will not ask your pardon, for that was unforgivable. In my defence I have only this to say: when you talk of becoming an actress, you lay yourself open to just such assaults.'

'From men like you?'

He flinched. Isadora was instantly contrite. She had not wanted to taunt him. But she could not help it. That he had dismissed the experience in such terms hurt so very much. What to her had been the culmination — or at least the beginning of an expression — of her love for him had been to him merely the sort of treatment a gentleman meted out to that kind of woman. The protest burst out from the pain of his rejection. 'You did it for that, I suppose? To show me the sort of attentions I am likely to invite if I pursue my ambition to be an actress?'

238

Roborough did not speak for a moment. He had not done it for that. He had not meant to do it at all. He had kissed her because he could not help it. And her response had so overwhelmed him he was within an ace of disgracing them both, right there in the open.

But nothing of that must appear in his face or voice. It was tempting to suppose her affections were engaged, but experience told him such an assumption might well be mistaken. He knew enough of women to understand that a first kiss — and he was certain it was Isadora's first kiss, if one discounted the Witheridge boy's juvenile attempt — could readily arouse passions innocent genteel females were not even aware of possessing. One could set no store by such responses.

He took a decision. 'That is exactly why I did it.'

Fire of a different kind swept through Isadora. The fire of pure rage. How could he use her so, and for such a reason? Sarcasm tore out of her throat as she rose from the tree-trunk. 'I must then thank you, Roborough, for demonstrating your libertine propensities. I only trust your real mistress will not take it into her head to become jealous. Oh, don't fear me. I shall say nothing. I would not wish to jeopardise your chances of gaining by the marriage — if you can bring yourself to marry her.'

Roborough was staring at her in the blankest amazement. 'What in the name of all the gods are you talking about? My mistress? What mistress, pray?'

But Isadora was already regretting her hasty words. Had she not known disaster would strike if she rode with Roborough? She must retract at once. 'It does not matter,' she said brusquely, pushing past him towards the horses.

He seized her arm. 'No, you don't. Explain yourself, if you please.'

'But I don't please.' She wrenched her arm out of his hold. 'I have said too much already.'

'You have not said nearly enough!'

'Well, it's all I am going to say!'

'Is it indeed?'

'It is indeed!'

He eyed her in frustrated silence. When she was in this mood, there was no doing anything with the wench. And he was too much moved himself to joke her out of it. He no longer knew what had or had not been said. Except — well, why the idiotic accusation of a mistress? She could not mean Ursula? Good God!

Isadora was already waiting at her horse's side. Automatically he went to help her. She accepted his aid in silence, settling herself on the back of the horse. She would not look at him, but immediately set off at a trot towards the mansion. Remounting, Roborough followed her more slowly, lost in thought.

This opened up a whole new line of enquiry. She had spoken in venom, but what she had said was open to interpretation. Had his caution been unnecessary? Had he been mistaken in his reading of her response to his embrace? Could it be —? Or was this merely wishful thinking?

Isadora, meanwhile, riding back towards the mansion ahead of him, was beset by far different emotions — all of them uncomfortable. Shame and anger were the least of them. But most of all she was conscious of a yearning ache — for the feel of Roborough's arms around her, Roborough's lips on hers. How she wished she had never experienced them. Yet how deeply satisfying it was to have had even that tiny taste of a wine she would never be permitted to drink.

The mansion loomed. Roborough caught her up, but although they rode into the stable yard neck and neck, Isadora kept silent just as he did. Vaguely she took in the presence of a familiar curricle standing in the yard by the stable-block.

Roborough regarded it frowningly as he swung out of the saddle. Forgetting what lay between them, he looked across at Isadora, who was dismounting with the help of a groom. 'Another visitor,' he said grimly.

Isadora, her consciousness receding as the same thought came to her, met his eyes in startled enquiry. 'Is it —?'

'Yes, I'm afraid it is. My good friend Syderstone.'

CHAPTER FOURTEEN

Isadora eyed Syderstone surreptitiously as he basked, urbane and fashionable as ever in a wine-coloured cloth coat, in the flattery of the elder Pusay exiles, who had invited him to visit this afternoon in Mrs Alvescot's private sitting-room. She had been trying for such an opportunity — impossible yesterday when everyone had to attend Sunday service — since he had arrived three days ago.

He appeared delighted to be in company with both the Pusay ladies again, exercising the charm that had worked so well before. To Isadora's intense annoyance, Matilda threw her a glance pregnant with meaning. No doubt she supposed, knowing nothing of the deceased Lord Roborough's debt, that they owed the doubtful honour of this visit to Syderstone's unswerving attachment to Isadora. A useful view now.

He was not in the least degree attached to her, she knew well. But that was not going to prevent her from carrying out the brilliant plan she had conceived.

It had come to her the morning he had arrived, as she had watched the bitter aspect creep into Roborough's countenance when he had thought no one was looking. Every other member of the household had been engaged in the presentations, which were performed with a slight air of patronage by Matilda.

From their demeanour, neither Lady Roborough nor Lady Ursula — and one would suppose Roborough must have opened his mind to her — could possibly be privy to the information Syderstone had fleeced the late master of the house of an enormous sum of money.

While the elder man had been enjoying all this feminine attention, Roborough had allowed his polite company mask to slip a trifle. Isadora, seeing it, had been conscious of the strongest desire to jump up and fling her arms protectively about him. Of course she could do no such thing. Embarrassment apart, it must be unwelcome to him. He might have conducted himself towards her in a manner scarcely befitting a gentleman — conduct which she would give anything to have repeated — but he had made clear his purpose in doing so. It had not been because he wished to.

Quite when the germ of her idea came to her Isadora was not sure. But once it had entered her mind it burgeoned swiftly. She could do it — yes, she could. And it would solve several problems at one blow. Roborough would be free both of the debt and the need to provide for herself, and she — perhaps more importantly — would be free of the misery of watching him enmeshed in the toils of Lady Ursula Stivichall.

Not, as she could plainly see, that he was suffering. Far from it. Anyone with eyes could tell how much he enjoyed her company. God knew what else he enjoyed with her in their private moments together. No, she must not think of that. The idea of the Ursula female being the recipient of such caresses as she had received — and more, if Matilda had gauged the matter rightly — was too painful to be borne. The longer she remained in this house, the worse it would become. Lady Ursula's year of mourning was almost up. What was to stop Roborough marrying her immediately beyond the moment when Society would deem it acceptable?

Nothing in the world. Certainly not Isadora Alvescot. She would be far away, pursuing that ambition she had long ago decided was the goal of her life. Only then she had not known she would meet a hateful, teasing wretch who made her laugh at every moment he was not rousing her to fury. A wretch who was never going to know she was doing this only so she might not be obliged to watch him making love to another woman.

With an inward sigh, Isadora thrust these uncomfortable thoughts to the back of her mind and threw herself into the role she had carefully worked out through the day.

Interrupting a nostalgic conversation about the days of their youth — for the two elder ladies were much of an age with Syderstone — Isadora claimed his attention. 'Oh, this is quite outrageous, Mr Syderstone, to be talking so hard to Mama and Cousin Matty about times which mean nothing to me. How can you?'

'It is indeed disgraceful of me, Miss Alvescot,' he agreed, the vivid eyes turning in her direction. They held a slightly questioning look. 'Besides, I am anxious to know how you go on. Do you miss your home very much?'

'Oddly, no,' Isadora replied. 'But our house, you must admit, had only the gardens to recommend it. You have not had a chance to see the gardens here, I think?'

Matilda jumped in immediately. 'Now why do you not show Mr Syderstone about the grounds, Dora? I am sure you must enjoy them, sir.'

Isadora rose with alacrity. 'I shall be very happy.'

'Why, this is most kind, Miss Alvescot,' said Syderstone, following suit. He added in an undertone, the moment they were outside the door, 'But why, Miss Alvescot? I cannot think you really wish to show me the grounds.'

'I don't,' Isadora agreed readily. 'But I could think of no other excuse to get you away from them.'

'This is most flattering, I protest,' he said, brows raised.

The implication of this was not lost on Isadora. She had done nothing to encourage him, and after his revelation of

Roborough's debt she had barely spoken to him again at Pusay. She assumed a look of troubled entreaty.

'Well, I hope it may be. I have been in such a quandary, you see, and could not think where to turn. Then you came, and suddenly I knew I was saved.'

She glanced at him as she spoke, still leading the way through the corridors towards the gallery, to find, to her satisfaction, that the bait had hooked. His eyes gleamed with genuine interest.

'You intrigue me greatly. Let us by all means hasten to the gardens that you may tell me how I may save — or at least serve you.'

The grounds about the mansion at Barton Stacey were extensive, with walled gardens and stepped lawns leading down towards an artificial lake. To either side of the unkempt lawns — another sign of the tightness of funds here — were intermittent alcoves behind wide beds of overgrown flowering plants where benches were set into the stone.

Isadora selected the first of these for her tête-á-tête with Syderstone. She sat, wringing her hands in an agitated way to show her supposed inner turmoil.

'Tell me all, Miss Alvescot,' invited Syderstone, watching her gravely as he took his seat beside her.

Turning to face him, Isadora put a piteous inflexion into her voice. 'It is Roborough. You were right when you warned me against him.'

'Was I?'

There was caution in his tone, but Isadora was ready for it. He must realise that by now she knew the truth. 'Oh, I do not speak of his father's gambling. He would not take that path himself.'

'You know, then?'

'That the debt to you was incurred by the late viscount? Yes, of course. No, no, this is much more painful to me, although the debt is significant in this.' She drew a breath as if she must determine herself to speak. 'You see, Mr Syderstone, I am wholly in Roborough's power. He — he is coercing me to marry him.'

Syderstone's eyes narrowed. 'Coercing? Come, come, my dear Miss Alvescot.'

She gazed at him, injecting a world of tragedy into her expression. 'I see you do not know him well. He is a hard man, sir. Why, do you not know he is selling our home from under us? As for repaying you from the proceeds, he has vowed he will die first.'

'Has he indeed?' said Syderstone softly, but with an edge to his voice.

Isadora seized one of his hands, holding it between both of her own. 'Oh, Mr Syderstone, dare I trust you? I have conceived such a notion — a way to enable us both to escape — well, perhaps that is not a word for you. But I, alas, have only that option before me.' Her eyes brimmed. 'Except that I cannot do so alone.'

He was eyeing her, she thought, with a good deal of misgiving, a little of his habitual urbanity deserting him. 'You are proposing I should aid you to run away, Miss Alvescot?'

'That is it exactly. Well, not entirely.' Releasing his hand, Isadora turned a little away, embarrassment in her tone. 'I — I hardly know how to say this. Nothing could be more forward, more — more unladylike, but —' she turned eyes she hoped were drowned in dread back upon him — 'I am desperate, Mr Syderstone.'

For a moment he stared at her in a horrified sort of way. It was working. He had taken her meaning. There could be no other way open to a chivalrous man than to offer for her at once. Was this man chivalrous? She watched him anxiously. Disappointingly, the expression of lively apprehension gave way to another look. One of — yes, calculation, as if he was weighing her words.

'Miss Alvescot,' he said, more in his usual manner, but with his eyes firmly on her countenance, 'if you do not wish to marry Roborough, why do you not refuse him? It is not so easy in these enlightened days to force a female into wedlock.'

'It is,' said Isadora mournfully, 'if she has a family wholly at the mercy of her suitor.'

A frown creased his brow. 'There is a threat there?'

'A very real one, sir. We are all dependent upon Roborough. He gives me two choices — either I marry him or he turns the lot of us out.'

'You shock me infinitely, Miss Alvescot.'

Isadora was not surprised. She was shocked herself by the dreadful things she was saying of the man she loved. It hurt her to speak of him so. Only if she was to convince Syderstone to rescue her she must do. She sighed dramatically. 'You can scarce believe it of him, I dare say. Then you will be even more dismayed to learn that his determination to wed me is for his convenience only. He may thus dispose of me suitably, without being obliged to expend one penny on either dowry or settlements, and at the same time provide himself with the means to supply an heir to his name.'

'My dear Miss Alvescot,' said Syderstone in accents of disgust, 'I protest this is callous beyond belief.'

'You see now why I turn to you, sir.'

She groped for her pocket handkerchief and made play with it, sniffing and dabbing at the corners of her eyes. Peeping through her lashes, she saw that Syderstone was now frowning heavily. It seemed as if he was convinced. But would he commit himself?

Abruptly, he reached for one of her hands and drew it to his lips. 'You did quite right to turn to me. I trust I may prove a more honourable man than Roborough.'

That, thought Isadora, was quite impossible. But she gave his fingers a grateful squeeze and smiled tremulously up at him. 'I knew you would not fail me. I promise you I will give you no cause for regret.'

'Oh, I won't regret anything,' he said on a cynical note that gave Isadora an instant's pause.

Had she misunderstood? She rushed into the clinching argument. 'You will not lose by it, Mr Syderstone. For do you not see that if I am married to you —?'

'Married?' He sounded almost amused. Then he smiled. 'But of course. Gretna, do you think?'

'Oh yes, for we must do it all in the greatest secrecy,' Isadora agreed. 'You need not concern yourself. I have thought it all out. We must take the main road which runs from Stockbridge to Basingstoke, and from there we can take the post road north.'

'That seems a sensible route,' he conceded.

'And when we are married you will be in a position to force Roborough into paying your debt. For he dare not refuse when he knows you may blacken his name with a tale of his wrongs to me.'

'Now why had I not thought of that? But of course you are perfectly correct. He will most certainly agree to my terms.'

He sounded so confident Isadora was shaken by doubt. Had he given in to her rather too easily? But next instant he was smiling again.

'Now we must plan the details of our escape. How soon would you wish to elope?'

The escape was effected with no difficulty at all. Summoning a footman to her bedchamber, Isadora instructed him to take her packed portmanteau down to the stables and place it in Mr Syderstone's curricle.

'The gentleman is passing by our previous home, and has very kindly agreed to take some items that Mr Thornbury, our man of business, has requested me to send as gifts for the servants who are leaving us.'

The Barton Stacey domestic staff being, like all servants everywhere, conversant with every detail of the family business, including the facts of the Alvescot inheritance, the footman took this without a blink. All that remained was for Isadora to rise at an early hour upon the following morning and slip off through the gardens to the road where Mr Syderstone picked her up outside the gates to the mansion.

It was with a heavy heart that she climbed up into the curricle. It was bad enough she had not been able to say a fond farewell to her mama, worse — infinitely worse — that she had seen Roborough only in company at dinner last night, when he and the Ursula female had their heads together at the top of the table.

Fearing her emotions would get the better of her if she stayed, Isadora had pleaded tiredness after the meal and retired before the gentlemen had come in from their wine. Tears had been shed into her pillows. Useless, stupid tears. For what was the point in crying when, if she did not do what she had decided to do, she had only despair before her? But that was all in the past.

The future, while it might not include her mama and Roborough, would be bright enough. For, little though he knew it, it did not include her escort. The letter she had left for Roborough — to be delivered by her maid, along with a note for her mama, once she was safely at a distance — would ensure Syderstone troubled none of them again.

Dear Roborough,

I have persuaded Syderstone to elope with me to Gretna Green. He believes marriage with me will enable him to blackmail you into paying his debt. But of course I will not marry him at all. You may then challenge him to dare to claim his debt, as you must say you believe he has ruined me. Pray don't concern yourself over my future. I shall be doing that which I have always desired.

Isadora

If that did not bring Roborough haring after them, then she was entirely mistaken in his character. He would be intent upon preventing her from going to Gretna. But it would avail him nothing, for when he caught up with them he would find only Syderstone. That would baffle him. He would not know where to look, and he would be looking for Isadora Alvescot. There was not going to be any Isadora Alvescot.

He would no doubt deal with Syderstone as he saw fit. She could guess how that might be, but of one thing she was certain: the man could not possibly have the effrontery to demand to be paid when he had run off with Roborough's cousin. As for Roborough, this time Isadora flattered herself that she had out-generalled him. He would think she was ruining herself one way, when in fact she would be busy ruining herself in quite another. That would fox him. And there would be nothing he could do about it, because by the time he did catch up with her — if he managed to do so at all — it would be too late to do anything to save her. Not, she reminded herself, that he had said he would save her. Quite the contrary.

Here a tiny voice at the back of her mind informed her she was dreaming if she supposed for a moment he would carry out his threat. Of course he would not set up as her protector. He had no desire to do so. He had only said it, and kissed her, to make her aware of the dangers of following her ambition. Instead, his kiss had precipitated her into taking the step that would push her into doing so — because she would rather die than live with the agony of seeing him married to another.

She had so much on her mind that the journey to Basingstoke hardly seemed to take any time at all. Syderstone being equally silent — was he perhaps having some doubts? — there was no difficulty at all in introducing her final ploy.

As soon as they were driving north out of Basingstoke, she began to moan softly now and then, putting a hand to her stomach. It was not long before Syderstone noticed.

'What is the matter?'

Isadora hoped she was pale enough from lack of sleep to lend credence to what she replied. 'Forgive me. I am a trifle queasy. The rocking —' she snatched at her mouth as if she were indeed about to be sick — 'I have never been a good traveller.'

'Lord!' exclaimed Syderstone, with all the horror of a man faced with such a domestic crisis. 'Just how nauseous are you?'

Isadora allowed her head to fall back, saying faintly, 'Don't concern yourself. I shall be —' Then, in a panicky tone, she cried, 'Oh no, I shall not! Do you think we might stop? If I could just lie down for a space…'

Pulling on the reins, Syderstone slowed the curricle, calling on his groom to keep his eyes peeled for a likely inn. A small tavern came into sight in a few moments, its swinging sign unmistakable. In a remarkably short time, Isadora had been escorted up to a little room on the first floor, with the landlady fussing over her and offering all manner of remedies.

'I want nothing, thank you,' Isadora said, collapsing on to the bed. 'Only, pray would you ask the gentleman to have my portmanteau brought in? I have some powders with me that will greatly reduce my sickness. I recall packing them.'

The portmanteau was duly brought up, and Isadora, waving away all offers of refreshment bar a glass of water, and pleading only for quiet, soon found herself left alone. She was up at once, darting to the door. Stealthily she opened it, but there was no one about. Breathing a sigh of relief, she closed the door and swiftly turned the key in the lock. Then she seized her portmanteau, hefting it on to the bed.

Ten minutes later, Isadora Alvescot had disappeared. In her place stood a young man, his long black curls drawn back and tied at the neck with a ribbon, and largely concealed by the round felt hat that partly shaded his face. Breeches of blue cloth adorned his slim thighs, and a waistcoat and frock in contrasting greys, although a trifle ill-fitting at the front, sat finely across his shoulders.

Isadora had not forgotten the necessary smallclothes, and only wished she'd had more practice in tying a cravat. She had secretly filched the entire costume for one of her performances, more than a year ago, from her papa's wardrobe. So amused had he been by his daughter's unexpected appearance he had permitted her to keep it for the future. Little had he supposed it would be used for this adventure.

Now it only remained to remove herself from the inn without being noticed. Which did not mean without being seen. It was a small place, but there were still people about. The thing was to step out boldly. No one would expect her, and therefore it was probable no one would challenge her. Or so she devoutly hoped.

Once she was outside the chamber, she took the precaution of locking the door from the outside and pushing the key under it. That would hold them. Then she squared her shoulders, took a firm grip of the portmanteau, and trod in a leisurely way down the stairs.

As she expected, neither the landlady nor Syderstone, who must have been refreshing himself in the taproom, was present in the little hall. A lad was engaged in polishing some brasses that adorned the walls, but he merely glanced about to see who had come down, and then went on with his work.

Isadora sauntered out of the inn, her heart hammering painfully the while, and struck out back towards Basingstoke. She had gone barely half a mile before she was able to get a lift with a passing farmer, spinning him a tale about her horse having gone lame. The farmer, a man of few words, merely nodded, asked where in Basingstoke the gentleman wished to be set down, and calmly besought his horse to proceed.

At Basingstoke, Isadora was obliged to wait for an agonising hour before the stagecoach arrived at the Green Man, at which hostelry the farmer had assured her it would stop on its way to Staines, and thence to London. But no irate Syderstone arrived to interfere with her plan, and she was able to remind herself that in all probability he was still waiting for her to emerge from the room at the little inn.

The stagecoach was noticeably slower than the curricle, and Isadora had too much leisure for reflection. But she had a role to play — for it was not to be supposed the other passengers, curious to a man, would ignore an obvious member of the quality travelling by the stage — and the effort of appearing as much like a youth as possible kept most of her inevitably dismal thoughts at bay.

When the coach stopped for the change, everyone alighted. Isadora would have liked to remain on it, for in spite of her confidence in her disguise she could not help a shiver of apprehension from rising in her bosom. Yet it would arouse suspicion if she did not get down like the others, at least to stretch her legs.

Ignoring the steps, she jumped down — as a young man would — and, adopting what she hoped was a male stride, marched towards the inn into which her fellow passengers had already filed, sparing no glance for the knot of people standing outside.

As she approached the door, a dry voice caught her unawares, one she had imagined to be miles away.

'Rosalind, I presume?' said Roborough. 'Or is it Viola?'

Isadora turned about. He was standing not two feet away from her, having stepped from out of the clutch of persons she had vaguely noted as she passed. And, for all the mildness of his tone, he was looking like a thundercloud.

'Oh, God help me,' she said involuntarily.

'You may well say so.'

Blank shock was swiftly succeeded by the rising tattoo of her pulse in her breast as she stared at him. Useless to pretend she was not herself. He had already recognised her. How had he come here? How had he known? If anything, he should have been wrestling with Syderstone's whereabouts. She found her tongue, in an inevitably blistering attack.

'What are you doing here? How did you know? You had no right. I am going to London and you cannot stop me.'

'We will not discuss rights at this present,' he said, his tone grim. 'But stopping you is another matter. Your journey is done — sir.'

Her attire! Glancing about, she realised they might easily be overheard, and flushed at this timely reminder. She saw a measure of satisfaction enter Roborough's features and her ire rose. She glared at him. 'We'll see about that.'

'We shall indeed,' he replied in a calm voice that belied the granite set of his jaw. 'I imagine you have a portmanteau in that coach. We will begin by extracting it.'

'You will do nothing of the…' Her voice died as she encountered such a blaze of fury in the light eyes as she had never seen before. A little shiver shook her, of fright and distress. It was hideous to have him in such rage with her.

'We will,' he repeated, the words weighted with menace, 'extract your portmanteau. Then we shall go into this inn, where you will change back into your proper raiment, which I make no doubt is contained therein.'

It was too much. How dared he take such a tone with her? Yet Isadora's voice shook a little. 'I will not!'

His eyes narrowed. 'My good *sir*, you endanger yourself more every moment. You will, for once in your life, do as you are told.' He paused briefly, then added icily, 'Or, if you prefer, take the consequences.'

Isadora hesitated, her heart beating rather fast. There could be no doubt she had driven him utterly beyond his patience. Moreover, dressed as she was, he might do anything he chose to her and no one would intervene. She looked every inch a young lad, and Roborough was her senior by so many years he might treat her as such with impunity. Discretion, on this occasion, must be the better part of valour. She bit her lip on any further protest.

'Very wise,' he said drily, and turned from her to address a lounging ostler to whom he had evidently been speaking before he had accosted her.

In a very short time indeed, Isadora found herself carrying her own portmanteau, and trailing in Roborough's wake — just as if she had been a youth and not the lady she actually was — up the stairs, to halt outside the chamber designated by the footman who had shown them up.

'I thank you,' Roborough said to him, nodding at Isadora to enter the room. 'Inform the landlord I shall require ale and coffee, together with a light luncheon — nothing at all elaborate, if you please — to be brought to the parlour I have bespoken.'

The footman, pocketing the coin Roborough handed him, confirmed he would relay these instructions, and went off down the corridor. Roborough followed Isadora into the room and closed the door.

'What now?' she demanded.

'Belligerent as ever, I see,' he remarked coolly. 'Now, ma'am, I will leave you to return to your true identity.'

'And what do you suppose the landlord is going to say when he sees you with a female instead of a youth?'

'I have not the slightest interest in anything he may say. The matter does not concern him.'

'He is bound to think it extremely odd.'

'Then he will have penetrated your character extremely shrewdly. No one could be more odd. If this escapade had been perpetrated upon anyone other than myself, I imagine you would by now have been carted off to Bedlam.'

'How dare you? Do you suppose I did this to play some sort of trick upon you?'

'We will argue the point when you have changed,' he said, moving back to the door. 'And don't think to try any further trick on me as you doubtless tricked Syderstone, for I shall be waiting outside the door. Don't take too long, either.' With which, he extracted the key from the inside of the door and, taking it with him, removed himself and shut the door.

He left Isadora fuming. How dared he treat her so? What, was she a child to be ordered this way and that? Let her but return to the mansion — which she could not doubt was just what would happen — where she was no longer vulnerable to his threats, and then they would see. She would tell him precisely what she thought of him.

Ripping off her jacket, she began savagely to undress, raging still. He was hateful. He was a beast. Great heavens, he was so angry! Tears started to her eyes, and her hands slowed in the act of tearing away her improvised cravat. That was the worst of it. God knew she had raged and ranted at him many a time, and once or twice he had hit back. But never like this. And he had called her *ma'am*. That, distancing her dreadfully, was so extremely painful the tears squeezed from her tightly shut eyes and trickled down her cheeks.

A rapping on the door brought her eyes flying open.

'A little speed, ma'am,' called Roborough from the other side. 'There is no necessity to titivate.'

Resentment flared anew. Titivate indeed. As if she were in the habit of spending hours on her appearance. But she began to hurry nevertheless, dragging her somewhat crumpled black gown out of the portmanteau and slipping it on over her chemise. She shook out the skirts, but there was nothing to be done about the creases. Nor was there anything she could do

257

with her hair, she thought despairingly. She had lost most of her pins so that her usual topknot was impossible. The best she could do was to pin back the front curls and allow the remainder to hang down her back. She stared critically at herself in the mirror above the dressing-table. It would have to do. Not that it mattered what she looked like. Roborough was intent only on punishing her. He was hardly likely to pay the slightest attention — even had he the least interest in the matter — to her appearance.

The thought caused her eyes to well again, and she realised her cheeks were a trifle streaked from where she had wiped away the earlier tears. Hastily rubbing her fingers over them, she removed what traces she could see. Then, seizing the portmanteau, she marched to the door and flung it wide, a touch of defiance returning.

Roborough was leaning against the wall outside. He turned his head, and his glance raked her from top to toe, resting briefly on the tresses curling about her shoulders, and then on her cheeks. Did he notice the tell-tale traces of tears? Apparently not.

'That's better,' was all he said, unsmiling. 'You make, I admit, a fetching boy, but I prefer you as a girl.'

Was that a gleam at the back of his eye? Or was she imagining it, only because it was what she longed to see? She looked down to hide any hope that might be reflected in her face, a faint flush staining her cheeks.

Roborough took the portmanteau from her hand, saying roughly, 'Come along.'

He led the way back to the main hall above the entrance where the footman had earlier pointed out the private parlour. The room was small, furnished with a table in a window alcove, already laid with a cloth and two places, and a couple of armchairs before the empty fireplace. Roborough set the portmanteau down against the wall near one of these, and turned to survey the table.

'I wonder what they will produce for luncheon?' he said musingly, and moved to the bell pull beside the mantel. 'Perhaps they have forgotten us. I had better ring and remind them.'

'Oh, for heaven's sake,' exclaimed Isadora, suddenly exasperated. 'Must you conduct yourself in this tiresomely normal fashion? I know you are angry with me, and if you mean to scold me I wish you will set about it immediately.'

He looked over at her. His voice was even, but she could hear the undercurrent of rage beneath. 'I dare not, ma'am, for if I start I cannot answer for my temper.'

'*Ma'am* again! How can you speak to me in that manner, after all that has passed between us? I must be the last person in the world to be troubled by a little loss of temper. There is nothing I hate more than waiting for a quarrel. Let us get it over with.'

'I don't wish to quarrel with you, Isadora,' Roborough said in a tightly controlled tone. Then, as if he could no longer contain himself, he burst out furiously, 'What I wish to do is to throttle you!'

'Throttle me? When all I have done is to try and help you to be rid of Syderstone?'

'This is your notion of helping me, is it? Doing your best to ruin yourself?'

'What do you care if I ruin myself?'

'I will tell you —' he began, but broke off as the door opened and one of the inn servants entered, armed with a laden tray. Roborough cursed inwardly. He had known what would happen if he allowed rein to the fury consuming him.

The servant, excusing himself, went to the table, casting as he did so a surprised glance at Isadora, who had flounced away to the other side of the room. Of course he had not been expecting a female. No doubt he had heard their voices, too. Not that it mattered. Better to be overheard here, where they were not known, than at home where the repercussions might be endless.

Although he was still excessively angry with the little monster, he was so relieved to have found her this easily his murderous fury was muted by now. Never in his life had he spent a more painful journey, racked both by rage and a very real fear for Isadora's safety. He could swear it was only the thought of the severe chastisement he planned to administer that had kept him from insanity. He had very nearly done it too — when she had dared to defy him even at the last. She must have known instantly the game was up. But no, Isadora could never give in without a fight. Which was why, of course, he felt as he did about her.

His rage began to slide away from him. But what other weapon had he? She must learn he was not to be trifled with, and only a fury greater than her own appeared to do the trick. He began to chafe. Damn the servant! Would he be forever at his work? He glanced across at Isadora. She had paced to the fireplace and was standing with her back to him, looking down into the empty grate.

At last the man finished laying out the luncheon, and Roborough slipped him a coin, saying, 'I do not wish to be disturbed again. Unless I ring let no one enter this room, if you please.'

That took Isadora's attention. She turned quickly, waiting only for the door to close behind the servant before rushing into speech.

'Roborough, you don't understand. I know you think I have behaved —'

'In a manner that reflects upon your sanity,' he cut in swiftly.

'— in a way that must seem as if I have tricked you,' she finished. Then she realised what he had said. 'What do you mean, reflects upon my sanity? It was a carefully thought out plot.'

'That is just what I mean. No one but a madwoman would devise such a plot. And do you know what lacerates my feelings the most? That you should so underrate my intelligence. How dared you, Isadora, suppose I might take on trust all that utter nonsense you wrote to me?'

'It was not nonsense. At least, I did not tell you quite all my intentions, but how dare you doubt my purpose after all I said?'

'I can't believe I'm hearing this. If I believed for one moment you meant what you said in that foolish note —'

'Why shouldn't I mean it?'

'Don't try me too far, Isadora.' He moved a few steps closer. 'If you knew what I itch to do to you!'

Isadora shifted back involuntarily. 'Are you daring to threaten me?'

'Yes, I am threatening you, and with good reason.'

'Oh! You hateful man! You had much better have gone for Syderstone and threatened him.'

Roborough uttered a short laugh. 'You don't imagine I would waste my time chasing after Syderstone, do you? I know you a little too well, my girl. Your letter reeked of some idiotic plan afoot.'

'It was not idiotic at all,' protested Isadora indignantly. 'It was a very clever plan.'

'It was an extremely stupid plan — besides containing a gross miscalculation.'

Isadora stared at him blankly. 'How so?'

He seized her shoulders and shook her. 'You little fool! Syderstone had never any intention of marrying you. He had his own axe to grind. Unfortunately for him, he is not as well acquainted with you as I am, or he would have seen through your game and anticipated this.' Releasing her, he made an airy gesture as if to encompass her escape.

The tiny doubts that had beset Isadora at the outset came hurtling back, in full flower. She had not convinced Syderstone. But why had he agreed to elope with her, then? And how was it Roborough knew all this? He meant, of course, that he had seen through her game. But not all of it. 'Even you could not have known I would disguise myself as a man,' she told him, with a resurgence of her usual defiance.

'I should have thought of it. I guessed you would give Syderstone the slip. Oh, it was not difficult to fathom that,' he added, seeing the frown of annoyance descend upon her brow. 'You told me, Isadora. I was not to concern myself over your future. You would be doing what you always wanted. There could be only one interpretation.'

She had not fooled him at all. He had outwitted her again. Disgruntled, she said, 'Well, how should I know you would read so much between the lines?'

'That is exactly what I complain of, but I dare say it is too much to expect your lunatic mind to encompass that I might add two and two to make four.'

'But how was it you tracked me here?'

'It wasn't difficult. Since I knew your purse could not possibly run to hiring a coach, or even a horse, the stagecoach was the obvious solution. London, given your ambitions, had to be your objective. I had only to check at each stage of the route. Fortune favoured me, however, for my coach must have passed you on the road. I arrived here ahead of you, and was thus able to search for you among the passengers as they alighted.' A slight quirk of his lips signalled, for the first time today, a smile. 'I confess I had not quite bargained for the sight that met my eyes.'

Isadora was silent for a moment or two, thinking it all out. She paced about the room, barely conscious of Roborough's gaze. She did not know whether to be glad or sorry her plan had been foiled. But a sneaking pleasure grew in her that he had cared enough to come after her. Not that she could set much store by it. He had made his views on her ambition to become an actress very clear indeed.

His voice recalled her. 'Why did you do it, Isadora?'

He was no longer angry. There was a touch of that gentleness in his tone she knew so well now. It caused her heart to swell and tears to prick at her eyes.

'I told you in my note.'

'And I told you,' he said in a harder tone, 'that I do not believe your sacrificial faradiddles about getting Syderstone off my back. Tell me the truth!'

The truth? Great heavens, how could she? Indeed, how could she get out of answering him on this head at all? Then his mention of Syderstone brought back to mind what he had said of him.

'What did you mean when you said Syderstone had no intention of marrying me? How can you know what he intended if you have not even seen him?'

Roborough's jaw tightened. 'I am indebted to Syderstone himself for the information. I received two notes, Isadora.'

'He wrote to you?'

'I don't know what you said to him, but he allowed you to believe you had won him over, and then —' He broke off and, coming up to her, took her by the shoulders again, gently this time. 'Isadora, I had hoped to spare you this. The fact is Syderstone wrote that he would ruin you if I did not follow. He meant it literally, for he used a low term which I shall not distress you by repeating. I was to catch up with you both, and write an undertaking to pay him his money from the proceeds of the Pusay house.'

Isadora stared up at him in mounting puzzlement. She saw the anger was back in his eyes, but she recognised that this time it was not directed at her. Only she could not understand Syderstone's reasoning.

'He must have been mad. How could he suppose you would agree to that? You would catch him up, of course you would. But surely you would call him out? Any man would.'

'Very true, but he had thought of that.' Roborough released her, his voice taking on an edge. He moved a little away, looking at some vision in his mind rather than at Isadora's face. 'He had, he said, no intention of making the matter public. It was enough I should know what he had done to you. He knew perfectly well I would pay. Either that or I would have had to kill him.'

Isadora stared. He spoke with an intensity that astonished her. 'I don't understand.'

Roborough turned to look at her. There was a look in his eyes that she did not recognise. 'Don't you? Let me see if I can make it clearer. It appears Syderstone saw which way the wind was blowing even before I did myself. That is why, I surmise, he set up a mock-rivalry between us for your favours, and told you of the debt.'

'Are you saying he set out deliberately to make mischief between us?'

'Exactly. I do not suggest he had it in mind even then to elope with you. I think he was rather testing my reaction to check his own judgement. Unfortunately, this time, he must have been certain of it — as who could not be? — and you, Isadora, played right into his hands.'

She scarcely heard the last. Testing what? Certain of it? Could he mean...? 'Roborough, don't trifle with me,' she burst out. 'Syderstone was right about what?'

The expression in his eyes was compound of entreaty and some species of pain. 'Can't you yet guess? Oh, Isadora, what is the use of concealment? If I distress you by this, I beg your pardon. The truth is that Syderstone guessed that I am in love with you.'

Isadora's knees almost buckled under her. It *was* what he meant. She had hardly dared to give room to the burgeoning thought. But now —! Her heart leapt. Her pulse throbbed painfully and her throat ached over a rising lump. 'Distress me?' she said huskily. 'I have never been so happy in my life!'

Then, as his features broke into a radiant grin, she flung herself across the room and burst into tears on his chest. She was clutched so tightly she scarce had room to gulp in her breath on the sobs that rose up to choke her.

Suddenly the hold relaxed, and her face was seized between two firm hands. 'I had not dared to hope. You can't imagine what I've been through, you wicked little devil!' He kissed her hard. 'I could willingly slaughter you!'

But his lips were again at her mouth as he dragged her back into his embrace. Isadora's tears were arrested. She was unable to utter anything at all beyond a hungry groan, and, conscious only of warmth sweeping through her, she gave herself up to the violence of Roborough's passion.

It was some time before he could abandon his repeated assaults upon her lips, punctuated with the most gratifying statements of his emotions towards her. At length he did stop kissing her, but only so he might look down into her wondering features.

'But what about Lady Ursula?' was the first thing Isadora managed to say.

Roborough, playing with her loosened tresses and smiling at her in a manner both foolish and endearing, merely uttered vaguely, 'What about Ursula?'

Isadora brought her hands up to grasp the lapels of his coat. 'Roborough, don't you see? She is the reason I conceived my plot.'

'Are you mad, Isadora?'

Her voice began to shake. 'I thought — I believed you were in love with her, and I couldn't b-bear to remain to watch you making love to her and — and marrying her when her mourning was over.'

His expression altered and his fingers closed over hers. 'Marry Ursula? You are joking!'

'I am not. Even your mother seems to think you might do so. And — and Cousin Matty is convinced Lady Ursula is already your mistress.'

'And you believed it?' An unmistakably astonished laugh shook him. Nothing could more surely have convinced Isadora of the folly of her belief. 'Now I see what you were driving at the other day.' Drawing her fingers up to his mouth, he kissed them, saying lovingly, 'You little idiot.'

Isadora heaved a sigh, protesting nevertheless, 'I don't see why you should call me an idiot. How should I have known? You certainly greeted her in a highly suggestive manner.'

'Ursula is a dear friend, Isadora, as was her husband. When my father was alive, their house was my second home — the only place I felt truly comfortable.' He cupped her face with one hand. 'I am extremely fond of Ursula, but I don't love her.'

'Don't you?'

'No, I love you. I want you, not Ursula. She would positively stare at the notion of becoming intimate with me. Besides, although she shows a laughing face to the world, she was broken by Stivichall's death, and mourns for him still.' He grinned. 'In any event, if you must know, she has spent the last few days carping at me for hesitating to tell you how I feel about you.'

'She — what?'

'Yes, I tell you. She guessed the state of my heart within minutes and I have been subjected to all manner of scolds. Although she was quite unable to discover, which she said she tried to do, what your sentiments were.'

So that was it. All those silly questions, which Isadora had been unable to understand, about the sort of man Roborough ought to marry her to. That was what Lady Ursula had meant. Then the thoughts flew out of her head, for Roborough drew her back within the circle of his arm, his fingers pushing up her chin so that he might look deep into her eyes.

'Speaking of your sentiments,' he said softly, 'am I to assume they are what your recent conduct in this room seems to indicate?'

Isadora gazed balefully up at him. 'If you mean what do I think of you, Roborough, let me tell you that you are a hateful wretch. In fact, you are the most abominable man in the world — and I love you to distraction!'

'Thank God for that,' he said, relieved, as he claimed her lips once more. He added, as he released her mouth, 'Because, you see, I am about to order you to marry me.'

Isadora giggled. 'What, now?'

'Not now, you little monster, but in the shortest possible order. You need not imagine I have any intention of waiting for our mutual mourning to be over. I swear I could not tolerate many more rides with you without abandoning all claim to be called a gentleman.'

Isadora blushed, but said shyly, 'Nor I prevent you from doing so, to be truthful with you.'

A remark which caused Roborough to seize her mouth in a very fever of passion. 'If you only knew the torture you have put me through.'

'You can't have suffered more than I,' retorted Isadora. 'I thought I had utterly alienated you by the horrid things I said. It did not seem possible I could ever inspire affection in you — especially after that dreadful quarrel in the library at Pusay.'

'Oh, don't speak of that. I left you in a mood of murderous rage, but barely had I shaken the dust of Pusay from my carriage wheels than I realised I had fallen hopelessly in love with you, Isadora.'

'What, even then? But you never showed by the slightest hint that you felt that way about me.'

'No, because I thought I had ruined any chance I might have had of attaching you. Nothing, I believed, would serve to eradicate your ill opinion of me. Even when you knew the truth, I could not begin to suppose you had changed towards me.' He hugged her tight. 'I am not even going to ask you when you began to care.'

When his hold relaxed, Isadora's brown eyes were moist as she looked up at him. 'I didn't know it then, but I think it was the very first time you smiled at me — for I find the way your eyes crinkle at the corners quite irresistible.'

Roborough, unable to help himself, did smile then. Sure enough, the corners of his eyes crinkled and the tingling warmth that Isadora had always felt — and which she only now recognised for what it was — swept through her.

She drew a breath of deepest satisfaction. 'You may plague me beyond bearing, but that teasing look will ever redeem you.'

'And you, my adorable Isadora, will undoubtedly drive me into an early grave. But I shall die the happier for having taken to wife a female that will bedazzle Society with her acting skills.'

Light flooded across Isadora's face. 'You will not mind it if I perform in public?'

'I shall take delight in showing you off — in your very own theatre. I shall build one especially for you just as soon as I have recovered the family fortunes.'

'Well, you may easily do that now for you need not provide me with either a dowry or settlements.' She gasped, reminded of the ramifications of her own plot. 'Great heavens, I used just that argument to persuade Syderstone you were importuning me to marry you.'

'Did you indeed? Pray don't ever hesitate to vilify my character any time it seems to you expedient to do so.'

'I won't,' Isadora promised.

'If I could stop kissing you for one moment,' Roborough told her ominously, suiting the action to the word, 'I should certainly slap you instead, you vile female.'

'Not if you don't wish me to scratch your eyes out,' she retorted. Then she frowned. 'But what of Syderstone? What are we to do about him?'

'You may leave Syderstone to me. When I have finished with him he will dare neither to utter a word in your disparagement nor to importune me for his debt — which I shall choose when to pay.'

'Yes, but he will have discovered my absence by now, and perhaps he may search for me.'

'Let him do so. He won't find you. Besides, after we are married, I will be searching for him. And he won't care for that, I promise you.'

He almost ground his teeth as he spoke and Isadora thrilled to the possessive intensity she sensed within him. How he must love her. She lifted a hand to touch her fingers to his cheek, her heart melting as she smiled.

'You will tell him, I hope, that your scheme to entrap me has succeeded? After all, he imagines you wish to marry me for convenience only.'

'Which I do, of course. Marrying you is much cheaper than throwing you on to the marriage mart. In fact, that is the real reason why I did not offer for you. You might have refused me. By ordering you to marry me, on the other hand —'

'Roborough, you are abominable,' interrupted Isadora, on a gurgle of mirth, 'and I hate you.'

'I know,' he said, the warmth crinkling at his eyes, 'and I shall be at pains to ensure you never cease to care for me in just that way.'

A NOTE TO THE READER

Dear Reader,

This story has one aspect that was a joy to me. I trod the boards for years before writing eventually took over, so it gave me a thrill finally to write about the experience of acting which had been so much a part of my life. I never left theatre entirely as I then went on to teach drama and direct plays.

Had Isadora realised her dream, she would have taken up acting in an environment where it was the norm to "declaim" rather than deliver the lines naturally. Actors of the day would strike a pose and say their lines with great enthusiasm and a good deal of unnecessary emphasis. What, in this day and age, we would call "ham acting". False, in other words. There's an episode of Blackadder III (set in the Regency period) which illustrates this overblown style hilariously well when Kenneth Connor and Hugh Paddick play thespians trying to teach the Prince to improve his delivery (and failing miserably).

An early actor of the 18th century who brought a more realistic style to the stage was David Garrick. He was renowned for being able to move an audience and his performances were apparently both electric and natural. He managed Drury Lane theatre for years and is said to be responsible for bringing Shakespeare back into fashion at that time.

From the theatrical family of Kembles rose Sarah Siddons, the great tragedienne of this era, celebrated for her emotional portrayals (especially of Lady Macbeth), but she also "cross-dressed" as many actresses did then, playing Hamlet many times. All the Kembles acted, toured and (some) managed theatres, but one of her brothers, Charles Kemble, achieved great success and was lauded when he acted in America.

In the early 19th century came Edmund Kean, whose fame rested on his Shakespearean portrayals, which it was said even surpassed those of John Philip Kemble, also renowned for such roles. Kean lacked height, though, and Sarah Siddons erroneously said of him that "there was too little of him to make a great actor".

I can't talk about actors of the period without mentioning Romeo Coates. An enthusiastic amateur, Robert Coates, having failed to make a career in the theatre proper, proceeded to use his personal fortune to mount productions of his own, playing the leading roles he loved. Because his most treasured role was Romeo, his critics, scornful of his pretensions to be a great actor, dubbed him with that name. He did gain notoriety and was at least successful in drawing audiences who flocked to his performances either to mock, or simply to find out whether he was as bad as reputation had it.

Actors of the day were not paid as such. If they had a share in the theatre company, they received a percentage of the profits. If not, they earned via "benefit" nights when the proceeds, after deduction for the costs of mounting the play, was shared among whichever of the players was named for that night. To attract a larger audience, managers would bring in top names to perform for just one night.

It was a precarious existence at best, which readily explains why actors needed patrons and actresses took up with a protector. One of the most famous examples of this form of supplementary income lies in the career of Perdita Robinson who, for a time at least, was mistress to the young Prince of Wales, earning him the sobriquet of Florizel, the name of the lover of Perdita in A Winter's Tale.

Our Isadora, being sadly ignorant of the seedier side of the acting profession, is thus perhaps fortunate not to have been obliged to take it up in earnest.

If you would consider leaving a review, it would be much appreciated and very helpful. Do feel free to contact me on **elizabeth@elizabethbailey.co.uk** or find me on **Facebook**, **Twitter**, **Goodreads** or my website **www.elizabethbailey.co.uk**.

Elizabeth Bailey

Sapere Books is an exciting new publisher of brilliant fiction and popular history.

To find out more about our latest releases and our monthly bargain books visit our website:
saperebooks.com